MURDER
at the
Gardens

BOOKS BY LISA CUTTS

A BELINDA PENSHURST MYSTERY

Murder in the Village

Murder at the Castle

MURDER
at the
Gardens

LISA CUTTS

bookouture

Published by Bookouture in 2022

An imprint of Storyfire Ltd.
Carmelite House
50 Victoria Embankment
London EC4Y 0DZ

www.bookouture.com

ISBN: 978-1-80314-203-6
eBook ISBN: 978-1-80314-204-3

For Tara Melton and Andrea Richards
(in no particular order of preference)

PROLOGUE

The most wonderful thing about the noises of the howler monkeys was that they covered the sounds of the break-in. Not a mean feat to get away with during an otherwise quiet late night in the Kent countryside. The two figures huddled together, crouched down away from prying eyes and the glare of the cameras.

There was little to worry about from the security men in their office, the lights from the television screen flashing between the gaps in the cheap, broken blinds. The sounds of a comedian, an enthusiastic audience and guffaws from the employees gave the intruders further reassurance they would remain undisturbed. While the security team ensured that no crimes were being carried out in the twenty square feet around them, the hooded trespassers crept along the edge of the formal gardens and on to the animal enclosures.

Each of them had a pair of bolt croppers in their gloved hands. Each knew exactly where they were going.

The route was one they had taken on a number of occasions, sometimes in the fog that swept across without warning from the marsh, mostly in the warmth of a summer day. This was a well-trod path with no room for error. These people weren't merely deadly serious, they were fanatical.

There were times that they didn't like what they had to do, but they did it for the greater good. It wasn't the first time they had broken into the zoo and caused problems, and it wouldn't be the last. They were acting under very specific orders and neither relished the idea of crossing their boss or running the risk of getting caught. There was far too much at stake.

Not a word was exchanged as, with heavy hearts, they went to carry out their task.

Any sound they made hacking through branches and sawing into fences was muffled by the primates' babble. They went about their covert operation completely unaware that they, too, were being watched.

Their every move was being followed as they crept along, scrambling in the shadows. Any thoughts they had of being top of the food chain in this murky enterprise were wrong. They were, in fact, the prey, their progress carefully monitored by someone capable of much more than they could ever imagine. If the whole sorry business wasn't carried out correctly, one murder wouldn't be the end of it. Nothing was being left to chance.

1

Belinda Penshurst watched her Labrador Horatio disappear into the distance. She whistled, knowing full well that he could hear her. She didn't really have time to chase him today, though it was a game they often played when they got a little further from the castle, to limit any damage and avoid a telling-off from the gardeners.

She managed to catch up with the young dog, his head in a bush, tail in the air, backside swinging like a pendulum. He wasn't even a year old, and had more energy than Belinda could cope with at times.

'We have to head back now, Horatio,' she said, trying her best to tempt him with a squeaky toy. It worked like a charm. He was all ears and paws as he turned to focus on the onion with its happy face. Inexplicably, it was his favourite.

With a teasing squeak, she turned and ran back across the field, toy held aloft. Her dog-walking shoes hit the ground as she went, the soles' Velcro-like grip preventing her from slipping on more than one occasion.

By the time Belinda reached the rear of the castle – its magnificence never something she took for granted – her shoulder-length black hair was a tangled mess, her face had a touch more sheen than she would have liked and her feet and legs were caked in mud. Still, she was head over heels in love with life.

She lived in a castle in the beautiful village of Little Challham with her scatty brother Marcus, their mostly absent father and her faithful Labrador, and to top it all off, her friend Harry Powell lived only a few minutes away.

For a moment, the figure at the double doors leading to the patio seemed like a ghost from another life. Belinda froze; Horatio, momentarily confused, came skidding to a halt, churning the grass as he put his brakes on. He barked at the stranger, then like most wayward puppies, hurtled towards him, irrespective of danger.

Belinda felt as if her nerves were on fire, despite the coolness of the morning. She stood on the edge of the patio and stared at her ex-boyfriend, the man who had broken her heart.

Ivan Brenner – still ridiculously handsome, still able to stop her dead in her tracks – was in her home. He stared at her, his deep blue eyes drinking her in, before he dropped down to make a fuss of Horatio who was close to hyperventilating at the utter excitement of a prospective new biscuit source.

Later, when Belinda looked back on the scene, she tried to convince herself that she had only stood speechless for mere seconds. She was occasionally kind to herself like that, but she suspected it was longer.

'He's my dog,' she said.

'The bag of his, er, stuff you're carrying is a giveaway,' said Ivan, his South African accent transporting her to a time and place she thought she had managed to leave behind. The palpitations said otherwise.

'What are you doing here, Ivan?' she said, dropping the bag and stepping towards him.

'I wanted to speak to you in person, Bel,' he said. 'After

Marcus persuaded me to pay you a visit ahead of my wedding, and then I cancelled on you, I felt bad. I wanted to come and clear the air.'

His words didn't tear her up as much as the surprise of seeing him had. She felt some relief at that.

'Yes, he told me that you're getting married. I... I... Congratulations.'

Ivan stood up, facing her, the intensity of his look making it a challenge not to shy away. She held her ground. He went to speak, then seemed to change his mind before finally saying in a sombre tone, 'It's not quite that simple: I've got a couple of things I need to talk to you about.'

'I'm hazarding a guess that Marcus knew you were heading to Little Challham,' she said, confused as to where this was going but trying to buy herself some time. He'd failed to respond to her well wishes about his impending marriage, so something was clearly amiss.

'To be totally fair to your brother, I only called him a couple of hours ago when I landed at Heathrow. It was all a bit last minute. Don't blame him.'

Belinda's stomach flipped. How would she feel if the next thing he told her was that he still loved her and she was the only one for him? She couldn't allow Ivan back in her life. He had hurt her in such an extraordinary and callous way. It was really unforgiveable.

'What's changed?' she found herself saying with passing curiosity rather than hope or desperation.

'I had business to attend to.' Ivan glanced down at Horatio who had rolled onto his tummy and was staring back, probably hoping the tall stranger had a pocket bursting with dog treats.

'You're avoiding looking at me,' said Belinda, with even more directness than usual. She surprised herself at her lack of subtlety; Ivan, too, judging by his expression.

'You never had mastered the art of beating around the bush.'

He smiled at her. 'There's a few things going on at your local zoo that I said I'd offer some advice on. You know, animals and suchlike.'

'I am aware of what's kept in a zoo.' Belinda grabbed at her hair, which was flying around her face in the breeze. 'Shall we go inside? The dog needs a drink and it's getting colder.'

Belinda walked across the patio, Horatio at her heels. At least he was showing his loyalty – not to mention that he always got a biscuit after his morning walk.

Ivan obediently trotted along behind the two of them across the patio and into the spacious drawing room. Belinda tried to hide her discomfort at having an unexpected house guest, especially one who had played such a mammoth part in her life. Now Ivan stood awkwardly beside the large, overstuffed green sofa, unsure what to do next.

'Ah, sis, there you are,' said Marcus, his blue eyes crinkling with delight at the sight of her. 'And you've already said hello to Ivan. Splendid.' He leaned forward to kiss Belinda's cheek and whispered, 'Sorry.'

At least he had the good grace to feel bad that he hadn't warned her; he knew that the sight of Ivan would knock the wind out of her.

'How long are you staying?' said Belinda, turning to face Ivan. The two men looked awkwardly at one another. The noisy slurping of a thirsty puppy draining his water bowl and drowning the rug at the same time was a strange background to a conversation Belinda never thought she would have.

'You're OK with me staying here?' said Ivan.

'Oh, thank heavens,' chortled Marcus. 'I thought she was talking to me!'

Belinda shot him a look; Ivan ignored him.

'Of course you can stay with us,' said Belinda, unzipping her coat. 'We wouldn't have it any other way, would we, Marcus?'

'No, no,' said Marcus with a dimpled smile. 'I've already put his bags in the front guest room.'

She nodded slowly, grateful that her buffoon brother had put her ex-boyfriend in the guest room furthest from her own. Perhaps Marcus was growing up at last. He was in his mid-forties, so it was about time.

'As soon as it opens, the three of us should go to the pub,' said Marcus, rubbing his hands together.

Ivan looked down at his creased beige trousers, with what looked to be tomato ketchup on the leg – Belinda hoped it wasn't blood as there was only so much shock she could take – and his faded black T-shirt and green waterproof coat, and shrugged. 'I could do with a freshen-up.'

'Absolutely,' said Marcus. 'What was I thinking? You need a shower. I mean, you possibly need a shower and a change of clothes.'

'In the meantime, we can sort you out refreshments too,' said Belinda, ever the hostess.

'And then we'll go to the pub,' said Marcus. 'Mind you...' He leaned in closer and glanced over his shoulder at the empty room. 'You'll have to have your wits about you in this village, Ivan. People keep managing to get themselves murdered.'

'What?' said Ivan. 'Murder? In Little Challham?'

'Marcus is exaggerating slightly,' said Belinda. 'One or two poor unfortunate souls met an untimely end.'

'More than one or two,' said Marcus. 'If you ask me—'

'And thank you, but we didn't,' said Belinda. 'How about we give you an hour to rest and if you're not too tired, we can decide what to do for the rest of the day? You're probably exhausted from the travelling.'

'Oh, come on, Bel,' said Marcus, determined not to let this one go. 'She's only being modest because she helped to solve the murders and work out who the killer was – both times.'

Belinda started to wave away his praise, sneaking a look at Ivan. His mouth was slightly open and his eyes wide.

'Really?' Ivan said. 'That's incredible, but also exactly the sort of thing I'd expect you to get up to. You've never been one to sit idle.'

'Although, let's be fair,' said Marcus, 'she had a tiny bit of help from Harry.'

'Harry?' said Ivan, blinking rapidly.

'Yes,' said Belinda. 'Harry Powell is a retired detective inspector who moved to the village several months ago. He's investigated more murders in his thirty years in the police than you can shake a stick at. He's a neighbour and very good friend.'

'Hang on a minute,' said Marcus, clapping his hands together. 'Harry's going for a job at the zoo tomorrow afternoon and Ivan's going to meet with the board members. He could put in a good word for him. This is going to be marvellous.'

Ivan's face was difficult to read. Belinda hoped it was the journey dragging his features down and not contempt. It would be hard for anyone to meet Harry and not take to him straight off, unless you happened to be the former lover of someone whose cheeks reddened at the mere mention of him. As things stood, there was little to tell, although Belinda had hopes that her relationship with Harry would extend beyond mere friendship.

'I'm sure that Ivan's got much more pressing matters to deal with than helping Harry out with a security job,' said Belinda.

'As it happens,' said Ivan, 'security is very high up the agenda. If he's a retired police officer and you can vouch for him, I'd be happy to put in a good word tomorrow.'

'Well, that's settled, then,' said Marcus, steering Belinda and Ivan towards the door. 'Let's get ready for a libation or three in the village, get you fully briefed on what a fine chap Harry is, and you can make sure he gets his dream job. It's not as if anyone is actually going to get murdered in a zoo, is it?'

2

Harry Powell had been a police officer for more than half his life. Now he was retired, he was learning to adjust. It was a slow process, one that had been helped by moving to Little Challham, getting reacquainted with Belinda Penshurst and their friendship blossoming, not to mention landing a job as a Doggie Delight delivery salesman. It wasn't a bad job, but after his time as a detective inspector, he felt that he needed something that would better occupy his mind.

As he drove his Audi through the gates of Brabourne Zoological Gardens on his way to his interview, following the signs for the staff car park as instructed, he took a deep breath. He allowed himself the luxury of dreaming that he would soon be on the zoo's security team. He needed something with a little more depth and responsibility than delivering dog food.

He parked and sat for a moment drinking in the views. The zoo was part of a hundred-acre site adjacent to Brabourne Gardens which was set within its own twenty acres. The impeccable gardens had won numerous awards, and the horticultural world was fiercely jealous of the never-ending supply of manure from the wild horses.

Harry got out of the car, brushed the creases from his trousers and straightened his tie. He knew he looked immaculate, having shaved minutes before getting dressed in his best pressed suit.

With unwelcome and unexpected feelings of nervousness, he approached the security office. He glanced at his watch; he was thirty minutes early, but hadn't wanted to take any chances with the traffic. Arriving after his appointment was hardly going to win anyone over. For a beat, he stood twenty feet or so away from the entrance, not sure whether he should knock.

The door opened and a slim woman in her mid- to late-thirties, with straight brown shoulder-length hair and a mouth too large for her face, stood in the doorway. Her brown eyes locked onto Harry's, and she smiled. The sound of raised voices behind her appeared to startle her. She pulled the door to and clipped down the three concrete steps in heels she seemed to struggle with.

'I hate dressing up for these formal things,' she said, coming to a clumsy standstill in front of Harry. 'You must be Harry Powell.'

Harry shook her hand and said, 'I am. And you are?'

'I'm regretting wearing these ridiculous shoes.' She pumped his hand up and down and then, as if remembering what she was supposed to be doing, added, 'I'm Estelle Samuels, owner and manager of Brabourne Gardens and Zoo, Chair of the Board of Trustees and all that other palaver. I prefer getting stuck in with the animals, you know, not tied down in the admin of it all. Still, it's hard to find anyone I can actually trust with looking out for the interests of the zoo. It's not as if I haven't tried. Sorry, I've gone off on a bit of a tangent, haven't I?'

Estelle's gaze wandered to the top of Harry's head. He stood at over six feet tall and much of his hair was still red, although a liberal sprinkling of grey was doing its best to infiltrate it. His build was on the generous side, too, making him someone that was difficult to miss in a crowd.

'It's great to meet you,' he said, his attention drawn to shouting coming through the open windows of the security office.

'Oh, don't worry about that,' she said, jerking a thumb in the direction of the noise. 'The last interview hasn't gone according to plan, but it'll be fine. Come and let me show you the sights.'

Harry allowed himself to be led away from the squabble that seemed about to end someone's chance of a job. It probably wasn't the best idea to *start* a fight when the security job spec included preventing and stopping altercations. He couldn't resist one more peek over his shoulder. The door opened once more and a thirty-something man in a navy suit stomped down the steps. He paused to make the sort of gesture that wasn't particularly welcome in a family-orientated zoo.

'We'll let you know,' a voice shouted from inside the building.

'I – er, is it always like this?' said Harry. A job at the zoo would completely satisfy his longing for a slightly more inter-esting working day, if this was anything to go by.

'No, it's usually fairly run-of-the-mill stuff,' said Estelle, pointing into the distance with what Harry couldn't fail to notice was a slightly shaky hand. 'That's the elephant house over there. We have a whole herd we're relocating back to Africa. You probably saw the demonstrators outside the gates?'

'Demonstrators?' said Harry. 'No, there was no one out there when I drove in. What are they demonstrating about?'

'Oh, you know, the usual,' said Estelle, her cheeks reddening as if she had said too much. 'Over there is the bear enclosure, and then the beginning of the African Savannah Experience.'

'What does that consist of?' said Harry. 'Being sent to the African savannah with the elephants?'

Harry laughed. Estelle didn't.

'No,' she said. 'It's our big new attraction, intended to rival Kent's other zoos and parks. We're very proud of it and its security will be one of your main duties. If, of course, you get the job. There's still so much work to do.'

He stopped himself from saying that provided he didn't pick a fight and storm out, vulgar gestures and all, he stood a better chance than the last candidate.

'I should probably get over to the office,' he said. 'I don't want anyone to think I was late.'

'Of course,' she said, guiding him back towards the office as if he was unsure of where he was going. 'I'm sure you won't mind if I don't sit in. It's the last interview of the day, and to be honest, I'm missing the animals.'

'It does make sense that you like animals,' said Harry, 'what with it being your zoo.'

'I love animals. They're so much better than people, don't you think?'

'That goes without saying,' said Harry, aware that she had a very strong grip on him as she delivered him back to the entrance. He supposed she was used to getting the chimpanzees in a headlock when they misbehaved, then dismissed the thought. He was fairly sure that the welfare of the inhabitants was second to none and no such thing ever happened while she was around. Estelle happened to be strong, that was all. Besides, chimpanzees could actually be very dangerous.

With that, the zoo owner was gone, leaving Harry to hope he was about to make a good impression and get himself a new job.

Straightening his tie one last time, he climbed the steps and knocked.

3

Belinda was driving herself and Ivan towards Brabourne Zoological Gardens in her Land Rover. He had got into the passenger seat without a word, but she saw the look of approval as he ran an eye over her car. For some reason she couldn't fathom, it pleased her that he liked it. Then it worried her that she was seeking any kind of endorsement from her former partner.

'You never really explained why you came,' she said, navigating a bend in the country road. Autumn was definitely on its way as the trees on either side of them dropped their leaves onto the road, one or two drifting onto the windscreen. 'You told me that you wanted to speak to me, and yet last night, you only talked about Estelle Samuels' plans to return a herd of elephants to Africa.'

'That's because it's easier to talk about a neutral subject than what happened between us,' he said. 'You're absolutely right, though: we need to get a few things out in the open.'

'Do we?' She risked a glance across at him. 'You're getting married. I don't see that we have that much to talk about.'

Belinda didn't want to have this conversation, least of all

now. The only reason she had agreed to drive Ivan to Brabourne
Gardens was because Marcus had persuaded them both that
Belinda was the best person to ferry him around. Besides, she
knew that Harry had his interview that afternoon and she was
hoping to bump into him. As soon as they got through the gates,
she was going to leave Ivan to it and head towards the security
office. As Belinda was on the board, she also wanted to catch up
with Estelle and go over the plans for one or two developments.

'The zoo is just up ahead,' Belinda said, indicating left. 'If
you really want to talk, we can do it later this evening.' She
slowed at the top of the approach lane of the staff entrance, her
attention drawn to a group of people fifty yards or so further
along the road.

The security guard, a man in his mid-fifties, moved his
weather-worn face so that it was level with hers. 'Hello,
Belinda.'

'Hello, Stan,' she said. 'Good to see you. We've an appointment with Estelle Samuels.' Her words were wasted as he had
already opened the huge black metal gates remotely and made
to step back. She had known Stan Whiting for years; he often
carried out security work at Little Challham castle when large
events were held there. Getting into a conversation with him
was fairly difficult. Even though she was aware that the odds
were against her, she tried.

'What are those people doing outside the main entrance?'
she asked.

Stan glanced towards the trees lining the bank on the other
side of the road, showing very little interest. 'They're
protesting.'

'About the zoo?' said Belinda.

The security guard scratched his head. 'Not exactly.
They've been here for the last few days on and off. They're
protesting about the animals in the zoo – the elephants, to be
exact.' He shook his head in disbelief, as if the elephants had

brought shame on everyone for something as un-British as attracting attention.

'*My* elephants?' said Ivan, stretching across to speak to Stan through the window.

'If you say so,' said Stan. He moved back a couple of feet, presumably to indicate that the conversation – short as it was – was not about to be prolonged.

With a wave at Stan, Belinda drove forward, barely reaching the other side of the gate before it started to close behind her. 'We'll find out more about the protestors and exactly what their issues are with the elephants from Estelle.' She stopped herself from calling them 'your' elephants. Ivan hadn't even got inside the grounds yet. Claiming ownership seemed to be jumping the gun a touch. Still, she didn't want to dampen his enthusiasm.

'You've been here before?' said Ivan as Belinda followed the road as it dipped down towards the back of the large modern offices and overnight staff accommodation huts, turning left into an almost hidden driveway.

'Yes, quite a few times,' she said, pulling into a space marked 'Reserved'. 'I've dropped by to see Estelle and a couple of the other board members over the years. She truly is inspirational. Her vision for this place is quite remarkable. It's really no problem to drive you here.'

This part she meant, although she could have done with longer to get her head around the fact that he was actually here, sitting in her passenger seat, breathing the same air.

'Anyway,' said Ivan. 'I'm grateful to you.'

With a smile and a total avoidance of eye contact, she opened the car door.

'I want to show you something,' said Ivan, putting a hand out to touch her shoulder, making her freeze in her seat.

'If it's the view across to the marsh, I've already seen it.'

'It's partly the view,' said Ivan. 'I asked Estelle not to

mention my involvement to you at all. I thought that if you knew, you might refuse to have anything to do with the zoo. I couldn't let that happen. She's too passionate about it and I know you are too.' He took a deep breath and continued. 'I wanted to make up for what I did – not that I ever expect you to forgive me, but see over there?' He took his hand from her shoulder and pointed. 'I'm going to advise Estelle on building a grand giraffe lodge for visitors to come and have breakfast on the top floor while the giraffes wander over and join the guests. Well, their heads will come through the open windows, not all of them, obviously. How amazing will that be?'

Belinda closed her eyes as he spoke quietly and passionately about a project that genuinely interested her. Not to mention, if he was going to be advising, did that mean he would be around for some time to come? She wasn't sure how she felt about that.

'Yes, it certainly would be astounding,' she replied in hushed tones.

'I'll never forgive myself for what I did to you,' said Ivan. 'That's the real reason I'm here: things ended so abruptly and I went into a new relationship with my eyes wide shut. I've known for a while that I was with the wrong person, when all along it should have been you. As awful as it was for Tanya, I broke off my engagement. I couldn't simply let you go without telling you how I still feel.'

Belinda felt as if her heart was racing. There had been a point when nothing would have made her happier than to spend the rest of her days with Ivan. Right at this moment, she couldn't think straight. She tried to steady her heart rate, not show how petrified she felt at what he was saying. Before she had a chance to answer, a figure appeared at the door beside her, dragging her back to the Kent countryside from her thoughts of a lost existence living in an African private game reserve with Ivan.

'Estelle,' she said, jumping out of the Land Rover and

greeting the zoo owner. 'Lovely to see you again, and you look, well... different. But stylish.'

Belinda stood back to admire the suit the younger woman was wearing, something she had never seen her in before, but had to admit, made her quite formidable. She watched Estelle's gaze move across to where Ivan now stood, having climbed out of the car, watching the two of them. The man knew how to track and hunt animals, so it shouldn't come as a surprise to her that keeping an eye on two women as well as surveying the landscape wasn't beyond his abilities.

'Hello, Belinda,' said Estelle, 'and hello to you, too, Ivan. It's a pleasure to actually meet you after all the calls.'

Belinda couldn't help noticing that Estelle was paying a lot of attention to Ivan. It wasn't jealousy she was feeling – which was a relief – but more intrigue. She had known Estelle for around eight years since their paths had crossed at a fundraising event, and what with Belinda's weakness for anything animal orientated and Estelle's passion for rescuing unwanted creatures, they had developed an acquaintance that didn't quite stretch to friendship, though they were more than colleagues.

'And you, too,' said Ivan, rushing around the Land Rover to grasp Estelle's hand in both of his. 'I can hardly believe I'm here. Thank you for asking me for my help.'

'First things first,' said Estelle. 'Let's get over to the office and I'll talk you through the developments with the protestors.'

'Yes, we saw them from the staff entrance,' said Belinda. 'What exactly are they protesting about? Surely it's a good thing that the elephants are being returned to Africa?'

Estelle stepped towards the small row of office buildings. Belinda walked a couple of feet behind them, running an eye over the fifty or so other parked cars. Harry's Audi was at one of the furthest points along the tarmacked area, neatly reversed into a space. She desperately wanted to ask Estelle how her friend's interview had gone. As Belinda had already put in an extremely good word for him, she expected nothing other than a very successful outcome. Harry didn't know Belinda had smoothed the way for his potential change of career. And if she had anything to do with it, he never would.

Belinda and Ivan followed Estelle into a large spacious office. The room was furnished with a desk against the far wall and a grey corner sofa with enough space for six people. Directly facing the double doors was a large television screen, currently switched off.

'Please take a seat,' said Estelle, indicating the sofa, and moved across to a coffee machine on a low table beside the desk. 'Coffee?' she asked and on receiving nods, she set about making their drinks.

As she did so, Estelle filled them in on the protesters. 'You both know that we've spent a long time studying the best thing for our herd of twelve? Plus we've had a lot of help from Ivan who's smoothed the way with the relevant wildlife services and wildlife trusts.' She carried two cups to her guests and placed them on the coffee table before making her own.

'And the protestors don't want to see the elephants leave the park?' said Belinda.

'If only it were that simple,' said Estelle with a sad smile. 'There are currently two groups of protestors at the gates: one that want the elephants released into their natural habitat, and one that want them to stay here in the zoo.'

'That sounds a little strange,' said Belinda. 'Why would they be objecting to their return to Africa? Surely they're better off in the wild than here in Kent?'

'That's not how some of them view it,' said Estelle, picking up her cup and gazing at the contents. 'That particular group have convinced themselves that the elephants will die in the wild, and I'm worried about what they'll do to make sure the animals stay here. And then, I'm driving myself insane over what the rival faction will do to ensure the herd gets rewilded.

There seems to be a deep-rooted belief amongst that gang that *all* animals should be returned to the wild and all zoos closed down permanently. Some of them are so radical that they would literally do anything to get what they want.

'If I'm being honest with you, I also can't rule out a few of them being troublemakers who would pick any cause at all – good or bad – to give themselves a cause to fight. Another reason we have to step up the security.'

'I'm sure some of the protestors have well-founded beliefs about the animals,' said Belinda, with more tact than she was feeling. 'What exactly are their objections?'

'The group who want them to stay claim that animals raised in captivity stand no chance on their own in the wild, when, of course, the evidence says otherwise,' said Estelle. She gave a nervous laugh and added, 'Not to mention people expect to see elephants in an African Savannah Safari Experience.'

'If I've got this right,' said Ivan, pitching forward on his seat, 'they're objecting to animals being released on the grounds that they want to go on an African Savannah Safari Experience and see animals kept in captivity?'

'Er, yes,' said Estelle. 'Baffling, isn't it? That's why I could do with as much help as I can get to ensure the swift but safe passage of the elephants. The increase in security is coming just in time.'

It was Belinda's turn to perch on the edge of her seat. 'I have to admit, I was expecting that your security staff deal with the odd bit of shoplifting, reuniting lost children with their parents and perhaps on a very bad day, a touch of pickpocketing. This is more than I anticipated.'

'As you know, Belinda, there are eleven other board members, with myself as Chair of the Trustees, and every single one of them wants to step up security,' said Estelle with a look that Belinda couldn't interpret. 'The only problem has been getting everyone to vote for more funding to do so. There's been pressure to expand the board – fresh blood, as it were – but I'm not convinced that's the answer.'

'Although you are taking on more staff?' said Belinda, now concerned that Harry had applied for a job that didn't exist.

'Oh, yes.' Estelle smiled. 'I've moved some money around, robbed Peter to pay Paul, that sort of thing. It's far from ideal but with Ivan's help here, I think we can bring in many other streams of revenue, not just from the African Savannah Safari Experience. Talking of which, Robert Piper, our head of security, should have finished the last interview. We'll soon find out who's got the job.'

Belinda had a sinking feeling that her glowing recommendation of Harry might have been a mistake.

'We need someone with a vast array of skills,' said Estelle. 'I hate to say it, but the protestors have been getting more and more vocal. The last day or so has seen a fairly charged atmosphere out there. Now, before I get called back to the gate again, how about a tour?'

Ivan jumped out of his seat, keen to see the sights. Belinda was a tad slower in rising to her feet, still getting her head around the idea that she might have talked her dear friend Harry into one of the toughest workplaces in the county.

4

Harry thought that the interview had gone reasonably well. He had answered all the questions with an ease that either meant he was self-assured to the point of arrogance, or they were ridiculously easy. It seemed that no matter what he said, the person interviewing him was paying little attention.

The five-foot-ten white man, aged forty or so, who introduced himself as Robert 'you can call me Rob' Piper when Harry had knocked on the door of the security office, seemed unperturbed by the shouting and earlier drama. He had ushered Harry inside, rubbed his hands together and started with, 'So, tell me about yourself and why you want this job?'

Harry had trotted out his well-practised answer and sat eagerly expecting the next question but he had very much got the impression that Rob was going through the motions. The last thing Harry had expected after fifteen minutes was for Rob to stand up, shake his hand and then offer him the position as deputy head of security.

'I don't know what to say,' said Harry, standing awkwardly, his head alarmingly close to the low ceiling.

'I'm hoping you'll say, "Yes," followed by, "When can I start?"' said Rob.

'Yes,' said Harry. 'When can I start?'

In response, Rob walked over to a bank of CCTV screens that Harry had been unable to see from where he had been sitting during the interview. Curiosity got the better of him now and he followed Rob, watching as he pointed to the screen on the top left-hand side. 'I see that Drew Matterson is having a bit of an altercation with a customer over by our Lemur Life Experience. How about you show us that Harry Powell magic I've heard so much about and see if you can help out? If your reputation is anything to go by, you'll manage our expanding team, help the elephants on their way to Africa, oversee any of the intricacies of animal and guest safety right here and be home in time for tea and medals.' Rob gave him an expectant smile.

'I – well, I...'

'Out the door, across the car park, straight down the path and it's the first large enclosure you come to on the left,' said Rob, rushing across to open the door for Harry. 'Then you can come back and let me know how it went while I sort out the paperwork and a security pass for you. See you soon.'

Before Harry knew what had happened, he was back outside in the weak afternoon sunshine, heading towards the primates to sort out a row. He hoped his animal knowledge wasn't about to be tested. He wasn't really sure what a lemur was, let alone what the problem might actually relate to. As Harry strode along, members of staff walking past him, a crowd of school children in the distance, he wondered if this was Rob's idea of in-house training. Surely there should be some formalities before he was thrown in at the deep end.

Harry knew he was getting close when he heard raised voices, one telling the other to 'Just calm down now, sir.' He rounded the corner to see two men, one wearing a Brabourne Gardens security tabard and holding a walkie-talkie in one hand. His other hand was open-palmed, perfectly executing the 'keep your voice down' gesture. A few people wandered past them, their attention drawn to the scene, but not interested enough to stop and listen or referee.

'Hello, gents,' said Harry. The two men were within striking distance of one another, which made him uneasy. 'Can I help in any way?'

Both of them paused and turned to look at him. Drew's face was a picture of surprise – something that Harry liked to see in his colleagues – while the features of the other party displayed pure annoyance.

'Help?' the other man said, turning his attention to Harry. 'Help? I'll give you help! I've been coming here for years, ever since this place went from a formal garden to somewhere that unwanted exotic pets were taken in, to a fully functional zoo.' He stepped towards Harry, his index finger extended and point mode fully deployed. 'And what do I get for my unerring support? I'll tell you what I get – chuff all respect, that's what!'

Even though the angry customer was a good eight or so inches shorter than Harry, he still tried his best to meet his eye, never blinking, never looking away. Harry, meanwhile, was wondering when and how zoos had become so toxic.

'Respect!' said Drew. 'Tell me why you think that us changing the feeding times of the lemurs without the zoo staff personally informing you is, in any way, a lack of respect.'

'Hang on,' said Harry, positioning himself between the two of them. 'You're arguing about the feeding times of the animals?' He had heard some very weird things in his time but he had never thought he'd see the day when two grown men were about to kick off over so trivial a matter as this.

'We pride ourselves on customer care,' said Drew. 'Only on this occasion, we had to change the time because one of our keepers has called in sick. Some of the crew are on double shifts and the schedule had to be changed. It really is nothing personal.'

'That's all very well—' said the extremely red-faced customer.

'So, tell me, Mr...?' said Harry.

'Carter, Simon Carter,' said Simon, making eye contact with Harry and appearing to take deep breaths.

'Mr Carter, what time was the lemur feeding supposed to be?' said Harry.

'It was scheduled for 1 p.m. and it was moved to 2 p.m.,' he said, narrowing his eyes.

Harry glanced at his watch. 'It's coming up to three o'clock now. By how long did you miss it?'

'I didn't miss it,' said Simon. 'I was here.'

Drew sighed and crossed his arms.

'I'm confused,' said Harry, running a hand across his face. 'You thought it was an hour earlier than it was – so if you'd been here at 1 p.m., you would have seen the sign moving it back an hour – yet you were here at the rescheduled time, and managed to see them getting fed?'

'Yes,' said Simon. 'It's not on.'

'Sir,' said Drew, palms still open in a non-aggressive stance that pleased Harry, 'what exactly is the problem?'

'Don't take that tone with me, young man,' said Simon. 'I'm a customer.'

Drew's hands were now more jazz hands than placatory at this stage.

'Where do we record official complaints?' said Harry to Drew.

'If Mr Carter comes with me to the—'

'I don't want to put in a complaint,' said Simon. 'The last six I lodged got me nowhere.'

'Then what do you want to do?' said Harry, thinking that selling dog food really wasn't all that bad after all.

'I want to let you know that I'm displeased, that's all,' said Simon, waving his annual pass at them both. 'VIP Priority Pass' was written along its entire length. 'I come here at least twice a week, buying your snacks and paying for raffle tickets. I've even started a JustGiving page for the orphaned giant anteaters, but does anyone bother to tell me when the timetable changes? Of course not. Now I'm off to see the penguins and I expect them to perform.'

With that, he turned on his heel and strolled off as if there was nothing out of the ordinary.

'Er... by the way,' said Harry, 'pleasure to meet you. I'm Harry Powell and I've just been appointed deputy head of security.'

They shook hands, Drew's face brightening. 'I can't begin to tell you how grateful I am that you're here. Someone needs to take the reins and start banning customers like Mr Carter.'

Harry glanced towards Simon's retreating back and said, 'That was a bit odd: he was complaining about missing something that he clearly didn't miss. I'm not sure I followed what just happened.'

'We get that a lot here. People whinging and not really knowing what the problem is. He's a particular challenge, that one. He was talking to the protestors outside the gate yesterday, so who knows what he was telling them. He's already tried to sue us once for selling anatomically incorrect orangutans in the gift shop. Apparently, their legs should be roughly the same length as their arms, and well, they're stuffed toys, so they aren't.'

'If he supports the zoo so much, why would he want to sue?' said Harry.

'He told me that he wanted to make a point,' said Drew, with a sigh. 'He wanted to sue and then donate the money and buy himself a place on the board.'

'That's one of the most ridiculous things I've ever heard,'

said Harry, scratching at his temple. 'Other than what he was suing over in the first place.'

'I'd love to be on the board,' said Drew, his eyes suddenly shining as if a light had been switched on. 'I have so many ideas about how to improve the place. That would be a dream come true.'

'One day, perhaps,' said Harry, pleased that at least one member of the team seemed to have ambition.

'Anyway, I suppose I should call up the penguins and let them know Simon's on his way – obviously not the actual penguins, that would be daft.' Drew chuckled at himself.

For a moment, Harry stood beside the Lemur Life Experience, a couple of cute big-eyed primates peering at him through the glass. He wondered what on earth this place was hiding beneath the family-friendly veneer and overpriced concession stands.

'When did you start work?' said Drew, bringing Harry back from considering why lemurs had evolved to look as if they had heavily made-up eyes. Exactly who were they trying to attract from the branches of a Madagascan tree? He knew that was where they came from as he'd watched the film. By film, he meant cartoon. No one seemed to be demonstrating outside the gates in aid of their repatriation, so perhaps they were just *too* cute.

'About fifteen minutes ago,' said Harry. 'I haven't even looked around properly yet.'

'Come on,' said Drew, 'we can walk over to the Safari Experience and I'll show you around. We can start with the lion enclosure. They're amongst our most popular animals, you won't be surprised to hear. It's a wonderful space for them, only don't be too disappointed if they aren't there. They should be getting checked by the vet, provided *that* schedule hasn't changed too. Their enclosure was designed with the animals on a lower level with several viewing platforms, and the first one we come to gives you one of the best views.'

As they strolled amiably along, Harry listened intently to Drew and his enthusiasm for the gardens and zoo.

A hundred feet or so from the lion enclosure, Harry saw a face in the crowd that jolted him. He thought he'd glimpsed a woman who looked remarkably like Belinda. He found himself edging through groups of people and elbowing his way amongst families. Only vaguely aware that Drew was struggling to keep up with him, Harry raced along the footpath that promised to take all and sundry to see the kings of the jungle. The woman seemed to be with a tall dark-haired man, so he knew it wasn't likely to be Belinda. If she were at the zoo, she would surely have told him. Today of all days, she would be here to wish him luck.

Two things happened at once: a gap in the throng meant that he saw her face clearly and realised it *was* Belinda, and a piercing scream went up from further along the path. There had only been a handful of people standing between him and Belinda but now many more flocked to the fence and leaned over, pointing open-mouthed at what was below.

'There's a child in with the lions!' shouted a man.

'It's a boy. He's fallen in,' said a woman, her hand to her forehead. 'Someone do something.'

Just as Harry was about to act – which in all honesty, really amounted to peering over the barrier with the rest of the crowd – the tall dark stranger who had been walking alongside Belinda suddenly put his hand on the rail and vaulted over the top.

With a morbid fascination, Harry watched as he landed hard on the floor amongst the bushes, only a few feet from the angry-looking lion.

5

'Oh, good grief,' said Belinda, clutching onto the rail with one hand and Harry's arm with the other. 'It's Ivan! He's jumped in to save that boy.'

'Oh, it's Ivan,' said Harry, trying not to sound in awe, but falling short. He was only too aware that he had witnessed one of the bravest things he was ever likely to see. He watched as Ivan stood slowly, only a pounce away from the lion. 'Does he know what to do?'

'Yes,' said Belinda, though her panic was obvious in that one word. 'As long as the lion feels intimidated enough, it probably won't charge. If it does attack, this won't end well.'

Harry didn't want to take his eyes off the horror unfolding thirty feet below him, but knew he had to look for Drew and get him to call for help. He frantically looked round, aware that the crowd had swelled, most of them videoing the sight rather than doing anything useful. One woman was frantically talking into her phone, alerting the emergency services that a child was about to get eaten by a lion, assuring the call handler that it wasn't some sort of hoax. The near-hysterical man being pulled away from the railings was probably the boy's father.

Drew's head appeared between two worried, yet intrigued faces in the growing masses around the enclosure. He waved at Harry, gave him a thumbs-up gesture and spoke excitedly into his radio, presumably telling the rest of the security team to summon the police.

Harry turned his attention back to the lion, Ivan and the small white-faced boy curled into a ball cradling his left arm. Ivan stood tall, waving his arms and shouting. The king of the jungle glared at him but mercifully remained lying down. Ivan called out to the boy, 'Get up, son, come and stand beside me.'

'The boy has to stand up,' said Belinda, the start of a wail to her tone. 'He can't stay on the ground and Ivan won't want to risk bending down to get him.'

'I can see a few of the keepers down there,' said Harry, pointing towards the metal doors to the rear of the enclosure. 'They're unlocking the outer door.'

Belinda tore her gaze from the spectacle below to the metal cage that two of the keepers had just locked themselves into. 'I can't stand it. If Ivan can't get them out of there, they'll have to shoot the lion.'

He could feel her fingers pinching his lower arm. 'Ivan has the boy on his feet,' said Harry. Ivan's shouts and waves at the lion were doing little to make it back off, but it hadn't got up either.

Ivan was leading the young trembling boy to the cage; the keepers had the inner gate unlocked and the one with the rifle had stepped inside the enclosure. She was calling something that Harry couldn't make out, but he heard Ivan call back. He was dragging the young boy by his good arm towards the keepers.

The entire crowd went silent as the lion slowly got to its feet, watching Ivan's every move. Harry's heart was in his mouth, Belinda's fingernails in his flesh.

They were still fifteen feet from the cage. The armed

keeper lifted the rifle and aimed. Harry heard a gasp and realised it was around one hundred bystanders who had been holding their collective breath. In one move, Ivan swung the child over his shoulder and stepped backward so that the keeper's aim was unhindered. He continued to edge slowly and carefully towards the safety of the cage.

Harry watched the keeper as her finger started to release the trigger. Then the lion yawned and sat down again. One hundred people said, 'Oooh,' in anticipation of a happy ending. Ivan was through the inner door, the boy was sobbing and the markswoman had made it back to within grabbing distance of the cage.

As she stepped back inside, the door was slammed shut by her colleague, and the crowd cheered and whooped. The lion looked up at the throng with indifference and rolled onto his side.

'I thought he was going to die,' said Belinda, at last releasing Harry's arm and dabbing at her eyes with a tissue. 'I really couldn't have stood it if he'd been attacked by the lion.'

'I don't think it would have been much of a result for the lion, either,' said Harry, rubbing his arm to get the circulation going again. Even though he was still wearing his jacket, Belinda had a pinch like a vice.

'Here he comes,' said Belinda, pushing past Harry to get to Ivan, which made Harry sad, followed by feeling guilty that he was being so daft. Ivan's actions had been truly heroic.

Harry turned to watch Belinda work her way towards Ivan. Behind him, the young boy was being hugged by his father while first-aiders tried to check the lad over for injuries. Harry's height meant he had a clear view as his friend ran the last few feet to Ivan and wrapped her arms around his broad shoulders. Belinda was looking straight into Ivan's extremely blue eyes. Eyes that, Harry couldn't help but notice, softened as he returned the embrace.

Not wanting to appear ungrateful that someone had just saved the day – not to mention the child and the lion – within minutes of Harry being appointed to the security team, he picked his way through to them.

As he got closer, Harry looked round to see if Drew was still nearby. He seemed to have made a hasty exit, security protocol undoubtedly meaning that he had called the police. Harry thought about following up but saw little point in doing so when Drew would be taking care of it. Instead, he concentrated on appearing warm and welcoming to the man hugging Belinda.

Harry stood in front of them, weirdly and uncharacteristically nervous.

'Are you OK?' said Ivan, placing a light but firm hand on Harry's shoulder. 'You look a bit on the pale side.'

Harry turned his attention towards Ivan, noticing his hairline was receding and it was shaved at the sides. He was sporting a very neat beard which gave him a casual jungle look. He wasn't sure whether to admire or hate the good-looking, brave South African.

'I'm doing fine,' said Harry, worried that it should have been *him* asking after Ivan. 'That was really something.'

'Bit of a strange thing to find myself doing today of all days,' said Ivan, frown lines rumpling his forehead – one that Harry couldn't fail to notice was large enough to project a film on.

'Harry,' said Belinda, 'I'm sorry to have to introduce you under these circumstances, but this is Ivan. Ivan, this is Harry, a dear friend of mine.'

Few things could have prompted Harry to push his chest out and swell with as much pride as those few words. He could have kissed her. The thought made him look down at his feet and he felt a blush appear on his face.

'Wonderful to meet you, Harry,' said Ivan, holding out his hand. 'It's great to know that Belinda has such great people around her.'

'Likewise,' said Harry as he grasped Ivan's hand in his.

One thing he did know was that no matter what came his way, he wasn't ever likely to impress Belinda as much as Ivan had by taking on a lion.

6

Belinda watched Harry and Ivan shake hands and felt slightly queasy. Her feelings didn't make sense – unless, of course, you considered that this was the former love of her life face to face with someone who could be the most important person she had ever known.

'We should really go and see Estelle Samuels and Robert Piper,' said Ivan, his blue eyes twinkling as he switched his gaze from Harry to Belinda. 'We can tell them all about Harry here and what a perfect match he'd be for the job.'

Ivan turned back to Harry and said, 'I hope you don't mind that Marcus told me all about the job you were going for here today. You strike me as the perfect person to be the deputy head of security.'

'You're so kind,' said Harry with a slightly modest smile. 'But good news – I've already got the job.' He winked at Belinda and for a second she wondered if he had any idea that she had already put in a good word. That was surely impossible. He was more likely to be annoyed at her interference than pleased. As long as he didn't find out, it really wouldn't matter.

'Congratulations, old man,' said Ivan, giving Harry a hearty slap on the back. 'Isn't it great, Bel?'

'That's amazing, Harry,' she said, moving forward and giving him a peck on the cheek, aware that she was being watched by Ivan. 'We'll celebrate properly tonight.'

'It's a date,' said Ivan, cajoling Harry in the direction of the security office. 'Let's find Estelle and Rob and you can tell us how it went, can't he, Bel?'

'Of course,' she said, falling into step beside them as they walked away from her, side by side like two old friends chewing the fat. 'It's all right, I'm coming. Honestly, don't wait!'

Belinda glanced around at the retreating crowd and hoped that the young boy was over his horrendous ordeal and that he and his father were being suitably cared for. Exactly how the child had managed to fall into the enclosure was going to cause enormous headaches for the zoo, not to mention give the protestors something else to protest about. This was bad publicity they truly did not need.

Before setting off after the two men, she scanned the crowd to see who else from the security team was around. The least she expected was to see the place crawling with security, but their presence was a touch thin on the ground.

She walked on regardless, keen not to lose sight of Harry and Ivan. She wanted to hear what they were talking about, especially if it happened to be about her. Then she heard a woman saying to the man beside her, 'I'm sure that boy said that he was pushed. He must have been mistaken.'

Feeling the hairs on the back of her neck stand up, Belinda turned on the spot to see who had just made such a worrying comment. But they had been swallowed up by the crowd.

Slightly perturbed that the two men hadn't waited for her, she set off at a pace to catch up with them. When she did, she was relieved to hear Harry say, 'I'm not sure what swung it for me during the interview, but Rob told me straight away that the job was mine.'

'When do you start?' she said, drawing level with him.

'It seems that I already have,' said Harry, moving to make room for a family with a pushchair to get by. 'I suppose that officially it's as soon as I get given the fetching uniform and a radio. A little training wouldn't go amiss.'

By now, they had reached the top of the tree-lined path back to the staff car park and the security office. The sky had begun to cloud over and the temperature had dropped considerably. Belinda shivered.

'Do you want to head inside?' said Harry. 'I think that Rob's probably in his office where I left him and it was definitely warmer in there.'

'No, I'm fine,' she said. 'I'll grab my jacket from the car if I need it. There's something much more important to take care of. I tried to catch up with you, but you'd rushed off ahead. A woman went past me in the crowd and I heard her say that the boy claimed someone pushed him.'

'Crikey,' said Harry. 'Was she talking about the boy in the lion enclosure?'

'Well, I'm not entirely sure,' said Belinda, tucking a strand of hair behind her ear. 'I'm assuming that she was.'

'Where's she gone now?' said Ivan.

'I – er... she went past me, and in all honesty, I couldn't tell you if she was young or old, tall or short or even the colour of her skin,' said Belinda, feeling slightly dejected.

'Look, don't worry,' said Harry. 'The police will be here soon. They'll ask witnesses to leave details on their way out and besides, someone will speak to the lad and find out what happened. I'll check with Rob that the police are aware if it puts your mind at ease.'

'Should we leave you to it if you're technically working?'

said Belinda. 'I don't think that any of us thought your first day would involve so much horror.'

Harry put a hand up to scratch at the advancing stubble on his chin. 'I expect Rob'll need to run through stuff with me, even if it's only when I need to be back here to officially start.'

'I'm sure he'll be only too pleased to have you get stuck right in,' said Ivan. 'If you two don't mind, I think I'll go and see if I can have a word with that keeper with the gun. I'd like to run over how many trained marksmen and women they have here and how often they deploy their firearms, that sort of thing.'

'Sounds interesting,' said Belinda. 'I'll meet you back at the Land Rover in an hour.' She was talking to Ivan's back as he waved over at her and all but jogged back down the path.

'Congratulations again on the new job,' said Belinda. 'If you have time, we could go for a celebratory coffee or something now rather than wait until tonight's festivities.'

Harry glanced over at the security office, giving the matter more thought than she would have liked. She had a sinking feeling that Ivan's appearance had knocked Harry for six. 'I'd love to, but I'm really not sure what I'm supposed to be doing. I tell you what, how about I have a quick word with Rob and then come and meet you somewhere?'

As Belinda was about to answer him, she was distracted by the office door opening. 'Someone's coming,' she said, indicating behind Harry.

Harry turned and waved at the man, who appeared a little flustered.

'Harry, there you are,' he said, stern expression set hard. 'I was coming to congratulate you on dealing with your first crisis but then saw the business with Gerald the lion. Good grief, what's this place coming to when small children fall over the rails and have to be rescued by the guests? The lion wasn't even supposed to be in there. He should have been with the vet. Can't anyone stick to a timetable around here?'

'Hi again, Rob,' said Harry. 'This is my friend Belinda. She's here with Ivan, the man who got between the lion and the young boy.'

'Yes, hello, Belinda,' he said with a curt nod. 'How are you? Good to see you again.'

'Oh, I wasn't aware that you two had—'

'Met. Yes. A fair few times,' said Rob, his attention clearly now waning. 'Belinda often meets here with Estelle to talk all things funding and finance. I need to get down there and see what's what, so if you'll both excuse me.'

'Rob, I'm not so convinced it was an accident,' said Belinda. Rob froze, his face a mask of disbelief. 'I overheard a woman say that the boy thought he'd been pushed.'

'This is horrific,' said Rob. His mouth hung open for a second or two before he added, 'This will get us shut down. We really can't take any more bad publicity. We're on the brink of disaster with so little money to go round and less and less coming in from sponsorships and donations, and this zoo is my life.'

Rob stood stock still, staring in the direction of the lion enclosure until Harry said, 'I'll come with you and you can fill me in. The least I can do is help you keep the place up and running with no more incidents like that one.'

For a moment, Rob peered at Belinda. With a lurch, she thought that he might be about to tell Harry that it was mostly her doing that he had the job in the first place.

'If we both walk with you,' she said, smiling, 'then you can tell Harry what it was exactly that made you decide that he was the right person for the job.' Without waiting for an answer, she moved towards the footpath, Harry and Rob closely behind her.

'He was unreservedly the right man for the job,' said Rob. 'I can't think of anyone with better credentials. We all agreed.'

With a sinking feeling, Belinda heard Harry's size tens come to a stop on the gravel.

'We all agreed,' repeated Harry.

'Figure of speech,' mumbled Rob. 'We – er... went through the applications long before we invited you in.'

Momentarily, Belinda felt relief that she could continue to hide the truth from Harry. But sooner or later he would find out. Besides, hiding the fact that she'd already pitched him for the job would only make her appear underhand. If Ivan showing up hadn't messed up any chance she had with Harry, this would be the final straw.

Content that she could now leave them to it, she said, 'I'll go and find myself a coffee shop and wait for you and Ivan to find me.'

Rob pointed through a gap in the evergreen bushes on their right-hand side. 'Over there – a little way past the brown bear enclosure – is the best coffee spot. Not all of the concession stands have the full remit of syrup shots and other goodies, but that's my favourite. After what's happened, the police won't hang around closing them all and emptying the zoo, so you'd better be quick with your order.'

'This one's closer,' said Belinda, indicating a more modest open-sided silver truck. Half a dozen bistro tables and chairs were dotted nearby, only two of them occupied and no queue at the counter. 'I'll grab a drink here and perhaps even take a look at the bears when I've finished. I see that the walkway starts over there past that viewing platform.'

Rob paused with his hands on his hips. 'You may see one of the four bears we have here. An entire family was rescued from another zoo that was about to close. Some of the work that goes on here is truly remarkable. As I've said, this place is my life. Anyway, mustn't dawdle.'

In half a mind to skip the coffee and see whether she could spot a bear, Belinda noticed that a crowd was forming on the viewing platform overlooking the enclosure. The platform was around forty feet high and unlike the lion enclosure, was set back a distance from the animals' habitat. The inside of the enclosure had enough of a drop to ensure that the bears weren't able to climb their way out and fences were kept to a minimum. Belinda knew it was all part of Estelle's vision for a better environment for the animals.

Just as she was about to make her decision, for the second time that day, a piercing scream went out. For a terrible moment, Belinda thought that someone had tumbled inside the brown bears' domain, probably spelling the end of Brabourne Gardens.

But the hullabaloo appeared to be coming from a hysterical woman standing between a large metal hay container and an electric buggy.

The woman was in her early forties, plump, with mousy blond hair bursting free from a baseball cap emblazoned with the logo Coffee Perks. Her legs were trembling so much, it looked as if she were jogging on the spot. Her eyes were wide open and staring behind the buggy.

Wasting no time, Belinda ran across to the barista.

Belinda reached the buggy and looked down to see the body of a man on the ground, an African Savannah Safari Experience bandana tied tight around his neck and his lifeless bulging eyes staring skyward.

7

Harry raced across to join Belinda. He could see from her demeanour that whatever she was peering at was not an everyday occurrence. Certainly, the distraught woman beside Belinda looked as though she were about to go into shock.

By the time Harry had covered the short distance, Belinda had moved herself between Susan, according to her name badge, and the corpse.

It didn't take long for Harry to recognise who was lying on the ground, having made his last complaint about the zoo – Simon Carter. His pass was still attached to the lanyard around his neck, which interestingly to Harry, hadn't been used by the killer to strangle him.

'Cheap material, I guess,' Harry muttered to himself as he kneeled down next to Simon.

'Oh, good grief,' said Drew, his Reebok trainers coming to an abrupt stop beside Harry, followed closely by Ivan's all-weather lion-challenging, crocodile-wrestling, hyena-kickboxing footwear. Harry returned his attention to the dead body and reminded himself not to be so petty.

'You're security, aren't you?' said Belinda. She had one arm around Susan and was trying to move her backwards. Her question was aimed at Drew, who looked at her, somewhat startled.

'Er, yes, yes, I am.' He automatically took his walkie-talkie out and waved it at her.

'Splendid,' she said. 'How about you get on that thing, summon help and escort Susan here away to, say, those empty seats over there?'

Drew stared at her.

'Provided, of course,' said Belinda, 'that you're feeling quite up to it? I expect that getting the police here right now would be extremely useful.'

'Right away, ma'am,' said Drew, frantically pushing the button on his walkie-talkie to get help and leading Susan away at the same time. Harry noticed Drew glance back a couple of times at Simon's body. He wasn't sure whether the young man's face showed relief, intrigue or revulsion at the sight of the previously troublesome customer's mouth hanging open and his tongue lolling to one side. Simon's face made it clear to Harry that he was dead but still he checked for a pulse. When he found none, he got back to his feet and stood beside Ivan and Belinda, looking down at the body.

Without warning, Ivan put an arm out and tried to draw Belinda to him, which took Harry by surprise and clearly annoyed her.

'What are you doing?' she said, pulling in the opposite direction.

'I was making sure you're OK,' he said, puzzlement running all over his face.

He really has got a massive forehead, thought Harry. 'Let's concentrate on poor Simon here, and not lose our focus,' he said, immediately distracted by Belinda stepping away from Ivan.

'How long do you think he's been here?' said Belinda, her arms folded, concern on her face and a sombre tone to her voice.

'I spoke to him only about forty or fifty minutes ago,' said

Harry. 'I'd been speaking to him and Drew after he created some fuss about the lemurs' feeding times. The last we saw of him, he was stomping off towards the Penguin Palace.'

'So, why did he end up here?' said Ivan, glancing to where Drew and Susan sat a few feet away, the young man consoling her.

'I've no idea,' said Harry. 'Often, the obvious suspect is the person who found the body.'

'Then that would more often than not be you or Ms Penshurst,' said a voice behind Harry.

'Vince Green!' said Belinda to the police officer who had appeared seemingly from nowhere. 'How wonderful to see you again, and this time you're back in your police uniform. Didn't CID work out for you?'

Harry moved out of the way to allow the PC to step towards Simon's body and crouch down to check for signs of life. 'The paramedics are on their way,' said Vince, avoiding Belinda's question. 'Has anyone else touched him or moved him?'

'He did,' said Ivan, pointing at Harry.

Harry added 'grass' alongside 'massive forehead' to his mental list of things to dislike about Ivan. 'Yes, I've already checked for a pulse, Vince.'

'I wouldn't have expected anything less of you, Harry,' said Vince. 'Sadly, he's gone. Let's move back and I'll get one of my colleagues to set up a cordon.'

Keen to do anything she could to help, Belinda stepped away, taking Ivan with her. Vince directed the other officers as to where they should attach their blue-and-white police tape, to preserve the evidence and give Simon Carter as much dignity as possible.

'Care to tell me what happened?' said Vince.

Harry thumbed in the direction of Simon's body. 'I've just been appointed Deputy Head of the Security Team.'

'They may well sack you after this,' said Ivan. 'It must be a world record.'

'Thank you, Ivan,' said Belinda.

'And sorry, who are you?' said Vince, pocket notebook at the ready.

'Ivan Brenner. I'm a friend of Belinda's, visiting from South Africa. Belinda and I used to run a reserve in South Africa. We protected wildlife, kept poachers at bay and created a safe haven for the animals. Created breeding programmes and ensured the survival of rare and endangered species too. It was something we were both extremely passionate about.'

Harry watched Vince eye him suspiciously and then glance at Belinda before returning his attention back to Harry. Vince nodded a 'go on' at Harry.

'As I was saying, I got a job on security an hour ago,' said Harry. 'My new boss Rob Piper said that one of the customers appeared to be arguing with Drew Matterson – that's Drew over there with Susan who found the body – and that I should get off to the Lemur Life Experience to handle it. Drew was in the midst of a heated debate with Simon Carter – the poor unfortunate who appears to have been strangled with a bandana.'

'So, they were arguing,' said Vince, scratching at his scalp with the tip of his biro. 'And then not long after, he was murdered.'

'That doesn't mean anything,' said Belinda. 'There are hundreds of people here and besides, Harry said he watched Simon walk away from both him and Drew.'

'Don't say any more, Bel. You'll incriminate all of us,' said Ivan.

'It's hardly a confession, is it?' she said, a touch of annoyance to her tone. 'Besides, we've all pretty much been together since the whole horrid lion business.'

'What about you, Mr Brenner?' said Vince, his eyebrows taking on their full interrogation mode.

'Me? Me?' said Ivan. 'After I saved a small boy from a lion and made sure everyone – including the lion and the markswoman – was OK, I doubled back towards the car to see if I could catch up with Belinda and Harry and chat things over. I'm here to help out with the elephants' repatriation and conservation development generally.'

'So you know all about the protestors at the gates?' said Vince.

'I've been given an idea of what they want,' said Ivan. 'Do you think they could have murdered that man?'

Vince tapped his pocket notebook with his pen. 'The reason we were here so quickly is because we're on standby in case the protestors kick off. You know, the ones for the elephants being returned to Africa versus those who want them to stay in Kent. I've been stationed up the road in a lay-by for most of this week and we were monitoring any of them trying to get inside the zoo, legitimately or otherwise.'

'I'd say one of them is the most likely to have done this,' said Ivan.

Everyone else turned to look at him.

'Why would you say that?' said Harry, a little curious as to why Ivan would make such a sweeping statement.

'Animal welfare brings out the worst in some people,' he replied, with a reluctant flick of his head towards Belinda.

'Who's this?' said Vince, nodding at Estelle as she stomped across the tarmac as quickly as her ill-fitting shoes would allow.

'Estelle Samuels,' said Harry. 'She's the Chair of the Board of Trustees, not to mention she owns the zoo and all of the grief that goes with it.'

'Remarkable person, though,' said Ivan.

Belinda turned her head sharply, a strange expression on her face.

'I got here as fast as I could,' said Estelle, standing next to PC Green. 'I heard that someone's been killed. Is it true?' She tried to peer over towards where the paramedics were moving around Simon Carter's body.

'Yes, ma'am,' said Vince. 'I'm sorry but one of the members of staff found a body and we've had to cordon off the area. Can I ask how you heard about it?'

Estelle gave Vince a wan smile. 'My head of security Rob Piper told me after Drew Matterson contacted him on the radio. I can't believe this. I really can't.' She appeared close to tears. 'This is the last thing that the zoo needs. I know that sounds incredibly callous but the last thing we need is bad publicity. If it holds up the elephants being moved, I don't think I can take it.'

'Hey, hey,' said Ivan, stepping over to Estelle and placing a hand on her shoulder. 'We'll get through this, don't worry.'

Harry would have found it quite touching if it wasn't so nauseating. Belinda looked a little green around the gills, too, and Harry knew it wasn't down to finding yet another cadaver.

'How about I take you to see Rob Piper?' Harry asked Vince. 'He's the head of security, and he can help with the CCTV system.'

'Great idea,' said Vince. 'I don't think it'll need all of us, so I'll leave Mr Brenner and Ms Samuels here to make statements.'

Belinda gave Ivan a triumphant look as she followed Vince and Harry towards the security office.

8

Belinda had been somewhat put out by Ivan's attitude towards Estelle, which she knew was ridiculous. Decades ago, Estelle had bought the land they stood on with her sights firmly fixed on a haven for unwanted animals. Over time, she had raised millions of pounds and had taken in abandoned and discarded creatures from all over Europe. Belinda reminded herself of how much she admired Estelle and all that she stood for.

As Belinda walked along, Harry having fallen into step to one side of her and Vince on the other, she pushed aside her petty thoughts and recognised the now familiar sensation of having another murder to solve seeping into her core. Even though she wasn't in any way grateful for something so sinister to happen only a stone's throw from her – again – she knew that Harry would need her help. He had been appointed to the security team only an hour before a murder. She would do everything in her power to make sure whoever was to blame faced justice.

'Heaven forbid that I tell you how to do your job, Vince,' she said with a dazzling smile, 'but Simon Carter must have annoyed someone to end up strangled. It can hardly be some sort of zoo rage incident.'

'It smacks of something personal to me,' said Harry.

'We'll certainly get on with finding out as much as we can about the victim,' said Vince, making a point of not looking at either of them as he spoke.

'I'm sure you're going to start with his family and friends, that sort of thing,' said Harry, a light tone to his voice.

'Er, yeah,' said Vince. 'That's, you know, standard.'

The office door opened as they got within a few feet and a startled-looking Rob Piper rushed down the steps towards them.

'I can't believe what's happened,' he said, flapping his arms around. 'What a day, what an absolute pig of a day. Officer, please come inside and I'll help you in any way I can, as will my staff.'

'I need to take a look at your CCTV system,' said Vince, indicating the security office, Belinda already on her way across the threshold. Behind her she could hear hurried introductions between Vince and Rob, plus Harry's less than dainty footsteps.

'Of course, of course,' said Rob, coming through the door that Belinda was holding open for him. 'I have to say it's patchy at the best of times. Prepare yourselves for disappointing news: Drew told me where Simon's body was found and unfortunately that part of the grounds isn't covered by a camera.'

'You're kidding me?' said Harry, following him inside. 'Why not?'

When all four of them were standing at the bank of twelve screens, Vince said, 'I would have expected many more cameras for a place this size.'

Rob breathed out slowly as he leaned across to tap his password into the control panel and said, 'The amount these animals cost to feed, it's a wonder we have any funding left at all.'

'What's the nearest working camera you have to the Coffee Perks stand?' said Vince.

'It's this one here,' said Rob, pointing at the top row of screens, second one along. 'It's camera fifteen – they record more than one view. That way, we don't need hundreds of them. We only leave the live feed on the ones with the most footfall and key areas of concern.'

'Concern?' said Belinda. 'What could possibly be of concern in a zoo, other than people getting murdered, obviously?'

'There's the protestors for a start,' said Rob, his focus on finding the correct timeframe for the footage. 'I'm sorry, but the footage closest to the scene of the murder doesn't seem to be here. The whole system needs an overhaul – it's not the first time I've flagged up these problems. I can't begin to tell you how frustrating it is. It's only showing the live feed at the moment. Look, here's Drew still sitting with Susan from the coffee shop. Sorry, but it's not recording. I've asked Estelle enough times to get this sorted and she never made it a priority.'

'I'll contact my sergeant and see if we can call someone out from our Digital Services Department,' said Vince. 'They might be able to work a miracle.'

As Vince moved back to make the necessary calls, Belinda ran an eye over the dreary office. There was little in the way of home comforts and it had a stale smell to it. It didn't seem to be concerning Harry. He leaned forward and took over the controls from Rob, demonstrating that he knew his way around the system.

'This one's interesting,' said Harry, peering a little closer at one of the screens. 'It's an external camera.'

'Now, that one is definitely recording,' said Rob. 'It's permanently trained on those protestors. We can't afford to let our attention wander from them at any time. They're an absolute menace.'

'Do you think that one of them is responsible for Simon Carter's murder?' said Belinda.

Rob replied with a shrug before adding, 'It wouldn't surprise me at all. If they can bring enough trouble to our door, the zoo's future might be in jeopardy and then the herd won't get sent back to Africa. On the other hand, I know that none of them entered the grounds today. The gate staff are under strict instructions to keep them out, and other than the interviews, I've not moved far from the screens today. I would have noticed any of them sneaking off from their gaggle of the great unwashed and trying to get in over or under the fence somewhere.'

'You don't appear to have all that much time for them,' said Harry.

'Neither will you in a few days' time,' said Rob, glancing at his watch. 'Look, there's going to be a mass exodus once the police start to move everyone away from the hay store and close the place, so I have heaps to do. Perhaps I can leave you here with the police officer and you can help him out with anything he needs?'

With that, Rob gave a wave at Vince and Belinda turned her attention back to the security camera feed.

'I've got a guy coming over to take a look at the system,' said Vince, finally ending his call. 'I'm not sure how long they're going to be, so can I leave you two here while I make sure the CSIs and CID officers know where they're going and start getting the place cleared? Here's a card with my number on it if you need me.'

Harry took the card and studied it. 'It takes me back, you know. When I was in the job, I— Oh, he's gone.'

'Nice work getting rid of him,' said Belinda, still giving the screens her full attention.

'Yeah, well, no problem,' said Harry, a slight puzzled tone to his voice. 'Why are you so pleased to see him leave?'

He stretched forward to see what she was looking at.

'This,' she said, jabbing at a figure on the screen. 'I didn't want Rob or our resident police officer to see this. I know that I don't owe Ivan anything, but moments ago I saw him on his way to the main gate. I'm a bit worried he's going to go outside and start trouble with the protestors.'

9

Harry wasn't sure how to react. He hadn't exactly warmed to Ivan but really didn't have him pegged as a murderer. He followed Ivan on the screen as he walked up to a group of protestors and started to talk to them. One or two even put their placards down and seemed to engage in conversation with him.

'I know that we need to tell the police about this,' said Belinda. 'But what exactly is Ivan up to?'

'I hate to state the obvious,' said Harry, 'but when they look at the CCTV they'll spot Ivan going through the gates.'

'He can't be in league with them, can he?' Belinda sat down in the worn chair, its wheels giving out a squeak in protest.

'No,' said Harry. 'There's no way Ivan's mixed up in this. He's only very recently got here for a start. All that's happened is we've seen him speak to the protestors.' He stopped in his quest to locate a pen on Rob's untidy desk. 'I want to write the time down for Vince to look into it later on, on the off chance there's something more sinister. Although that's only my cautious police training kicking in. I'm sure it's all fine.'

As Harry pushed papers aside on the desk, he tried to let feelings of jealousy go. He should be pleased for Belinda, if, after all this time, she was getting back together with Ivan. He saw no point in letting Belinda see the crushing disappointment that was drilling through his heart. How would that help? She already seemed agitated. He still hadn't worked out if it was the visit from Ivan itself that had riled her or whether it was finding another dead body.

'Ivan hadn't even met Simon Carter before he was murdered. He couldn't possibly have had any reason to want him dead. The man was a little on the annoying side, but he spent a lot of time and money here. He seemed to be a huge supporter of everything Estelle's doing. Even if it was in a roundabout way. I can't see that anyone at the zoo, Ivan included, would have wanted to harm him, let alone kill him. It would only mean publicity for the wrong reasons and a loss of income.'

Belinda pushed herself out of the chair – with a little difficulty. The mechanisms were so defunct, the seat tipped up as she tried to stand, and the squeaking was painful to hear.

'Ivan has quite the temper at times,' she said, facing Harry. 'You heard about Simon's attempts to sue the zoo. That would mean financial hardship which would put the future of the animals, especially the elephants, at risk.'

'Enough of a temper to fly across continents at this news and strangle him?' said Harry. 'Surely not? That's a little bit extreme even for Little Challham.'

'We need to find out if anyone else had any problem with Simon, not just the staff whose livelihoods would be in jeopardy because of him,' said Belinda.

'It sounds as though Estelle would have the most to lose,' said Harry. 'She's built this zoo up from nothing to a huge tourist attraction. She knew it would attract bad publicity, although not as much as going broke.'

'What are you looking for?' said Belinda. 'Other than a murderer, I mean.' She pointed at the desk.

'I'm after a pen, but I can't seem to find one in all this clutter. I suppose that I should carry one at all times, except I...'

Harry stared down at the printed pages lying on the solid oak desk, at odds with the rest of the room's cheap décor. His fingers grasped one of the sheets.

'What is it?' said Belinda, moving around the desk so that she could read whatever he was holding.

'When I got here earlier for my interview, there was already someone in the office. It clearly wasn't going very well at all. I'm trained to pick up on these things. You know, the tiny signs such as shouting, doors slamming, people storming off and rude gestures.'

'That must have been intensive training,' said Belinda, taking the paper from Harry's hand.

'My failed marriage was a perfect place for first-hand experience,' he said. 'Anyway, this afternoon, the last candidate before me was Edward Logan. Here's his CV, a photo and also a warning. According to this, the gardens and zoo had already offered to interview him but he'd been fired from his last security job – which didn't come to light until he was due to have an interview.'

Harry put the paper back down. 'Wow, no wonder I got the job as easily as I did. I'm mustard compared to him. I thought for a moment that someone had bribed Rob. Whatever I said to him, he wasn't fully listening. Well, I'll be.'

'And you think that perhaps Edward Logan had something to do with Simon's murder?' said Belinda. 'I can't see why he'd commit murder simply because he didn't get a job on the security team and was trying to prove a point by strangling someone. No, it's too ridiculous.'

Harry leafed through the papers again for any more of Edward Logan's file. 'You're right, it is. Even so, I can't leave it there. I work for Brabourne Gardens now, I have to find out who did this.'

He glanced across at her. 'I don't suppose there's any chance you'd...'

Belinda raised an eyebrow at him. 'What are you asking? Let me guess: you, me and the whiteboard?'

Not for the first time, Harry thought that Belinda really was perfection itself.

10

Belinda and Harry left the security office to find somewhere to talk over what had happened so far. Belinda wanted to help Harry find out who was behind Simon Carter's death, especially as she felt a degree of responsibility for landing Harry with the job in the first place.

'What shall we do about locking up?' she said, as Harry closed the office door behind them.

'Good point,' he said. 'A murder and a walk-in theft on my first day and I really would be the worst security guard ever. I've got Vince's number. Perhaps I can call him and he'll get someone over here.'

Harry took his phone out of his pocket as Belinda tapped his sleeve. 'Look, H. Here comes that other fellow. Did you say his name was Drew? He's bound to be able to help us.'

As soon as Drew saw them both standing by the office, he hurried over. Belinda thought he appeared a touch too keen, but possibly that was his nature, rather than anything suspicious. Even so, Belinda had caught the expression on Drew's face as he glanced back at Simon's body a couple of times, and she was still having trouble interpreting it. She kept this to herself, making a mental note to mention it to Harry when they were alone.

'Hello,' said Drew. 'I was hoping that Rob was here. Have you seen him?'

'Not for a while,' said Harry. 'He went off to see how the police were getting on clearing the grounds. Although I'd love to lend a hand, I don't have any official identification, uniform or even a radio so I'd most likely hinder them. Besides, Belinda and I need to find her friend Ivan. Could we leave you in charge of the security office while we go and look?'

'Er, yeah, sure,' said Drew. He ran up the steps once they were clear of the door. 'Someone should be monitoring the CCTV anyway. I'm not sure exactly what Rob was thinking. It's supposed to be staffed at all times. It's not like Rob doesn't know that.'

He gave a sad little shake of his head as if this news really had ruined his day.

'How long have you worked here?' said Harry. 'I could probably learn a thing or three from you over the coming weeks.'

Drew's face brightened and he said, 'I've been here eight years and this place is my absolute world. I love it. I'd come to work for free if I didn't have rent and bills to pay. I've offered to permanently live in and have them take it from my wages, but Estelle wouldn't hear of it.'

'That's quite a commitment,' said Belinda, watching the young man closely.

A slow smile crept across his face. 'When you love something as much as I do, you'll do anything to make it a success.'

'How's Susan doing?' said Belinda.

'Oh, I've left her with a couple of detectives. They were taking her away to make a statement. I told her to have the rest of the day off.'

'That's very generous of you,' said Harry. 'We'll be off now.'

They walked a few feet away and Drew disappeared into

the office. 'He seemed a little intense about the zoo,' said Belinda, as they made their way back across the car park.

'How about we go and sit in my car?' said Harry. 'We can talk in there with less chance of being overheard.'

The two of them made their way to where Harry had left his Audi.

Even though Belinda knew where Harry's car was parked, she let him lead the way. She didn't want him to think that she kept tabs on him wherever he went. Once they were on their own, it would be best if she came clean about a couple of things, including her influence in his job success.

As she was a few car lengths away from Harry, she saw him turn his head sharply towards a blue Ford Mondeo. The driver's door opened and a man jumped out. His face was contorted in rage and he shouted something at Harry. Belinda saw a flash of a navy suit jacket as he raced towards Harry, slamming the car door behind him as he went. He had his fists raised and for a moment, she thought he was going to launch himself at her friend. The hostility had altered his features so much, it took her a moment to recognise him from the photo that she and Harry had been looking at only a short while before. It was Edward Logan, the unsuccessful job candidate.

'Whoa,' said Harry, palms open towards the clearly angry man, whose messy brown hair, greying at the temples, and loosened tie knot added to his 'I've lost everything today' air. 'Can I help you?'

Belinda was by Harry's side in record time. 'Yes, can we help you?'

The irate man glared at each of them in turn. 'I said, you got the job, then?'

'Sorry, but you're acting a little aggressively for someone who wanted a job stopping altercations,' said Belinda, wondering exactly what was going on to bring about such volatile behaviour.

'I'll prove to them that you're the wrong person,' Edward said. 'It should have been me.'

'I'm sorry that you feel that way,' said Harry, 'but we both went through the interview process, fair and square.'

'Like a mug, I turned up here today when the job had clearly already been promised to you,' he said, spittle flying in all directions.

'What makes you think that?' said Harry.

Belinda cleared her throat.

'Because you're an ex-copper, aren't you?' Edward said, his shoulders sagging as if he'd expended his fury and the fight was leaving him. He dropped his hands down to his sides. 'I was early and when I got here, I heard that Estelle woman say it right before I came in for my interview. From what the two of them were discussing, it was already in the bag before I walked in the door. I've been waiting to speak to you and tell you how gutted I am.'

He took a step nearer. 'I wouldn't really have minded so much, but I have to cover the cost of the petrol to get here and I'm broke. If they'd have simply not interviewed me, I'd be better off now than I was this morning. It's a fifty-mile round trip.'

'I'm sorry, Edward,' said Harry.

Edward's face had been in the process of softening, when the use of his name prompted his eyes to narrow. 'How do you know my name?'

'You left the office as I got there and Rob mentioned that a guy called Edward was the last interviewee before me, that's all,' said Harry. 'Be fair – you did storm out so you can't have thought it had gone all that well.'

Edward looked over towards the marshland and blew the air from his cheeks. 'I really wanted this job. Visiting this place is a form of escape for me, not that I can afford to come here at the moment. I shouldn't have got my hopes up. When I heard

Estelle Whatshername talking about an ex-police officer coming in and how he should get the job, I saw red. I blew it, so I've only got myself to blame.'

Feeling as though she should say something, Belinda was about to offer a few words of comfort when Edward turned back to face Harry. The look of hatred had returned. 'They'll be very sorry they gave you this job instead of me. And for wasting my time on a bogus interview for a job that I was never in hell going to get.'

He walked away from them, still muttering to himself as if he were rehearsing for an argument.

'You have to feel a bit sorry for him,' said Harry, watching Edward get back into his car.

'He all but threatened you,' said Belinda. 'Besides, there's been a murder here so we should at least tell Vince what he said. I'm less inclined to believe that he wouldn't do something so extreme to punish you for getting the job. He might be the murderer.'

'It's a possibility, I suppose,' said Harry, chewing the inside of his mouth. 'Now the police are emptying the place, they'll get his details at the gate anyway.'

'And if he is the killer,' said Belinda, 'you're always telling me how important early forensic capture is. Shouldn't the police arrest him now?'

'He'd have to have been pretty upset about not getting the job on the security team to attack a random person in the gardens and strangle him post interview,' said Harry. 'No, I think we're barking up the wrong tree there. Edward is simply extremely upset that he failed to get a job he'd set his heart on.'

'I have to tell you something,' said Belinda, steeling herself for Harry's reaction to what she was about to tell him. She heard him turn to face her and made herself do the same. 'This is my fault – well, not the murder, but that nasty brush with

Edward then and when he stormed out earlier. I feel dreadful about it and I promise I was only trying to help.'

She forced herself to look across at him.

'Go on,' he said.

'I-I— Oh, goodness.' She bit her lip. 'I put in a good word for you with Estelle and... the other board members.'

Harry let out a long slow breath and gazed over her head into the distance.

'I'm sorry,' she said. 'I really am so sorry. I thought that I was doing a good thing for you, I had no idea that someone as desperate as Edward would get turned down when money is clearly so tight.'

'I appreciate that you thought you were doing the right thing,' said Harry. 'Except you live in a castle. When was the last time you had to worry about getting a job or having a tenner to put petrol in your car?'

With that, he stepped round her and said, 'I'll see you later. I'm going to find Rob.'

It had been a long time since Belinda had felt so truly devastated.

11

Belinda's instinct was to go after Harry, reassure him that she had done it for the right reasons. The only problem with that would be telling him the main reason she had done it was to ensure he didn't leave Little Challham, and most importantly, didn't leave *her*. Now she stopped to think about it, it sounded very manipulative and calculating. That thought left her cold, so she could only imagine how he felt about it. If only Harry would forgive her, she would never do anything as controlling again. Belinda knew that she sometimes got people's backs up, but coming across as overbearing usually stopped people from taking advantage of her.

For several minutes, she stood in the car park and really analysed what she'd done. It made her feel incredibly selfish. She could have asked Harry if he had wanted her to put in a good word, except she knew that the answer would have been no. He wouldn't have wanted either her charity, or an unfair advantage over the Edward Logans of this world.

Heck, she felt stupid. Not to mention lonely. Here she was in one of the county's busiest family attractions, even if the police were emptying the grounds, and all she could feel was isolated. And she only had herself to blame.

Unsure what to do – the police would need to speak to her again, but it wasn't as if Vince Green had no way of getting hold of her – and feeling a spare part standing in the car park, Belinda decided to find Ivan and Estelle. At least she hadn't upset either of them today.

Belinda followed the pathway down to where she had last seen her ex-boyfriend being asked to make his statement about the murder. She was surprised that no one had as yet collared her for her official written account. She knew well enough how these things worked, having managed to get involved in several suspicious deaths since Harry had arrived in Little Challham.

She arrived at the spot where she had last seen Ivan, torn between whether she should seek him out outside the gates after all, or try to build bridges with Harry. Ivan was nowhere to be seen but there in the distance, past the animal balloon stall, she was sure she could see the back of Harry's head, the grey streaks in his red hair clear in the weak sunshine. She struggled to peer around a clutch of parrot-shaped balloons as Harry rounded a corner. Mind made up that Ivan could wait for another time, she took a left and hurried after Harry.

A couple of minutes later Belinda thought about giving up: he had clearly disappeared and, not wanting to appear desperate, she could only hope he would find himself at a loss and call her. At the very least, she would pay him a visit at home and apologise for interfering.

Realising that she was standing beside the walkway that would take her to the giraffe house, Belinda decided to make the most of the time she had left in the zoo before the police made her leave or Ivan rang to find out where she was. That thought made her stop in her tracks: she could simply have called Ivan from her mobile rather than return to where she left him. If that had been her preferred course of action, she would have done that in the first place. The penny dropped that all along she had wanted to bump into Harry again in the hope he had forgiven her.

'Fat chance of that,' she muttered to herself as she slowed her pace and calmed her breathing. Although she knew very well where the giraffe house was, she took a slightly longer route than necessary. She wanted to savour the relative peace as the day began to draw to a close. It was her favourite time to visit Brabourne Gardens and she was determined that she would be a more frequent visitor from now on. It would also hopefully have the added bonus of meeting up with Harry on his lunch break. If he decided to turn the job down because she had got involved in something that she should have steered well clear of, she would never forgive herself. With a deep sigh, she realised that even if she hadn't had said a word to Estelle or the rest of the board, Harry would probably have got the job anyway and this would all have been avoided.

At least she would get to see the giraffes in all their majesty.

Belinda climbed the last few steps to the top of the viewing platform and leaned her forearms against the first safety rail. The enclosure was their last stop before being bedded down, so the keepers could ensure they were safe for the night having roamed the fifty-acre wilderness of their area all day. It was one of Belinda's favourite places – at least while she wasn't in Africa watching them where they should be. She bit her lip at the thought. That's where she would have preferred them to be, but with an estimated population of only 2,500 in the wild, she accepted the reality that the species wouldn't outlive her without a conservation programme.

With a feeling of excitement that never went away, she spotted two of them in the distance, closely followed by another one. There were only six in total, so she expected the remaining three – they were never far from each other – to come ambling into view before long.

A noise to her left-hand side made her heart drop: it was either visitors disturbing her tranquillity or staff members about to move her in the direction of the gates. She was surprised it had taken this long for them to clear the park after finding a corpse. Still, she had had a few moments of peace so she should be grateful for that. She gazed over at the giraffes.

'I thought I'd find you here,' said a voice a couple of feet from her.

Belinda's smile spread across her face, mixed with joy and relief. 'How did you know, Harry?'

He shrugged and said, 'Lucky guess, I suppose.' He winked at her. 'That and the fact you've told me that giraffes are your favourite.'

'Oh, yes, I did, didn't I?' Belinda gave a laugh that sounded uncharacteristically nervous. 'I'd forgotten.'

For the briefest of times, they both stood watching the animals chew leaves from the trees, Belinda awash with gratitude that he'd come to find her.

'Look,' she said, attention still on the giraffes, 'I'm so very sorry for sticking my nose in where it wasn't wanted. I only wanted to help and I can't tell you how terrible I feel.'

Harry sidled along the railing until their elbows were touching. 'You're forgiven. I can't stay mad at you for long.'

'Thank you. You don't know how relieved I am to hear you say that.' Belinda turned sideways, taking in his profile. 'I know how much I—'

His forehead had creased into a frown and a look of concentration gripped his features. Belinda briefly thought that he was angry with her once again, although this time, she definitely didn't know what she'd said. Then she realised that he was staring into the enclosure.

'We have to call someone,' said Harry, as he grabbed for his mobile phone. 'That giraffe looks as though it's about to keel over.'

Belinda watched in horror as one of the giraffes collapsed to the ground.

12

It didn't take long before several keepers rushed into the enclosure; the vet was on her way and Harry and Belinda were heading towards the secure staff access area. Harry called, 'This way,' over his shoulder and hurried to the restricted road past the sign politely informing the public that they weren't welcome.

Harry spoke urgently into his mobile as he led the way, Belinda close behind him. He was well aware that she hated any sort of suffering to animals so this would be especially difficult for her. He had been about to tell her that they shouldn't row over such unimportant personal matters, especially when it was clear she had his best interests at heart. He understood that the giraffe's welfare would be most prominent in her mind now, so her apology – and his acceptance of it – would wait.

They managed to reach the staff entrance at the same time as Rob Piper, who was driving one of the electric buggies. He pulled to a stop and jumped clear, cutting through the gaggle of worried keepers and members of the security team.

'It's Sabbie,' a distraught-looking keeper said. 'She collapsed. I need to get in there.'

'OK, OK,' said a woman in her thirties, dark hair swept from her face in a ponytail, her scrubs and calm manner making it clear she was the attending vet. 'I'm going to take a look at her now. Let's go.'

Harry and Belinda hung back as the vet and the keeper made their way inside the enclosure. A couple of other members of staff were making sure the remaining giraffes were all safe and kept away from their collapsed family member. Belinda gave Harry a look of bewilderment: he didn't think that he had ever seen her appear so lost.

'She'll get the very best care,' said Harry, stepping towards her and gently taking her by the arm. 'How about we leave them to it and take a walk around the far side of the enclosure? We can talk on the way.'

With a wave at Rob, Harry guided Belinda by the elbow, taking them further along the restricted pathway. 'It really is fine, you know?' he said. 'What you were saying earlier. I've had a chance to think about it and now I've put things into perspective, I should be saying thank you for trying to get me a job. My pride got in the way.'

Belinda glanced across at him, a smile playing at the corners of her mouth. 'I should have checked with you, but I only wanted you to stay in Little Challham, that's all.'

'Why would I leave Little Challham?' he said. That truly puzzled him; why would she think such a thing? The more pressing question was whether she was going to hang around now Ivan had showed up.

'I thought you might be bored.'

He gave a short laugh. 'Bored? Apart from the inexplicably high murder rate for a small village, how could life ever be boring with you in it?'

They had slowed their pace, and Harry felt Belinda come to a stop beside him. He too stood still.

'I was hoping you were going to say that,' she said.

Harry stared at her, unblinking, not even sure he was breathing. He forced his eyes to look away. Her stare was so intense that it was too much. They stood silently amongst the quiet chatter of birds in the trees that flanked the pathway, the watery sunlight breaking through above their heads. The earthy scent of the nearby pine trees mingled with an occasional waft of wild animal dung. It was very romantic.

'So, getting back to the business of Simon Carter's murder,' said Harry, in a lame attempt to distract himself from his emotions. 'I think we need to look at who had the most to gain from his death.'

'Oh, of course,' said Belinda, sounding a tad confused at the rapid change of subject. 'Well, if he was going to sue the zoo, we know that Estelle and Rob have the most to lose. Estelle in particular.'

'We also shouldn't overlook the super-zealot Drew Matterson,' said Harry. He dropped down to his knees and began to pick up pinecones and stones. 'OK, this one here, this is Estelle.' He placed a pinecone closest to his knee. 'And this one is Rob.'

'Lovely improvisation,' said Belinda, crouching down to join him. 'Why have you put them next to each other? You don't think they're working as a team, do you?'

'No, not at all,' said Harry, then paused to consider what she'd said. 'There's too much at stake for Estelle to be involved. The police have closed the zoo, for a start, so that's a loss of takings. Rob keeps going on about funding for security, but murdering someone to prove you need more money to protect people is hardly a motive for him either. I've put them together because although Simon was threatening to sue the zoo, killing him would outweigh the benefits.'

'Right, but what about Drew? I'd say he seems a bit on the immature side, so perhaps it's something he'd do without thinking the consequences through,' said Belinda.

Harry moved a smooth stone near to the pinecones. 'Mm,

same really, though, don't you think? He's worked here long enough to know how important it is to keep people coming through the gates. Although, Drew did seem to have had enough of Simon's complaining.'

Belinda gave a delicate cough and rolled a mishappen rock towards Harry. 'As much as I want to avoid going over old, sensitive ground, there is the matter of Edward Logan.'

'OK, we'll speak to him first,' said Harry with a sigh. 'I'm not convinced he'd...'

From the corner of his eye, Harry saw a movement. He was staring over Belinda's shoulder and towards the bushes and shrubs near the inner perimeter fence. The foliage was trampled in places, pushed at unnatural angles, and one of the saplings was bent in the opposite direction to its neighbours.

'What is it?' said Belinda, a sharpness to her tone. She turned to see what had grabbed his attention.

'That's not right,' said Harry. 'It has all the signs of someone coming through from the road. I don't like this at all. Wait here.'

Harry knew he had wasted his last two words: he headed for the break in the line of plants and bushes, closely followed by Belinda. He crouched down and peered into the undergrowth. 'Yes, as I thought, there's definitely a trail in from the inner fence.' He crawled a foot or two inside the opening.

'Can you see anything?' called Belinda.

'Someone has cut a hole in the wire fence,' he said. 'The gap's big enough for me to get through. Give me a minute.'

The last thing Harry wanted to do was to drag himself along in the dirt and the plants in his interview outfit. Even so, he knew that he couldn't ignore damage that was likely to have been caused by an intruder. He hadn't exactly covered himself in glory by allowing a murder to take place within an hour or so of being appointed to his new role. This was worth a dry-cleaning bill. He made slow progress, keen neither to rip the knees out of his trousers, nor disturb what could be vital forensic evidence. After catching his elbow on a prickly branch and putting his hand in what might be scat, he decided he had had enough.

As Harry started to wriggle backwards, he turned his head to the right to avoid getting an eyeful of vegetation. A movement several feet away past the outer fence caught his attention. He squinted and tried to concentrate. He knew that the country lane ran the other side and there was a drop of four feet from the bottom of the metal chain-link fence to the road. Traffic passed by from time to time but the main gates were on the other side of the park, as was the staff car park, so vehicles were at a minimum. He convinced himself he must have imagined it, or seen a distant squirrel or bird.

Harry was about to carry on with his undignified retreat when he saw the same flash of something stirring. He kept still and waited.

Voices, Harry could definitely hear voices. Although he couldn't entirely make out what they were saying, he was sure it was two men. Something was unusual about one of them. Then he realised what it was. A South African accent.

Harry held his breath as he tried to make out what they were saying. The only words he could fathom sounded very much like 'Little Challham' and he wasn't completely sure which one of them had said it. As Ivan took two or three rapid steps forward, the person he was talking to came into view.

From the clothing, dreadlocks and badges adorning his every spare inch of material, Harry would have happily put money on the other person being one of the protestors. It was why he was talking to Ivan far from the main gates and rest of the animal welfare groups that intrigued him.

It didn't interest him half as much as Belinda's urgent whisperings as she knelt down and said, 'H, get up. There's something going on at the edge of the giraffe enclosure. I think they've found something.'

Whether it was the sound of Belinda's voice or another distraction, Ivan and the person he had been talking to glanced towards them and started to walk off in the direction of the main gate. Realising he was now gaining nothing from lying on the cold, damp ground, Harry made an ungainly exit. Wiggling on the ground like an obese worm gave him a chance to think about what he was going to say to Belinda. Ivan was back and Harry didn't like it, but he shouldn't let that get in the way of his feelings for her. If he shared her ex's suspicious behaviour with her, it would only make her think less of Harry. If Harry couldn't have the sort of relationship with her that he really wanted, jeopardising their friendship would be extremely foolhardy.

'Any idea what they've found?' said Harry.

'No,' she said, shaking her head, black hair framing her face. 'I can hear people rushing around and what sounded like "police". We're too far away. Let's find out.'

They hurried back to where they'd left the others dealing with the poorly giraffe to see a flurry of activity. Several of the keepers were milling around and members of the security team were running from one place to another, seemingly achieving little except burning off energy.

'What's going on?' said Harry when Rob rushed by, radio in his hand.

'I simply don't believe today,' said Rob, his face deathly white. 'I hope you're OK to put in a long shift, Harry.'

Harry opened his mouth to speak.

Rob held up a hand. 'OK, OK, double time it is, but you're on the clock as from now.'

'Er, all right,' said Harry. 'Don't tell me it's another body.'

'Worse,' said Rob, twisting his mouth. 'Someone's cut through into the enclosure to get to the giraffes. They've deliberately hurt one of my animals. I'll kill them if I get my hands on them.'

13

Belinda watched Rob as he spoke. He appeared on the verge of tears and glanced repeatedly over to where the police were examining where the fence had been sliced through.

'How's Sabbie doing?' she asked, worried what the answer might be.

'According to Dee the vet, not too bad,' he said, moving his radio from one hand to the other. 'As you know, the unique way that giraffes walk means that they move both legs on one side, followed by the other. It seems that someone placed a rope across part of the enclosure, tied it between two trees and tripped Sabbie up. She knows this area and wouldn't have been expecting it.'

Belinda gasped and put her hands up to her cheeks. Harry tutted and mumbled something about 'poxy oxygen thieves', but she was too horrified by what Rob was telling her to pay much heed.

'I know,' said Rob. 'It could have been worse, I suppose – they could have used wire and cut her leg.'

'We saw her collapse,' said Belinda, a little of her composure regained. 'Though Harry was probably paying more attention as I wasn't entirely focused on the animals at the time.' She obviously didn't want to tell Rob that she had been in raptures over Harry's acceptance of her apology.

'Absolutely,' said Harry, 'although I don't remember there being a rope. Like the animal, I wasn't expecting there to be one.'

'That's because they used a green rope,' said Rob. 'Who ever heard of anything sicker than a green rope?'

'To be fair,' said Harry, hand up to his chin ready to scratch his stubble until he caught a whiff of his palm and dropped it back down again, 'I've worked on many murders where the depravity of people never ceased to revolt—'

'Not now, H,' said Belinda. 'Rob, tell us what we can do.' She watched him look from her to Harry and back again.

'Well...' Rob said.

'We're a very good team, you know,' said Belinda, crossing her arms and tapping a foot. 'Simon Carter's murder wouldn't be the first one we've worked on together, so we can definitely help you establish who did this to Sabbie. Besides, I can always check with the board that it's perfectly acceptable for me to be made an honorary security deputy.'

Belinda heard Harry's deep intake of breath. Yes, she knew that she was abusing her power again but what was the point of having connections if she didn't use them?

'Well,' said Rob again. 'OK... As long as you can work for free. I've already promised Harry here double pay. I can't afford you too.'

'Two for the price of one,' said Belinda with a wink at an exasperated-looking Harry. 'What could possibly go wrong?'

'Indeed,' said Harry.

'You know how to get hold of me if you need me,' said Rob. 'Failing that, I'll see you at the security office at eighteen hundred hours.'

Once Rob had made tracks for the giraffe enclosure again,

Belinda stepped closer to Harry and said, 'Sorry about that, but I was desperate to help out here. You know, find out who's behind Simon's murder as well as who would deliberately injure Sabbie. There is, of course, a chance that the two dreadful incidents are connected. We're clearly dealing with despicable people.'

'Here's what I think we should do,' said Harry. 'We should take ourselves off somewhere and talk through what we have so far. We didn't finish before I got distracted, and besides, we need to discuss the injury to the giraffe. All we'll need is some paper to write a few things down.'

'May I suggest serviettes?' said Belinda.

'Mm, good idea, good idea. I like the improvisation,' said Harry with what she could only describe as a twinkle in his eye.

'Never mind that,' she said. 'You can use a couple to scrape the dung off your hands. It really is quite revolting.'

A few moments later, the two of them had stolen around the back of the nearest coffee stand after pilfering a handful of paper serviettes. Staff and service crew were locking up, although many had been told they couldn't leave before the police took their details. Mercifully, Harry had found the public toilets and washed the living undergrowth out of his pores. Meanwhile, Belinda had somehow charmed two large lattes from the coffee stand before it was boarded up for the day.

The two of them sat in companionable silence, sheltered from view. The land train, empty but for the driver, went by on its last journey of the day, cut short by Simon's murder. Harry and Belinda sat next to one another at a round metal table behind the originally named Coffee Spot, their paper cups holding down the edges of their makeshift whiteboard.

'So far,' said Belinda, 'we have Simon Carter strangled with a bandana, a child thrown into the lion enclosure, which was supposed to be empty of lions, and now poor Sabbie injured. Do we think they're connected? It could be a coincidence these things happened here today.'

'Simon's death *could* be completely unrelated to the other two incidents,' said Harry, 'but all three things in one day?'

'I think we should assume Simon was killed by someone he knew, rather than a random person who happened to be here,' said Belinda. 'The police will look into his friends and family, so we should start on those in the zoo.'

Harry nodded and wrote the heading 'Suspects'. 'Earlier on, we'd discussed Estelle and Rob, but said they had more to lose than gain, what with the bad publicity and all. So other than Drew, who again is unlikely to hurt a giraffe, we come back to Edward Logan,' said Harry, scribbling down his name beneath Drew Matterson's. 'Edward would be very stupid to hang around that long after the murder, and also, we'd have to ask why he killed Simon in particular. Still, it's best we check that out.'

'Agreed,' said Belinda. 'It would be extreme to kill someone just because you didn't get a job on the security team, but we shouldn't totally rule it out. In isolation, Simon's death was one thing, but now with the attack on the giraffes, perhaps the bigger picture is that it's more about threats to the zoo and the same person or people are behind the whole thing. An attempt to ruin it or shut it down through a series of awful incidents. And not forgetting the protestors: there are those who are against the elephants being returned to Africa and those who are for it. Again, it's a little much that they'd break into the zoo to do such a thing, but we mustn't overlook anything.'

'If we want to err on the side of caution,' said Harry, 'we'd have to include every member of staff who was working here today – or anyone here who had anything to do with Simon.'

'This could take forever,' said Belinda, chewing on her bottom lip. 'Perhaps it is connected to the damage to the fence by the giraffe house. Rather than someone coming through the gate and risking being seen, they broke in through the fence to get to Simon, knowing he would be here.'

'Something tells me otherwise,' said Harry, picking up his drink and taking a tentative sip before giving a slow nod of approval. 'It would be easier to murder him elsewhere than in a zoo with CCTV everywhere, even if the security system does need some serious maintenance.'

'Anyone else we should add to the list?' said Belinda, her attention drawn to a police officer a little distance away. If she wasn't mistaken, it was PC Vince Green coming towards them with a purpose to his step. He probably wouldn't be too pleased that she and Harry were drawing their own conclusions about who had strangled Simon Carter to death with an African Savannah Safari bandana.

Harry's face was doing something awkward: he appeared to be a tormented man, what with all the fidgeting and narrowing of his eyes.

'What's wrong, H?'

'I'm not sure,' he said, wiping froth from under his nose. 'Perhaps we should just leave this to the police. After all, Vince is on his way. We could let him know our theories and hand it over to the professionals.'

'We're only trying to help catch a killer.' She sat forward on the chair, her attention split between Harry and the business-like march of the police officer drawing near.

'Simon must have had family and friends – or at least acquaintances,' said Harry. He swallowed and dabbed his lips with a spare serviette again. 'This foamy stuff gets everywhere.'

Belinda made a 'go on' gesture, keen not to allow him to go off on a tangent again.

'I think, at the very least, we should ask Vince to let us know if there's anything suspicious about Simon's family or back-ground,' said Harry.

Belinda glanced up at the officer who was only a couple of steps away from being able to hear their conversation.

'All right,' she said, leaning across to place her hand on Harry's. Her friend looked completely overwhelmed. She had to cut him some slack when the first day of his new job had brought a murder to his door, only this time without any police powers or colleagues to back him up. 'Vince is right behind you, so we'll ask him to help us out.'

A look of relief came over Harry's face. 'This is the right thing to do, Bel.'

Belinda broke into a grin and she called out, 'Hello, Vince. Why don't you join us? We were hoping you'd show up.'

14

Belinda and Harry made space for the young officer whose shift was once more prolonged by a suspicious death in their vicinity. Belinda didn't doubt that at some point Vince might suspect the two of them if the murderers remained at large.

'Any progress?' she said, not expecting him to share too much, but feeling it was certainly worth a try.

'Not really,' said Vince, trying to sit down, the bulk of his stab vest and all of its attachments hindering him slightly. He fidgeted until he could move back into the seat. 'We're still speaking to Susan, who found the body. We've taken a statement from Drew, but we'll need to speak to him again. I know you said that he and Simon Carter were arguing shortly before Simon was murdered, but early indications are that he was elsewhere at the relevant time.'

'So, very little in the way of developments,' said Harry, playing with his paper cup of dwindling froth.

Vince let out a breath. 'This is looking very bad for Little Challham and the usually peaceful people of this manor. The Chief is *not* happy.'

'Neither is the dead bloke,' said Harry. 'Or his family.'

'Yes,' sighed Vince, 'that's a given. How are we going to find who's responsible?'

While Vince's sad brown eyes were looking down at his boots, Belinda and Harry exchanged a glance.

'Oh, let me think...' said Belinda, not quite able to believe what she was hearing. 'We could, er, put our heads together and try to come up with a list of suspects.' As she spoke, she slowly pulled the serviette towards her with its tell-tale 'Suspects' heading.

'That's not a bad idea,' said Vince. 'The thing is, my mum lives just outside Little Challham and I wouldn't let my sergeant hear me say this – the sarge is quite scary and loves a bit of protocol – but I'd say my mum's peace of mind would be vastly improved with you two helping out. In an unofficial capacity, obviously.'

'Oh, obviously,' said Harry. 'We were thinking of leaving it up to you – as in, the police.'

'No, please don't do that,' said Vince. He looked from Harry to Belinda. 'I want to tell you something, but I don't want to get fired. If I help you out and you tell me what you know, we could probably catch the killer before anyone else gets hurt. Do you think it would work out without me getting the sack?'

'Probably not,' said Harry.

'Absolutely it would,' said Belinda, glaring at Harry, then making her face a mask of tranquillity as Vince turned her way. She waved her finger back and forth between herself and Harry. 'We are the souls of discretion, aren't we, Harry? No one would ever know.'

'No, no one will ever know,' said Harry, 'providing we don't get caught. If we do, me and Bel might end up getting nicked and you'd be disciplined, no doubt you'd end up at a gross misconduct hearing, disgraced—'

'Yes, thank you, H,' said Belinda, knowing that Harry had a fair point but not wanting to put Vince off from assisting them.

After all, this wasn't just for her and Harry's benefit: it helped everyone in Little Challham. The sooner they could apprehend the killer, the sooner Estelle would be able to put it behind them and move on with positive press for the zoo.

An expression not unlike relief passed across Vince's face. 'You'd really do that for me? Help me out? I'd like to get onto CID, you know. This might help get me on a murder squad.'

'Oh, yes, I remember my first posting to Major Crime,' said Harry. 'It was very strange weather for the time of ye—'

'We don't have time,' said Belinda. 'You mentioned your mum. Family is important, so we need you to tell us if there's anything else about Simon we should know, or anyone outside the zoo who could have been a threat. In exchange, we'll let you know if there's anything on the inside you should be aware of.'

'I don't know if—' said Vince.

'Is that your sergeant coming over?' said Belinda. 'Mum's the word.'

Vince turned his head with whiplash-inducing speed, shoved his hat back on his head and jumped up. His baton got caught on the chair, and on the first attempt to move away, he took it with him.

'Look, I'll catch up with you two later,' he whispered, before adding in a slightly forced tone, 'OK, then, folks, thanks so much.'

'Oh, yes, thank you, officer,' said Harry. 'Sorry that we couldn't be more help.' He added an over-the-top wink at Vince which made Belinda sigh.

How Harry had managed as a police officer for thirty years was sometimes a mystery to her. Even so, where would she be without him? The thought of another murder was a tiny bit petrifying and Vince had hit the nail on the head regarding how scary this must be for the villagers. If she and Harry could surreptitiously help Vince out, perhaps things would return to a degree of normality for them all.

As she mulled this over, Vince wandered off to speak to his sergeant who glared at them from afar but didn't venture closer.

When they were alone once more, Belinda took the serviette from her pocket and placed it back on the table just as Ivan appeared from around the corner of the Meerkat Mansion. His forehead was furrowed and his mouth downturned. His purposeful walk was made all the more formal by his hands thrust deep in his pockets, a quirk that Belinda recognised as a sign he had things on his mind. That this memory had come flooding back momentarily stunned her: she hadn't thought about his idiosyncrasies for so long, she had assumed that she was cured. Apparently not.

'It's Ivan,' she murmured, more to herself than Harry.

'Perhaps he can share his forehead – I mean, foresight with us,' said Harry.

'Hello, Ivan,' said Belinda as he joined them. 'Everything OK? What have you been up to?'

Her questions earned her a sideways look from Harry, who was back to fiddling with his polystyrene cup.

'I've been talking to the police and Rob,' he said, taking the seat Vince had vacated. 'That poor guy who'd been strangled, it turns out that he was here a lot and caused lots of problems, such as threatening to sue for ridiculous stuff.'

'Is that so?' said Harry, swirling the last of his latte in his cup.

'We were aware of some of the issues,' said Belinda, seeing Harry's head snap up as she spoke. 'Anyway, how about you? Are you doing OK, considering all that's happened?'

'Yeah, yeah,' said Ivan, at last taking one hand out of his pocket and bringing his mobile phone with it. 'I really should give Estelle a call and make sure she's OK.'

Harry raised an eyebrow, a gesture that Belinda couldn't have failed to notice. She did, however, pick up the folded serviette complete with scribbled murder musings from the table and put it back in her pocket. She was happy to talk suspects with Harry, but not Ivan. A touch of a childish reaction, but one she couldn't help.

'It's good you're looking out for her,' she said, recognising the smallness of her own voice.

'She's been under a lot of pressure lately,' said Ivan.

'Murder will do that,' said Belinda, feeling more put out than she had a right to be.

'I've already told a couple of the police officers that they could clear this up in no time if they got on and interrogated the protestors,' said Ivan, with an edge to his tone and a scowl in the direction of the gates. 'A quiet word with one or two of them would soon get results.'

'That's not how we do things here, Ivan,' said Belinda. 'The police are perfectly capable of investigating a murder without resorting to anything of the kind.'

She locked eyes with him and wondered, not for the first time, whether she had overreacted to the way he had treated her back in Africa. He loved animals, that much was true, and yet here he was in her home county, only a couple of carnivore pens away from a murder, talking about forcing information out of the animal protestors.

'I was talking to one of them earlier,' said Ivan, shoving his hands back into his pockets. 'They all knew Simon Carter. He used to raise money for animal charities by doing all sorts of sponsored activities – walking for sloths, swimming for whales, jogging for jaguars, reading for pandas—'

'Sorry? What?' said Harry. 'Did you say, "reading for pandas"?'

'Yeah,' said Ivan, his brows drawing together. 'I was a bit surprised by that one but I suppose pandas might appeal to the bookish types. And they *are* black and white, so it kind of makes sense. If it raises money for a good cause, I'm all for it.'

'Well, I'll be,' said Harry. 'What else did the protestors have to say?'

'About the only thing I learned was that they knew him,' said Ivan. 'I've made up my mind not to get involved.'

'We understand your reluctance,' said Belinda, in a concerted effort at keeping her tone light. 'After all, you came here for the animals and they come first.'

Ivan glanced across at Harry, and without meeting Belinda's eye, said, 'Yes, it should always be about the animals.'

There was a short, awkward silence before Harry said, 'If you're done here, Belinda, I can run Ivan back to yours a little later.'

'That would... that would be good with me,' said Ivan. 'Only if it's not too much trouble.'

'In that case,' said Belinda, standing up, 'I'll see both of you later on.'

Without waiting for either of them to say a word, Belinda made her way back to her Land Rover, leaving behind the man who had once broken her heart and another who was helping it to heal again.

15

Harry spent several more hours with Rob and other members of the team assisting the police in any way they could. Progress was slow and by the time he was allowed to leave, Harry was exhausted. He had forgotten the sheer slog of a murder investigation, especially when he wasn't the one leading it.

As much as he tried to keep an eye on Ivan, there were many times when he didn't know where the South African had taken himself off to. It shouldn't have made Harry as edgy as it did, especially when he couldn't tie his suspicions down to anything concrete. Ivan had, after all, freely volunteered the information that he had spoken to one of the protestors, although he hadn't mentioned that he had done so out of earshot of the others. Harry didn't want to tell the police before he had a chance to think it over. He didn't honestly know if his judgement was clouded by jealousy and that certainly wasn't a reason to label Ivan as a murder suspect.

Rob had been showing Harry the CCTV system when the night shift turned up to take over. PC Vince Green stuck his head in to let Harry know that he could leave for the day and take Ivan with him. By that time, the sun had begun to slip from the evening sky and with little else in the way of background noise, the howler monkeys were in fine voice.

'Do they do that *all* night?' said Harry, not sure he was looking forward to his night shifts.

Rob chortled and said, 'You get used to it. Listen, Harry, thanks so much for your help today. I'm sorry you've been thrown in at the deep end, and I apologise if I've come across as a bit short. I've only been abrupt because you've years of police work behind you: you're used to taking and following orders, but let me know if I step over the line. I respect your opinion. If I'm terse, it's only because I'm under pressure trying to keep a wonderful animal sanctuary going. Most of us – including me – would give anything to keep this place afloat. It's obvious someone's out to cause as much grief for the zoo as possible.'

'Forget about it, I'm glad I could help,' he said, checking he had his phone and keys before heading towards the door. 'All I have to do is find Ivan before I go home.'

'The last time I saw him, he was heading back towards the main gate,' said Rob, with a wave in the direction of the CCTV screens.

'In that case, I can pick him up on the way out,' said Harry, hand already on the door, keen to get going and find Belinda so they could continue to discuss the day's events. 'What time do you want me back here tomorrow?'

'Tomorrow?' Rob paused from tidying the papers on his desk and glanced up at the clock. 'Don't go nuts, let's say 10 a.m.' He returned to thumbing through the files in front of him and muttered, 'See you then.'

Harry wasn't about to argue, so headed out of the door, mobile in hand to call Ivan. It took him a few seconds to find Belinda's message forwarding him Ivan's number, by which time, he was a little distance from the security office. He saved the number into his contacts and wandered towards his own car.

With one hand on the driver's door, the other holding his phone to his ear, Harry ran an eye over the offices as he waited for the call to connect.

'Hello,' said Ivan.

'Hey, Ivan, it's Harry. I'm about to leave. Shall I pick you up by the main gate?'

'Oh, yeah, I... I'm... Yes, that's perfect. See you then.'

Harry shrugged as Ivan ended the call. 'Well, that was to the point,' he murmured to himself, about to get into his car when a flash of something on the other side of the offices caught his eye. By this time, the light was weak and Harry was convinced that he had seen something green. In amongst hundreds of trees with a moderate breeze stirring the branches, that was hardly conclusive. Nevertheless, Harry was reluctant to leave it there. There had just been a murder after all, not to mention someone cutting a hole in the fence.

Making as little noise as possible and trying to keep away from an obvious approach path, Harry made his way across the hundred feet towards the edge of the tree line. The three offices were nestled on his left-hand side, the view across the marsh to his right and an acre or so of woodland in front of him.

As he walked, Harry concentrated on the gap where he thought he had seen movement. Suddenly, someone stepped out into a clearing.

'Ivan,' called Harry. 'What are you doing over there? I thought you were down by the front gate?'

Ivan jolted as he heard his name being shouted and sported an expression of the guilty. His lips moved but someone had hit the mute button. Eventually, he waved and gave a silent laugh. He ambled over and said, 'You're probably wondering what I'm doing here?'

'Er, yes,' said Harry. 'The clue being when I asked you, "What are you doing over there?"'

'I was taken short. Sorry for the detail, but I think the truth is always best, don't you?'

'That's a good philosophy,' said Harry, not entirely convinced that he was being fed anything other than lies. 'Why didn't you come over to the security office and use the facilities there?'

Ivan placed his hands on his hips and said, 'Apart from not wanting to disturb the very important work you're doing – there's no messing around when it comes to a murder investigation – I've spent a lot of time far away from any type of facilities. It comes naturally to me.' Ivan stepped forward and placed a hand on Harry's shoulder. 'From what you said on the phone, I'd got the impression that you were already at the gate, that's why I agreed to meet you there. I didn't want to put you out any more than necessary. Come on, let's go.'

Ivan made his way over to the car park, leaving Harry puzzling over exactly why the South African had been loath to disturb him in the security office when he thought he was at the gate. More pressingly, as Harry wrinkled his nose at his shoulder, he hoped that Ivan was lying about what he'd been doing, otherwise, come 5 November, there was going to be one very well-dressed guy on the bonfire.

16

Belinda had got home feeling dejected. Since Ivan's revelation that he had ended things with his fiancée and travelled across continents to get to Belinda, she had failed to summon the courage to speak to him about it again. Little things kept stopping her, such as Ivan jumping into a lion enclosure, Simon Carter's murder and then someone deliberately injuring a giraffe. Now she was at home, unable to rest and keen to find out where she stood.

Realising that she was chewing on her fingernail – a sure sign of stress – she dialled Ivan's number. He answered on the third ring.

'What time are you likely to be back?' she said. 'I think we need to have a talk.'

There was a brief pause. 'Harry's giving me a lift now. Providing the police allow us in the zoo tomorrow, I'm planning on being there for a few days at least. Otherwise, I'll be at yours, if that's OK with you?'

'Yes, yes, of course it is,' she said. It cheered her that he would be around long enough to put a few ghosts to rest. At least, that was what she told herself. Was she really conflicted over Ivan when she and Harry had become so close? She would never do anything to jeopardise what she had with him. Although, when she stopped to think about it, what exactly did she have with Harry other than a very solid friendship? Still, she couldn't afford to give that up.

Belinda realised that the line had gone quiet. She imagined the scene as Ivan sat beside Harry as he navigated the country roads, completely unaware that her ex-boyfriend was trying to rekindle their relationship. At last, for want of something better to say, she asked, 'What are your plans for this evening?'

'Once Harry's dropped me off, I have a few calls to make so perhaps we can catch up in the morning?'

'That should be all right,' she said, wondering why Ivan wasn't keener to talk to her sooner. 'Would you please let Harry know that I'd like to speak to him once he's dropped you off?' She heard Ivan relay the message and Harry's reply that he'd wait for her at the front door.

Belinda hovered nervously by her own front door. She knew that it made more sense to speak to Harry in private about Simon's murder. She couldn't rely on Ivan giving them the space she wanted without having a plan. Luckily, Marcus had come home just as she was ending her call with Ivan. Unwittingly – as was frequently her brother's way – he had helped her out by promising to ensure that their house guest was fed after Ivan had made all of the calls he needed to.

With the housekeeping matters taken care of, Belinda had one less thing to think about, leaving her with the bigger issue of a murder to occupy her thoughts. Talking it through again with Harry would help. It always did.

The shrill ringing of her phone brought her instantly back to the present. Belinda grabbed it from the wooden table beside the front door and answered it.

'Hey, Belinda,' said PC Vince Green. 'I tried Harry but he didn't answer.'

'Hello, Vince. He's driving at the moment. Is everything all right?'

'I've done a little digging and it turns out that although Simon Carter had family, they didn't have all that much to do with him. They weren't exactly estranged – there were a few text messages and other group chats on his phone – but everyone is either out of the country on a Mediterranean cruise or accounted for at work today. Sadly, he didn't seem to have any friends really. Sorry.'

'Thank you so much for that, Vince,' said Belinda. 'You've been very helpful. I'll let Harry know as soon as he gets here.'

Belinda's nerves calmed when she spotted Harry's Audi heading up the driveway towards her. She stood rubbing her hands, her shoulders hunched against the bite of the early evening autumnal chill.

Harry glanced at her waiting in the doorway, a look of surprise on his face. Ivan turned his head in her direction and gave her an empty smile. The two of them got out of the car and walked up the steps to her. 'Good to see you both,' she said. 'Ivan, Marcus is inside and has quite the evening planned out for you. He mentioned poker and snooker, and had a glint in his eye. Best of luck.'

'Thanks for the lift, Harry,' said Ivan. 'Bel, I'll catch up with you in the morning when we can have a proper chat.' He joined her on the top step, gave her a peck on the cheek and left them to it.

'Are you all right?' said Harry. 'I couldn't hear what you were saying on the phone but I could make out your tone and it sounded a bit frantic.'

'Remember... oh, I don't know... a lifetime ago when you found out that you'd got the job and I said I'd take you out to the pub to celebrate?'

'Before we got involved in another murder? Of course, but I wouldn't hold you to it now, not after the day we've had.'

'To be fair, H, you've had a much longer day than I have. I expect you're hungry – you usually are – and I'm famished.' She watched him rub his stomach and contemplate her offer.

'Sounds too good to be true. What's the catch?'

Belinda raised an eyebrow and said, 'We talk all things murder and suspects and you listen to my theories. I've given this a lot of thought and we need to clear this up before the bad publicity has a negative impact on what should be a family attraction. The murder is bad enough but this could be the end of the zoo.' She steered clear of adding that she didn't want the ending of Simon Carter's life in such a brutal manner to tarnish Harry's reputation in any way. He wouldn't take kindly to her motivation being about his professionalism.

'The pub it is, then,' said Harry, gesturing at his car. 'We may as well drive, especially as I have to be up for work in the morning.'

It didn't take them long to travel the very short distance to the end of the driveway, around the village green, past the shops, eateries, microbrewery and Little Challham's two pubs. They parked behind the New Inn. It was partly owned by Belinda who had invested a substantial sum of money in it, and the venture had been quite the ride. Things were improving however, especially with the recent appointment of her bar manager Freddie Laker.

They walked inside the seventeenth-century pub, its black-and-white frontage welcoming and unremarkable at the same time. A fair few tables were occupied and a handful of regulars were standing at the bar. The clientele was a mixture of couples, families and men partaking in a silent pint before heading home for the evening.

'Fredders,' said Harry when the tall, thin, almost gangly young man dressed in a white shirt and orange tie leaned across the beer pumps to greet them. 'How's things? Love the outfit. Have you followed your calling for a life on the airlines and got a job with EasyJet?'

'I never tire of hearing your hilarious wisecracks, Harry,' said Freddie in his startlingly deep voice. He pushed his glasses up the bridge of his nose. 'Hi, Belinda. What can I get you two?'

'A small Sauvignon Blanc for me, please, Freddie,' she said. 'Whatever Harry would like, and two menus.'

Harry clapped his hands together and examined the beer taps. 'A pint of Hopping Mad, if you would. Oh, and let's not forget that the emergency exits are here, here and here.' Harry made an exaggerated arm action of pointing in front, to the side and behind him.

'Take a seat. Please,' said Freddie, 'and I'll bring them over.'

Belinda made her way to a table at the rear of the pub, saying hello to a few more of her friends, neighbours and potential local murderers as she went. Most of the tables towards the back were empty and she made a strategic choice of one that was partially shielded by the screen to the side of the kitchen door.

As soon as they were seated side by side, Belinda leaned in to Harry and said, 'Guess what I found out?'

He shrugged. 'Marcus has had another terrible business idea?'

'That's a given. No, first of all, Vince called and we can rule Simon Carter's family out. They're completely alibied.'

'Fast work,' said Harry. 'I hope he doesn't get in hot water for telling us.'

'I'm sure he'll be fine,' said Belinda, wanting to avoid Harry giving her a run-down of police professional standards. 'When I got home, I thought I'd use some time to find out what I could about Edward Logan. And what I discovered was a bit of a game-changer. Ah, Freddie's coming over. Wait until he's gone and I'll tell you more.'

The bar manager placed their drinks in front of them, left two menus and told them he'd be back shortly.

'He's shaved his goatee off,' said Harry. 'I must remember to mention it when he comes back to take our order.'

'I think he knows,' said Belinda. She touched Harry's shoulder. 'Oh, that smells a bit funky, if you don't mind me saying.'

'Good point. You'd be wise to wash your hands before we eat. Anyway, never mind my jacket, what did you find out?'

'Edward Logan, as we know, worked in a supermarket and was sacked. A little bit of online research and bingo! What we didn't know was *why* he was dismissed.' Belinda made an open-palmed gesture with both hands. 'The reason was because he threatened a customer. And that customer was Simon Carter.'

'I'll be,' said Harry. 'Any idea why Edward threatened him?'

'As it happens, yes. Simon apparently slipped on a slick of spilled yoghurt in the chilled aisle and claimed he'd broken his ankle. It wasn't the first time he'd been in the store and caused problems – according to the one hundred per cent infallible accuracy of the internet – and Edward had had just about enough of him. He grabbed him by the lapels and hauled him to his feet.'

'Hmm, not sure about the complete reliability of that,' said Harry. 'Simon didn't strike me as the sort to wear a suit.'

'It's purely a minor detail,' said Belinda, picking up her menu even though she knew it off by heart.

'The devil is in the detail,' said Harry, following her lead. 'Although I get your point entirely.'

'We're running out of other suspects,' she said, 'if we follow the line of thinking that Simon's murder would damage the zoo. My money is currently on Edward Logan. I strongly suspect that the little boy was thrown into the lion enclosure as a distraction before someone tied a bandana around Simon's throat. Where Simon was found was close enough for the culprit to get from the lion enclosure to the rear of the hay store, provided Simon was definitely going to be there.'

'Who else could have been nearby?' said Harry.

'We know that Edward was there,' said Belinda. 'He's fit enough, strong enough, knew Simon and had a reason to kill him. As they say, job done.'

'He's certainly looking favourite,' said Harry, studying his menu.

'We should pay him a visit in the morning,' said Belinda before glancing up at Freddie who was approaching with the order pad. 'I'll have the chicken salad, please.'

'Pie of the day for me, Freddie, and don't be shy with the chips,' said Harry. 'And what about the incident with the giraffe?'

Belinda turned to face him. 'I don't think we should rule out the possibility of Edward doing both.'

'Strangling a man and tripping up a giraffe are hardly in the same league,' Harry said after considerable consideration. He picked up his pint and took a glug. 'But I'll grant you, they're clearly not your everyday activities, so, yes, very possibly they were done by the same person or people. You were closer than me to the lion enclosure when the boy went in. Was there any sign of Edward Logan then?'

'No, no, I didn't see him,' she said, picking up her glass and swirling the wine. 'But then I was too distracted by what was going on feet below us.'

'Perhaps if we rattle him enough, Edward might tell us anything else he knows about Simon,' said Harry. 'At least we'll be making progress. By the sounds of it, Vince hasn't turned up anything else.'

With a satisfied nod, she chinked her glass against Harry's. 'Thank you. You know talking things through with you always reassures me. Not to mention, you've completely alleviated any ideas I might have had about Ivan talking to the protestors.'

'Pray tell.'

'Ivan knows how much I love giraffes and one of the few things we have found the time to talk about was how he's going to help Estelle Samuels with the design of a grand giraffe lodge. He wants to make up for what he did.'

'I see.' Harry fiddled with his knife and fork. 'Can I ask... Do you want to tell me— No, I'm sorry, it's none of my business.'

Now was the moment for Belinda to unburden the secret she had been keeping to herself for so long. With a deep breath, she gazed down at her hands. 'Ivan and I had always agreed that the animals came first and we would do all we could to prevent poaching and hunting.' She let go of her wine glass, fearful she might snap it. 'So, we helped establish the reserve for visitors to come and see them in their natural habitat, running free. I loved the giraffes, and he loved the lions. We had one male lion, Lennie. Don't be fooled by the daft name: he was ferocious. One day, while I was on a trip to the city, Ivan arranged for some hunters to come onto the reserve and hunt Lennie. They shot him dead.'

Silence followed. Harry reached over and took her trembling hand in his. 'I'm so sorry, Bel. That must have been terrible. What did Ivan say?'

She gave him a startled look. 'Say? There was nothing to say. He'd allowed something that he knew I would never have agreed to, and made sure it took place when I was out of the way. I only came back early because there was a travel mix-up, otherwise, I might never have known how Lennie died. Ivan tried to justify what he'd done but I saw red, packed and got out of there as quickly as I could. What else could I do?'

'I hate to state the obvious,' said Harry, 'but if Ivan was

instrumental in allowing people to shoot a lion, why wouldn't he injure a giraffe?'

'He stayed at our home last night and had no way of getting to the zoo and back without us knowing. He couldn't have done it today because he was already inside the zoo, so why would he cut his way in? Not to mention, he didn't know Simon and has no interest in harming the zoo, financially or otherwise.'

Harry let go of her hand to scratch at his stubble. 'All good points. Look, I tell you what, I start work at 10 a.m., so how about an early start? The only problem is, we don't know where Edward Logan lives.'

'I do,' said Belinda. 'It was on the top of his CV in the office.'

'We can't use that information,' said Harry. 'It's a breach of data protection.'

'Oh, we'll say we looked him up on the voters' register.'

'Except we haven't.'

'Then we will,' said Belinda, feeling much more positive now she had told Harry the reason she had walked out on Ivan and what he'd done. 'And look, here comes your pie.'

Belinda knew that would give her the final word.

17

At 8 a.m. on a bright, crisp Thursday morning, Belinda walked to Harry's home. He lived in the Gatehouse at the bottom of Little Challham castle's driveway. He had rented the property from Belinda a few months earlier, neither of them realising who the other one was or remembering that their paths had crossed many years ago when Harry had arrested her for demonstrating against live animal exports at the Port of Dover. She was happy to have him as both a tenant and as a friend. That he lived within walking distance from her front door was another advantage.

Belinda made her way along the edge of the green, past the Gatehouse and to the rear garden where they had agreed to meet. Harry was already next to his car, about to get in.

'Morning,' he said. 'I hope that Edward Logan's in a good mood today. I'm still not entirely sure how you managed to talk me into going to his house without telling the police what we found out.'

'Providing they've heard of the internet at the police station, they're equally as informed as me.' She winked at him and got into the passenger seat.

. . .

For the next twenty minutes, Belinda directed Harry towards a small village complete with a community centre, doctors' surgery and a part-time fire station on the outskirts of Ashford. They turned into a long straight road, fields on one side, a row of houses on the other. Harry drew up outside number eighty-two.

'I'd suggest that we go for a subtle approach,' said Harry as Belinda opened her door.

'I wouldn't have it any other way,' she said, a smile tugging at her mouth. 'Come on.'

They had only taken a couple of steps along the pathway of the three-bedroom semi-detached house when the front door opened. Harry stopped on the broken concrete, and put an arm out to bring Belinda to a halt.

'It's all right,' called out Edward Logan, his voice gruff. 'I've not long been up and saw you pull up. Come on in.' He walked back inside, the back of his hair still ruffled from sleep and his tartan pyjamas testament to his words.

Warily, the two of them entered the house.

Edward reached the kitchen and, indicating the kettle, said, 'Just about to have a brew. Do you want one?'

'Er, no, but thanks,' said Harry.

'We'd like to ask you about yesterday,' said Belinda.

The pyjama-clad young man held his hands up. 'Sorry, sorry, sorry. I shouldn't have stormed out of the interview and I shouldn't have shouted at you.' He addressed the last part of his comment to Harry and lowered his hands. 'I was completely out of order. I'd lost my security job at the local supermarket for... I suppose you could call it being a little overzealous at dealing with the troublemakers. It's certainly not an excuse, but you see, the day I got fired, I'd worked a double shift from eight o'clock the night before and I was drained. I threw someone out of the supermarket and when I got home, I had a postcard from the wife telling me that she'd left me. The last couple of weeks have been total hell.' His face dropped and his shoulders sagged. He had the air of a broken man.

'I'm very sorry to hear that,' said Belinda. 'That must have been a terrible shock.'

'It was.' He sighed and picked up the kettle. 'She'd only popped out to return a library book. Meanwhile, I'd got out of bed, worked a double shift, and then a postcard of Bognor Regis appeared on the doormat to tell me she wasn't coming back.' He shook his head as he ran the tap, filling up the kettle.

'Look, I feel really bad that I got the job when things are difficult for you right now,' said Harry. 'How about I put in a good word? There's bound to be other openings soon.'

Edward moved to the counter. 'Cheers, pal, but don't worry yourself. As it happens, after I left the zoo, an old school friend of mine called. He runs a casino down on Margate seafront. I drove straight over to see him, and he offered me a job. It's better money, better hours and members only, so I won't have to put up with the likes of Simon Carter.'

While he busied himself taking a mug, coffee jar and sugar from the cupboard, Belinda gave Harry a 'go on' gesture.

'About Simon Carter,' said Harry, clearing his throat.

'You know him?' said Edward. 'Hang on, you're not about to serve a court order or writ or something on me for hurling him out of the store, are you? There was absolutely nothing wrong with that weasel's ankle. I watched him walk up and down the aisle a number of times looking at the spillage before he decided to fall over. His fall was about as genuine and unscheduled as canned laughter.'

'No, we're here about something else entirely,' said Harry. 'Simon's dead.'

'Wow,' said Edward, leaning back against the edge of the worktop. 'I wasn't expecting you to say that. How did he die?'

'He was murdered,' said Harry.

Edward put a hand up to cover his mouth. 'Get away! Murder. Who'd do something— Hang on.' He dropped his hand and the anger he'd been so quick to exhibit the day before was back. 'You think I killed him? Get out of my house.'

'We're only trying to find out if there's anyone you can think of who would have wanted him dead,' said Belinda, her uncharacteristically softer tones halting Edward as he pushed himself away from the counter.

'You're an ex-copper, aren't you? You should be able to work it out. Try taking a look at the so-called security team at Brabourne Gardens and ask yourself who was last seen with Simon. Why would I turn up, not get a job, kill someone and confront you? All I'd have done is draw attention to myself. How much of a cretin do you think I am? I didn't leave the area around the security office before or after my interview because I was waiting to have a word with you. Besides, I just told you that I drove straight to the coast to see my mate who runs the Margate Royale. He can vouch for me.'

Harry opened his mouth to answer him. Before he had a chance to speak, with unusual tact, Belinda said, 'We'll see ourselves out.'

18

The traffic was kind, allowing them to make it to the zoo in plenty of time for Harry's shift. He tried his best to persuade Belinda that she would be better off at home, but she was having none of it. Harry had come to terms with the idea that Ivan was back in Belinda's life, so she may as well go and have 'The Chat'. He had a sinking feeling that now Ivan was here, in her home, trying to save giraffes and the local zoo from an untimely end right before her eyes, she was going to forgive him. Would Harry make a complete fool of himself if he told her how he felt about her?

'If we're ruling out Edward Logan for lack of opportunity,' said Belinda, breaking into Harry's thoughts, 'where does that leave us?'

'It'll be easy enough to track his movements around the security office,' said Harry. 'That's the one bit of the CCTV that does seem to work. We can rule him out with his arrival and departure times through the gate too. I'll mention it to Vince as soon as I get to work.'

'So, we're back to who wants to cause damage to the zoo,' said Belinda.

'As I'm early,' said Harry, driving past the staff entrance, 'let's go to the main gate and see if we can catch the protestors before they start arguing with one another about elephant welfare.'

'That one with the dreadlocks is on his mobile filming the traffic,' said Belinda. 'How's that going to save the elephants?'

'Perhaps he collects number plates,' said Harry, slowing the car and indicating. He stared at the man, his clean, smooth face at odds with the tangle of mousy dreadlocks that reached to his waist. He was in his late twenties, dressed in a dark blue anorak, tweed trousers held up by braces, and black boots.

'He seems the ideal person to talk to first,' said Harry, pulling the car to a stop. 'He looks like the one Ivan was talking to and, with any luck, it might even give us an idea which group is on which side. I'm clueless.'

They walked back onto the main road, one group of protestors on one side of the gate, their rivals on the other. Harry and Belinda turned right and approached the dread-locked man eyeing them with interest. He was so intrigued he lowered his phone for the briefest of times before remembering what he was supposed to be doing. A couple of his comrades stepped closer.

Harry swept the gathering crowd for signs of trouble. He didn't want to create a situation on his second day, and most certainly didn't want to cause any upset while Belinda was beside him. More because he had an inkling that she might hurt someone. There was a touch of the Mrs Emma Peel about her.

'Morning,' said Harry.

'If you say so,' said the protestor, his grey eyes fixed on Harry.

'Well, it is morning, so I don't see that as a point of contention,' said Harry. He reminded himself that he had dealt with the chopsy public for thirty years, so he was certain he could hold it together for another ten minutes.

'You OK there, James?' said a young woman with short black hair, a tattooed neck and a scowl. Beside her stood a much older man who could have been her grandfather: he sported the same disgruntled facial expression, which appeared to have been handed down through the generations.

Harry counted another five people behind the three immediately in front of him and Belinda. He turned ninety degrees and took stock of the opposing team. 'There's three more of them than there are of you. Still, at least you've got enough for a five-a-side game if the weather gets a bit parky and you have to run around to keep warm.'

'Did you actually want something?' said James. He placed his feet square with his hips and crossed his arms. The woman behind him tried to do the same but she had difficulty keeping her placard upright. Its slogan read 'Elephants never forget'.

'We wanted to talk to you, that's all,' said Belinda.

'Why?' said the woman with the placard.

'Not all of you,' said Harry. 'I'd appreciate a couple of minutes with James.'

'OK,' he said. 'But I'm not getting in your car.'

'Good,' said Harry. 'I've just had it valeted.'

'You're not taking me to a police station or away from this demonstration,' said James. 'I've got work to do.'

'We can see that,' said Belinda, 'and we appreciate what you're doing for the elephants, but you must be aware of what happened here yesterday?'

'With that giraffe, you mean?' said James, his face clouding over. 'Me and Carmel lit candles and stayed awake all night sending positive thoughts her way.'

The placard-carrying woman behind James nodded vigorously and said, 'All night, all night.'

Harry held back from asking if it was the chanting and hoping that had done the trick or the veterinary care and medical treatment. Other than wanting these people to help him, he knew from previous experience that animal rights protestors were frequently some of the most extreme when it came to the life and liberty of any living creature, as long as it wasn't human.

'No,' said Harry. 'I was referring to Simon Carter's murder.'

'Oh, yeah,' said James, stepping towards Harry and Belinda. 'That was sad. Simon was a decent enough sort. He raised a fortune for so many voiceless souls.'

'Er, thanks for speaking to me,' said Harry. 'I'm part of the security team and if you knew Simon, anything you can tell us would be very helpful.'

James contemplated Harry's words as he stared up at the trees; a robin spied down on them from a branch, and cocked its head.

'Even that small bird up there deserves a chance to live a free and unhindered life,' said James. 'Humans are ruining this planet. We breed animals – poultry, livestock, fish to feed *us* – and in order to feed those animals, we have to breed animals to feed *them*. How screwed up is that? Breeding animals to feed animals to be fed to us? That's not sustainable. That's why I'm a raw vegan.'

'That's terrific,' said Harry, not having the foggiest idea what the man was talking about. 'When did you last see Simon Carter?'

'Shouldn't you be leaving this to the police?' said James.

'Yes, and we are,' said Belinda. 'This is our way of helping them out and learning anything that we can about poor Simon. I'm sure you understand.'

James pursed his lips and said, 'He used to come and chat to us from time to time when we were at demonstrations – anti-live animal exports at the docks, stuff like that. He didn't want to get involved in anything too active, but I do know that he gave money to various charities. He raised a lot of cash and made people aware of how endangered some species are. Simon didn't have any children but had a number of nieces and nephews, although he didn't see them from one year to the next. Even so, every Christmas, as well as giving them presents, he would sponsor an animal for each of them, the same on their birthdays. He was a very generous man, if a bit odd.'

'Did Simon have a problem with anyone at the zoo?' said Harry.

'Not that I know of,' said James. 'He used to get people's backs up: he was irritating and according to him, he was always trying to wind up the trustees on the board. He used to try and provoke me by telling me that we're wasting our time here and should be on the other side, joining forces, that sort of thing. But keeping these elephants here is the worst idea ever. They should be back in Africa where they belong.'

'Oh,' said Harry, suddenly realising that James, Carmel and their six amigos were against the elephants staying. 'I see, because I thought—'

'It's such an emotive subject, isn't it?' said Belinda, whose attention was drawn to Carmel edging closer to them. 'Why are you against them staying here?'

'Because they never forget!' said Carmel, thrusting her placard in between Belinda and James. 'That lot over there are crazy if they think these animals can live happily here when the knowledge that they should be on another continent is in their very core. It's barbaric. They need to go home and we're here to make sure this project actually goes ahead. We heard whispers that this was purely publicity for the zoo and the animals aren't going anywhere. It's all to make money and enslave more animals. All zoos should be closed and the animals freed. It's our mission statement, everything we stand for. How would you like to be kept in a cage your entire life?'

'And you? Carmel, is it?' said Harry, easing her placard out of his eyeline. 'How well did you know Simon Carter?'

'Me?' she said, pushing her bottom lip out, her breath

coming in short rasps after her outburst. 'I only spoke to him once. That was yesterday when he turned up here with his poncy VIP pass. The next I'd heard, he was dead, so don't look at me.'

An electric buggy charging down the driveway towards them caused the group to pause their conversation. While everyone else's attention was on Rob Piper and Estelle Samuels and their hasty approach, Harry took the chance to study James and Carmel. Both were dressed in clothes with more wear than a bald tyre and looked as if they'd spent at least one night sleeping in the elements. He was more than a little curious as to where James charged his mobile phone. *Perhaps he has a room in a Travelodge*, he thought as he weighed up James's motivation. How radical were they in their quest to have the zoo closed down?

Rob brought the buggy to a rapid stop inches from the garden's gateway and jumped out, followed by Estelle. She was dressed in a Brabourne Gardens polo shirt, lightweight beige trousers and black heavy-duty boots, her hair secured in a messy plait. Her movements were much more fluid than they had been when wearing her interviewing outfit the previous day.

'Harry, Belinda,' said Rob. 'Glad to see that you've turned up early. Let's get you both inside so we can run over a few things.' He shot a look of utter contempt at both Carmel and James before turning his attention to those on the other side of the gates. 'Waste of space, all of them.'

'I can drive Belinda to the office if you and Harry don't mind the walk,' said Estelle. 'We've got a couple of things to talk about – Ivan, in particular.'

Belinda opened her mouth to speak, then a cloud passed over her face. 'I'm not sure that Harry and I have finished here.'

'We've certainly got nothing else to say,' said James, re-adopting his wide stance and hands-on-hips pose.

'Then it looks as if we are,' said Harry. 'I'll see you in the office in a while, Bel.'

'OK, then,' said Belinda, not able to resist a backwards peek at James and Carmel. 'I'll see you there.'

The two women walked towards the buggy, Harry and Rob a couple of feet behind them. 'Listen,' said Rob when they were out of earshot of both sets of demonstrators, 'I know that you've plenty of experience behind you but watch yourself around that lot. I particularly don't trust James Kara. Even before they all turned up, waving their banners and spouting off about anything that avoids having to actually get a job, I'd seen him around the zoo.

'I'd be the first to admit that security hasn't always been the best. We had a couple of penguins escape from the Penguin Palace and one of our rhinos went missing for a day – don't worry, he came back. Needless to say, shortly before these things happened, James was here. We can't afford any more bad publicity, and we can't have the animals roaming around the Kent countryside. That's why we need you heading up the security, especially with Drew Matterson going AWOL on us.'

'To be honest with you, Rob, I'm not sure I know much about chasing down a rhino but I'll give it my best shot,' said Harry. 'Have you told the police about James being around whenever something worrying happens?'

'We didn't really want anyone to know about the penguins or the rhino, so we've managed to keep it low-key.' Rob lowered his voice before adding, 'I hope I can rely on you to keep schtum about this?'

'I'm not sure that I'd pretend all's well on the rhino headcount if it's not. That wasn't what I signed up for. And what's happened to Drew?'

'Never mind about Drew, he's bound to turn up. Yesterday just scared him. Look, you won't have to do anything dodgy. For a start, what are the chances of any of the animals getting lost again? Besides, we're thinking of asking Ivan to be a consultant on a more permanent basis, until things are fully up and running. We have big, big dreams of rivalling zoos across the country, not just the county.' Rob stopped and put a hand on Harry's arm. 'I know that I won't find a better person to help us. Someone is trying to make the zoo look very bad and it'll put the lives and futures of all the animals in jeopardy if I don't take action. We won't get another shot at this.'

Harry saw the electric buggy as it rounded a corner to the left of the main entrance, the sign welcoming everyone to Brabourne Gardens, a queue already forming at the kiosks. The back of Belinda's head was just disappearing from view, her shoulder-length black hair the last thing he saw as Estelle trundled them to the staff entrance.

Ivan had already let her down over the death of one lion, and years later she couldn't forgive him. It was little wonder that Harry felt obliged to stay and do everything in his power to ensure that nothing else terrible happened. The last thing he had wanted was the fate of hundreds of creatures to rest with him. Even so, he found himself saying, 'Of course, I'll do whatever I can.'

19

Belinda was keen to catch up with Harry, but equally pleased to have a chance to wheedle information out of Estelle.

'So, tell me how things are really going,' said Belinda, her tone as nonchalant as she could manage while her fillings rattled as they bounced over speed humps.

Estelle gave a shrug, worryingly accompanied by taking both hands off the wheel and flapping them in the air. 'I have such plans, especially when it comes to animal conservation. But it's difficult to show the board how I'm going to save a species when the blessed creatures keep breaking free. The buck stops with me and, if I'm frank with you, I've seen Harry as a kind of saviour. Security was damn awful. I'd placed a lot of faith in Rob and Drew, something I'm starting to regret.'

'Drew was the last person to be seen talking to Simon Carter yesterday,' said Belinda. 'How long have you known him?'

'Drew's worked here for years and years.' Estelle slowed down as they neared the security offices. 'I trust him completely, yet he seems to have taken his eye off the ball. He loves it here so much, it's his entire world. He wanted to live on-site, but I thought that wasn't a great idea. I don't think he would ever have switched off, and I couldn't have him working twenty-four-seven. And he would have done. I found him sleeping in the security office once and had to tell him to go home.'

'That sounds a bit worrying,' said Belinda, relieved the buggy was now stationary.

'It was, especially when he told me that he thought someone was getting into the office in the night and moving his stuff,' said Estelle. 'I wasn't sure if he was saying it to prove that the place was insecure or whether it actually happened. Anyway, the reason he was sleeping here was because one of the gorillas wasn't well and Drew told me that he was setting an alarm to go and see him every ninety minutes to make sure he was doing all right.'

'Wow.'

'Wow, indeed,' said Estelle. 'As I said, he would be here permanently if I let him, so I have to put my foot down. That's why it's very odd he's not here today. Before you say it, I can't see that he's involved in Simon Carter's death. The man was a total pain, but Drew's not capable of murder.'

'Even if Simon's threats to sue jeopardised the financial security of the very thing he adored?'

'No,' said Estelle, giving a firm shake of her head, 'not Drew. Definitely not Drew. I'll tell you how much faith I have in Drew – I've nominated him to join the board, not that he knows about it. I thought it would be a lovely surprise for him. If I had my way, I would have him with us in a heartbeat. Though it's not gone down well with everyone.'

Estelle started to get out of the buggy, thought twice and added, 'Drew's proactive when it comes to security. So much so, he's always scoping areas for new cameras to go up. He knows how patchy the coverage is. On more than one occasion, he's come to find me to let me know where an ideal spot would be. He's an absolute darling. You remember the report I gave you when you were considering investing in the security system? The one that showed the problem areas? Drew helped me put that together.'

Belinda waited until Estelle climbed out before doing the same. 'Is there anyone else you can think of who would kill to protect the zoo?'

'Absolutely not, Belinda, absolutely not.' Estelle walked around the buggy to face her square on. 'I've ploughed everything I have into this place, raised so much money, begged for funding, put my life on hold, and I wouldn't take another life to protect it. To even contemplate that Drew would kill someone, that's insane. Now, if you'll excuse me, I have a zoo to run.'

For a few seconds, Belinda watched Estelle walk away before she set off in the direction of the adjacent security office.

The moment Harry and Rob stepped through the door, Belinda sprang up from the uncomfortable, wonky office chair beside the bank of CCTV screens and said, 'H, I know that you officially start work in about twenty minutes, but any chance I can buy you that coffee I promised you? You know, the one before your first official shift?' She beamed a smile at Rob and added, 'I'll have him back by 10 a.m., I promise. And by the way, the door was unlocked when I got here.'

Rob bristled but said nothing.

'Oh, OK, then,' said Harry, allowing himself to be propelled back out through the door. 'What did you find out?' he said as soon as they were a little way from the offices.

'You and I weren't given a chance to discuss anything that James told us, before Rob and Estelle arrived,' said Belinda. 'Drew hasn't turned up, according to Estelle. He's fanatical about the place and was even sleeping here at one point, keeping watch on a poorly gorilla.'

'Drew?' said Harry, following Belinda to the nearest coffee stand. 'But he told us he wasn't supposed to stay here overnight.'

'Exactly, and yet he did,' she said. 'He was last seen speaking to Simon before his death, he was near the lion enclosure when the boy fell or was thrown in, and if he's been staying overnight, he might have caused damage to either get inside or make it look like someone was breaking in. Perhaps he's been causing all these problems to show up Estelle or Rob. He told Estelle that he thought someone was getting into the office where he was sleeping and moving his stuff. She wasn't convinced, figuring it was his way of justifying sleeping on-site. Despite her reservations, Estelle adores Drew so much, she wants him on the board. I think it's clouding her judgement.'

Harry waited until Belinda had placed their order and they had stepped away with their two takeaway cups of steaming black coffee before speaking. 'Rob mentioned on the way to the offices that some of the penguins and a rhino were having a game of hide and seek.'

'That's pretty much what James told us,' said Belinda. 'That is all so bizarre. I had no idea all these things were going on. Imagine opening your bedroom curtains one morning and seeing a bear or a buffalo on your front lawn. Has this ever been reported anywhere other than internally?'

'Not from what Rob's told me. It seems that they've tried to hush it up and now that Drew's not turned up for work, from everything you've said, I think he's our number-one suspect.'

Belinda lifted her polystyrene cup to her mouth and blew on the surface of the hot liquid. 'Everything that's happened seems to have been allowed to go on due to a very poor security system in place. Rob already explained that the CCTV isn't up to much and the area where Simon's body was found is in a blind spot.'

Harry winced as he took a sip of his coffee. 'Strewth, that's hot. Exactly, and Drew would have known that. He didn't seem too bad when it came to attempting customer care. However, he did tell me that he knew Simon and he was always in here complaining. His last complaint was about the lack of proportionality of the toy orangutans' arms and legs.'

'Wow,' said Belinda. 'Simon really did have too much time on his hands.'

'Or he simply liked to moan about things for the sake of it. We know he spent many hours raising money for good causes, so he couldn't have been navel-gazing all day long.'

'Didn't you tell me that Simon said something about coming here for years?' said Belinda, with a quick check of her watch, aware her time with Harry was coming to an end.

'Yes, he told Drew and me that he'd seen the gardens go from taking in rescue animals to the family attraction it is today. Why do you ask?'

'Our list of suspects consists of security-aware Drew, who knew and probably loathed Simon; the protestors, particularly James and Carmel, who want the zoo shut down and the elephants sent somewhere – presumably their hopes being that they'd end up in Africa; and then there's Rob and Estelle,' said Belinda.

'Neither Rob nor Estelle would make any sense,' said Harry. 'They'd both have too much to lose if the zoo closed. Estelle – and Drew, come to that – would be devastated if anything put the animals in danger.'

'Perhaps Drew felt he had to impress Estelle in some way,' said Belinda. 'She hasn't yet told him that she's nominated him to join the board.'

'One theory could be that he's been causing lapses in security to show how integral he is. But I'd say murder is a step too far.'

'Tell you what,' said Belinda, 'I'll ask around the park about Drew, see if I can track him down and see what he knows about the roving rhino and wayward penguins, and we'll meet up later.'

Harry drained the rest of his coffee, seemingly in discomfort as he did so, and launched the empty cup at the nearest bin. 'There's always the chance that it was someone completely unconnected to Simon. A passing stranger who was here yesterday, and who knows where they are by now.'

'That's even more disturbing,' said Belinda, shuddering and wrapping her arms around herself, her long-sleeved blue-and-cream jumper doing little to keep out the chill of a September morning. 'I like that option least of all. If it's someone who's here now, at least we stand a chance of working out who it is.'

'That's why we need our wits about us – we simply don't know enough at this stage,' said Harry. 'I noticed quite a few unmarked police cars in the car park this morning and a number of people wandering around in suits. I'd bet that there are a dozen or so detectives here today and soon enough, we'll see our old friend PC Vince Green. I'd guess there's no police presence at the front gate today because they're all in here.'

'With luck, I'll bump into him,' said Belinda. 'See if he'll tell me anything new that we haven't worked out yet.'

'How about we meet back here in a couple of hours?' said Harry. 'That should give me time to work out what Rob wants me to do.'

They said their goodbyes and Belinda's feet took her towards the scene of Wednesday's murder. She wanted to cast an eye over the layout once more in case there was something she had missed.

Belinda stood at the edge of the thoroughfare that led from the brown bear enclosure to the large metal hay store where Simon's body had been discovered. There were a couple of uniformed police officers keeping the public away from the area. 'Still a crime scene, then,' she muttered and tapped her fingernail against her chin, wondering what it was that she was missing.

It was absurd to think of Simon being strangled with an African Savannah Safari Experience bandana, away from the crowds. In the distance, Belinda heard the land train making its way across the zoo to the other side of the hay store. The paths leading from and to the store on Belinda's side weren't wide enough to allow the land train and its carriages to manoeuvre in and around, making it a reasonably remote spot. Coffee Perks was a hundred metres away, displaying a sign announcing 'Closed from 1 October'.

All of this begged the question of why Simon had been round the back of the hay store in the first place. There weren't any enclosures nearby and other than the part-time coffee stand, nothing else in the immediate vicinity. Had he been lured to the rear of the store? If so, what or who had enticed him?

Belinda's curiosity was piqued and she found herself following the footpath to the farthest side of the hay store just as the land train went by. It was travelling at quite a speed, and while not exactly a blur, she wasn't paying all that much attention to the passengers, so had she really seen Ivan in the last carriage? Why would he be on it in the first place? It took a circuitous route around the zoo and gardens, making numerous stops. If he wanted to see various parts of it, surely he would take an electric buggy? When they had spoken last night, they had left it so that they would speak again at some point today, but without confirming a time or place. Ivan couldn't have known Belinda was going to be at the zoo, and sitting on the back of the land train in all its zebra-striped glory wasn't going to help him track her down.

She watched it disappear into the distance and felt her attention drawn past the brown bear enclosure over in the direction of the main gates. The train's first stop was a short distance inside the entrance, a stone's throw from the protestors. Ivan admitted himself he'd been speaking to them. What was he up to?

Out of curiosity, Belinda headed for the train's last stop, retracing its route to the gates. From previous visits, she was familiar with its timetabled stops and knew that between the entrance and where she had seen Ivan, there was only one other stop – the hyenas. They were most definitely not on Belinda's list of favourites, but it was another big attraction for Brabourne Gardens. Quite why, she wasn't sure, as, in their natural habitat, their attacks on humans were alarming and frequently fatal. That obviously wasn't ever going to be a problem when they were in a secure compound and were well fed and looked after.

Belinda reached the end of the pathway and strolled across to the primary viewing platform. There was a walkway along the side of the high fencing to Belinda's right-hand side, next to a bank of trees shielding the perimeter of the zoo from the road.

She stood for a minute or two watching as a few of the animals paced up and down the fence while others lay on the dry, dusty ground. They didn't exactly make her blood run cold – they were, at the end of the day, scavengers and a necessary part of the food chain. Yet she would rather face a lion or a tiger than a hyena.

While these thoughts were going round her head, Belinda peered at one of the larger carnivores as it played with a tatty black object, pushing it through the scratchy earth and tufts of grass. It looked like... It couldn't be a shoe, could it? The only way a shoe would get in the pound was if someone had thrown it in or had walked in still wearing it. That was too absurd. How would anyone get inside, get themselves attacked and not be noticed? She scanned the top of the fence and the tree line beyond. One or two of the branches in a beech tree overhanging the hyena enclosure appeared to be misshapen and out of line with the neighbouring ones. It was as if something or someone had fallen from the tree, breaking its limbs as it went.

Belinda made her way through the small crowd that had joined her in the viewing area, several staying only seconds, others taking their time and lining up their photos. No one else seemed to notice the black shoe or sensed that there was anything potentially wrong. Until she was sure, she didn't want to waste anyone's time, and yet Harry worked in security. She should at least speak to him about it.

Although if she were wrong, he would think her daft and probably feel a little miffed that on his first official day of his new job, she was calling him to tell him that something that looked like a shoe was in with the hyenas. For all she knew, they were given shoes to play with.

It didn't take Belinda long to make her way to the base of the beech tree with its bowed and crooked branches. She scouted around behind its trunk, peeked into the nearby shrubbery and gazed at the canopy above. To begin with, she couldn't spot anything out of place, and then she peered closer at the undergrowth. At first, she thought it was a piece of litter, and then she saw it was a lanyard caught in the thorny thickets of the hawthorn.

Holding her breath, she crept closer, one hand out to grab the lanyard, the other over her hammering heart. She took hold of the thin cord with trembling fingers and yanked it towards her, pulling the shoots with it. As she did so, two things became apparent to her at once: the security pass attached to the cord showed a photograph of a smiling Drew Matterson, and the gap created as she tugged it towards her revealed Drew's very dead body lying inside the hedge.

20

'Today isn't going awfully well,' said Belinda to herself, feelings of nausea rising up. She took a step backwards. The last thing she wanted to do was touch the body, and the angle of his neck and limbs, not to mention the mask of horror on his face, made it clear he was beyond helping.

Belinda took her mobile out of her pocket and called Harry. He answered on the third ring with a cheerful, 'That was quick. Can't bear to be without—'

'Harry, listen. Call 999 or grab one of the police officers who are already here. I've found a body. It's Drew.'

'Good grief, Belinda. Are you OK? Who's with you? On second thoughts, never mind. *Where* are you?'

'I'm beside the hyena enclosure, between the fence and the railings that run alongside the road. I think he fell from the tree into the thorns below. At least, that's what it looks like.'

'Listen to me: I'm on my way.'

Belinda could hear Harry grabbing whatever he needed to come and stand beside her and look at a corpse. From the amount of noise he was making, it seemed like a lot of gear to gather for a task with little activity. Not that Belinda cared, just as long as he got to her, and quickly.

'I'm jumping into an electric cart,' said Harry. 'Rob said it's the quickest way to get to you.' He sounded as though he was running and his breathing was definitely getting heavier. A door banged and the noise of shoes hitting a hard surface was unmistakable. 'I'm leaving the line open, but I can't really speak while I drive this stupid tiny toy-town cart.'

'I'm not going anywhere,' said Belinda, a chill running along her spine, making her feel as though someone had walked over her grave. There was little in the way of sunlight where she was, most of it blocked out by the trees, and the day was a touch on the chilly side. Other than Harry pushing the buggy to its limits, with a liberal peppering of profanities, the only other sounds were of a small child crying in the distance and the ice-on-the-back-of-the-neck laugh of a hyena.

For what seemed like an inordinate amount of time, the noise went on, Belinda listening in morbid fascination. When it stopped, she gave a long slow breath, shook her head and then froze again as she heard the indisputable sound of a twig snapping only feet from her.

She whirled on the spot and came face to face with PC Vince Green. She screamed and he shouted in surprise at her reaction. 'It's only me,' he said. 'What are you screaming for?'

'Why are you sneaking up on me?' she said. 'You scared me half to death.' Her heart felt as though it was running at double its normal beats per minute.

'Are you all right?' said Vince. 'If you don't mind me saying, you look a bit peaky, and what were you staring at?' He covered the distance between them in a couple of strides and stopped, rooted to the spot. 'Oh, I don't believe it. He's dead.'

Vince turned to Belinda and asked, 'Was anyone else here when you found him?'

She shook her head. 'I've only been here a short while.' She held her phone up. 'I called Harry as soon as I saw Drew lying there. Harry's on his way and Rob Piper is calling the police. Or contacting whichever of your colleagues are already in the zoo. You didn't know what happened before you crept up on me?'

The officer grabbed at his radio to call in an update. 'Have you touched or moved him at all?' He stared unblinking at Drew's broken body.

'In this outfit? In those thorns? Don't be absurd, Vince. Besides, the poor man is clearly dead.' She raised an eyebrow at the young man who gave a sigh and put through an urgent message to the police control room.

Belinda watched him give his hurried message, then pull a pair of latex gloves from one of the many pouches that were dangling from his belt. He began to wriggle into the prickly shrub. She was still watching him try to find a pulse on Drew's neck – or lack of pulse as it turned out – and listening to him stifle cries from kneeling on a thorn or snagging some part or other on the spikes, when Harry drew up in his buggy.

'Are you— Oh, is that Vince on the floor with Drew?' said Harry, coming to an abrupt stop next to her, having sprinted from the abandoned buggy as fast as his not-very-svelte frame allowed. 'How come he's here already? I left Rob on the phone to the police, so I really didn't expect anyone to have got here yet.'

'He was passing by,' said Belinda. 'What with the cadaver and all, we didn't really establish why he was on this particular route.'

'And why were you down here?' said Harry. 'It's a bit remote and I didn't think that the hyenas would have been one of your go-to animals.' He glanced over to where the sound of a laughing hyena was coming from. 'That is not a good backdrop for another dead body. It's enough to give anyone the willies.'

'I know,' said Belinda, half distracted by the grunts and murmurs from Vince as he tried to reverse himself out of the crime scene. 'I came over here because I noticed something in the hyena enclosure. I was convinced it was a shoe.'

'A shoe?' said Harry. 'Why would there be a shoe in there?'

'I don't have the foggiest,' she said, 'but it looks as though Drew's missing one. Look.' She pointed to his navy-blue sock and then to the branches above.

'He's definitely dead,' said Vince, standing up and brushing leaves and twigs from his uniform.

'It's lucky you came along when you did,' said Belinda, giving the officer a withering stare. 'The twisted limbs and lack of movement and breath were useful clues, but I value your second opinion.'

'There's no need for sarcasm,' said Harry. 'Let the lad do his job. Besides, there's always a chance that he was still breathing.'

'I'd say he's probably been there for a couple of hours at least,' said Vince, peering in the direction of the main footpath. 'I can see a flash of green uniforms coming towards us, so the paramedics are here.' He followed Harry and Belinda's gaze as they cast their eyes up towards the top of the beech tree.

'It's more difficult to tell from here,' said Belinda, raising a hand to support her neck. 'From the viewing platform for the hyenas, I had the impression that a few of the branches were broken. It was as if something had dropped through the trees.'

'I'm no pathologist,' said Vince, pulling an iPad from yet another pocket, 'but Drew must have fallen from quite a height to cause that much damage. What was he doing up the tree?'

'What about his missing shoe?' said Harry. 'The reason Belinda was over here in the first place was because she thought she'd seen a shoe in the hyena enclosure.'

'That's right,' she said, watching Vince tap what she was telling him into his iPad. 'I couldn't be one hundred per cent certain as I was some distance away, but that's what it looked like.'

'And if Drew had been up the tree, lost his footing and a shoe, he might have slipped and fallen to his death,' said Harry, moving away out of the ambulance crew's way.

'Here comes my sergeant,' said Vince. 'I'll catch up with you two in a moment.' He paused and stared at them both. 'I was going to say, don't wander off or touch anything else, except I suppose you know the drill by now.'

Belinda and Harry turned to watch the paramedics as they checked for signs of life. The paramedic closest to Vince beckoned him over and pointed to a piece of paper that had fallen to the ground. The police officer dropped to his haunches to read what was printed on it.

With a sigh, Vince got back up and walked over to Belinda and Harry. 'It's a ticket made out to Simon Carter for a VIP Safari Experience one-day extravaganza. Despite my lack of CID training, I'd put money on Drew luring Simon to the hay store to give him the ticket and killing him.'

'Well,' said Harry, a grimace on his face, 'are you saying Drew murdered Simon and then later fell out of the tree?'

'That seems a bit unlikely,' said Belinda, hugging herself. 'What was he doing up the tree in the first place?'

'If he was damaging the fences to let others inside,' said Vince, 'then perhaps he was seeing if he could get them in through the trees. Protestors love a tree, don't they? They're always chaining themselves to them and living in them.'

'In that case,' said Harry, 'thanks so much. We'll leave you to it.'

Belinda was about to protest but felt a tiny nudge from Harry, something Vince failed to spot as he hurried away to his sergeant.

'Oh, yes, we'll get out of your way. Good work, officer,' Belinda called after him.

'I've got a security office now,' said Harry. 'And it's got its very own whiteboard. There's no way this is the end of this.'

She turned to him and smiled. 'You really know a way to a woman's heart. Come on, I'll even let you drive your buggy.'

21

Harry had to admit that he was worried about Belinda. He was used to seeing dead bodies often in a more alarming state than Drew's or Simon's had been, but perhaps this was one too many. She didn't talk to him until he had driven her back to the security office and parked alongside the other buggies lined up in an orderly row.

'H,' she said, as he went to get out, 'something's bothering me.'

'The bloke with several mangled limbs, I'd guess. I think we need to talk this over, make sure you're all right.'

Belinda gave him a grateful smile. 'I know you're looking out for me, but truly, I'm OK. Besides, I wanted to speak to you about Ivan.' Harry turned, which made the lightweight cart bounce up and down as he caught his knees on the console. 'Just before I went to the hyena enclosure, I saw Ivan on the land train. That was why I walked in that direction in the first place.'

'Go on,' said Harry, not wanting to say too much before his friend unburdened herself. He was steeling himself to hear that she was going to make another go at a lasting relationship with the enormous-foreheaded South African. If that was what she wanted, as painful as it would be for Harry, he would put Belinda's happiness first.

'Ivan was already on the train when it went past me – I was over by the brown bears. Please don't look at me like that: I wanted to see if I could pick up on anything we might have missed yesterday. It struck me as strange that Simon was around the back of the hay store, somewhere he really had no business to be. But if we're to take the VIP Safari Experience ticket found beside Drew's body, I guess that would explain how he was lured there.

'Anyway, as I didn't know about the ticket then, curiosity took me towards the train's first couple of stops. The first being the gate, where we know James, Carmel and their rivals are camping out, the second about a hundred yards from the hyenas. That's when I saw the shoe, followed by the damaged branches, and then, well, the rest you know.'

'There's something bothering me about the shoe,' said Harry. 'Other than it being nibbled at by a hyena, obviously. Yesterday, Drew was wearing Reebok trainers. Today, he put on black slip-on shoes and climbed a tree. No wonder he lost his footing and fell.'

'It does seem odd,' said Belinda.

'It still doesn't help us work out what he was doing up the tree in the first place,' said Harry.

'I agree,' said Belinda, a look of concentration on her face. 'I don't buy Vince's idea that he was trying to help the protestors.'

'If our theory is correct that Simon was killed because he was a threat to the future of the zoo,' said Harry, 'it wouldn't make sense that the murderer is also trying to sabotage it at the same time.'

'Perhaps we're looking at two different people,' said Belinda. 'We might have someone who's letting the animals out, causing general mayhem and bringing the zoo's downfall, as well as whoever murdered Simon.'

'Drew might be the sort of person who was trying to put Estelle or Rob in a bad light,' said Harry, 'but I'm not sure he'd commit murder *and* try to get the zoo closed. He thought too much of the place and the animals.'

'It seems a little too convenient that Drew killed Simon because he was a threat to the zoo, and then Drew fell from a tree and conveniently died,' said Belinda.

'So, we're now facing the possibility of two murders,' said Harry, 'as well as whoever wants to discredit the zoo. All in a day's work for your average deputy head of security.'

Belinda peered around Harry at the security office's front door. 'How about we... you know? Go inside and take a tiny look at the CCTV and see if we can find out when Drew decided it was a good time to climb a tree.'

Harry nosily blew the air from his cheeks and slowly shook his head. 'That would no doubt be well outside the terms of my employment and all sorts of naughty breaches of stuff.'

'Naughty breaches of stuff?' she said. 'Is that a term often used in a court of law?'

'Noooo. Oh, come on, you're right. Let's take a look. The worst they can do is sack me.'

Harry unlocked the security office door and glanced over his shoulder at Belinda. 'Rob must have gone out to meet the police. You can keep a lookout in case he comes back and wonders what on earth we're doing.'

Ordinarily, Harry wouldn't have allowed Belinda into the office to view the CCTV. It was likely to get him into a lot more trouble than he'd let on to her, but he really didn't want to let her out of his sight.

It didn't take long before Harry had fired up the system with his recently issued password and found the cameras pointing at the hyenas and surrounding area. He could hear

Belinda moving around in the office, making her way back and forth to the window to keep an eye out for Rob or anyone else returning.

'I've found a pen, H,' she said. 'Can I wipe this whiteboard clean? It looks like a shift pattern from months ago.' When she received no reply, she walked across to the monitors and waved a hand between his face and the screens.

'Er, sorry about that,' said Harry, 'but we have a problem.' He chewed his bottom lip and turned to face her.

'What sort of problem?'

'Unfortunately,' said Harry, fighting down annoyance, 'we're not likely to find out what Drew was up to before he climbed that tree. Rob showed me how to use the system only this morning and it was working fine. Since then, someone's wiped the footage.'

22

Try as she might not to overreact, Belinda was certain this was someone sabotaging attempts to track down the killer or possibly killers. She felt fury rising.

'Who else has been in here this morning?' she said.

'Other than me and Rob, I don't think anyone since the night shift,' said Harry, pushing the sturdier of the two office chairs Belinda's way.

'Thanks, but the last thing I want to do is sit down. We should go and do something. Who else could have got in here to erase the CCTV footage? We need to speak to them.'

'OK,' said Harry. 'First things first: apart from myself, Rob and the night shift, Drew could have sabotaged the system before he went off and climbed a tree. You found the door unlocked earlier so we can't rule out the protestors sneaking in. Then there's Estelle who has an "access all areas" pass.'

'We could go and find her,' said Belinda, with a sudden wild-eyed alertness.

'I can't simply leave when I have a job to do and there's been another murder or terrible accident, whatever it's officially going to be called,' said Harry. 'The police will want to talk to night security but their report from overnight is very bland and, if they're to be trusted, they didn't note anything untoward. Besides, Stan was one of the night security called in to help out due to the staff shortages.'

'Oh,' said Belinda, taking a seat despite her earlier protestations. 'I've known Stan for years and I'd trust him with my own life.' Her earlier fury had been replaced with despair that they were getting nowhere. 'I'm working myself into a state because other than the hideous loss of life, this threatens the zoo, and ultimately the animals. The worse the publicity, the more money's lost. Estelle is going to be beside herself. She adored Drew.'

She forced herself up from the chair, propelling it backwards.

'That's the thing,' said Harry, glancing up from the screens. 'Simon's murder and now Drew's suspicious death – murder if you're not fluent in police-speak – both point towards bankrupting the zoo. Add to that, the rhino that went AWOL, the awayday penguins, a boy being literally thrown to the lions and the giraffe incident, this is about causing shame and horror.'

'To the extent of stopping families coming here, plus sponsorships and financial backing being pulled,' said Belinda. 'That all points to the protestors. I'm going to find Ivan and see if he can coax information out of them. We know he's been speaking to James.'

'Vince asked us to wait for him,' said Harry in a tone she recognised as his placatory manner. 'I know you're worried, but don't lose focus. Please.'

'Vince is a sweetheart, he'll understand.' She gave Harry her winning smile, the frown gone; her composure was back. 'Besides, I've already told him all I know.'

Harry was stopped from speaking by Belinda waving her

palms at him. 'Whatever you're going to say, you're not going to be able to prevent me leaving. Nothing you can say will change my mind.'

'You don't have your car here,' he said.

'Oh, nuts,' she said with a sigh. 'That is going to hinder my escape.' Then her face brightened. 'I'll ask Estelle if I can borrow one of the safari jeeps. Or I could nab your car for a bit.'

Fortunately, their friendship wasn't going to be stretched beyond its murder-solving limits to whether Harry trusted her with his Audi or not. He pointed back to the CCTV screens.

'There's no need for you to go and look for Ivan,' he said. 'He's still here and he's heading towards the Meerkat Mansion.'

'And it's absolutely not a problem for me to borrow the electric buggy,' she said, straightening the sleeves of her Breton top. 'And the keys are...?'

'In my pocket, where they're staying,' said Harry.

'Don't sulk, H,' she said. 'I'm doing this for you, too. Your second day as deputy head of security and there's been another *suspicious* death. It can't be doing your probationary period the world of good, after all.'

'Ah, but no one's actually been killed *in* the African Savannah Experience,' he said with a slightly pompous air.

'That's the best you've got?'

After the briefest of hesitations, Harry said, 'Fair point. But I'm driving.'

They trundled along at a speed that infuriated Belinda. Still, she knew Harry wasn't about to break the speed limit for anyone. The notion of putting his foot down to speak to someone about a murder they shouldn't be investigating had clearly not occurred to him.

Harry spotted Ivan before Belinda. He stood, hands by his sides, his attention on the elephant house. Belinda looked across at Harry in surprise as he slowed the vehicle between a block of public toilets and a staff-only storage area. As soon as she saw her ex-boyfriend just thirty feet away, she muttered her thanks and jumped out. Whether Harry was taking an age to crowbar himself out of his seat or was simply adopting discretion in hanging back, Belinda wasn't sure. All she knew was how guilty her feelings for Ivan were making her when Harry was probably the most decent person she had ever had the pleasure of knowing.

She circumnavigated a group with half a dozen prams and as many toddlers rushing and hollering their way across the clearing, two of the boys with candy floss as big as their own heads, and sauntered up to Ivan. She stood beside him, drinking in the view. 'Elephants are amazing,' she said.

Without looking at her, he nodded. 'They certainly are. How did you know I was here?'

The last thing she wanted to tell him was that she and Harry had been monitoring him on the CCTV. Even without two deaths within the grounds, it sounded a little creepy and intrusive.

'I saw you earlier on the land train and guessed that you'd be heading this way. What with all the elephant business you have to attend to.' Belinda heard Harry give a discreet cough. 'Harry here gave me a lift over from the security office.'

Ivan turned to face him so that the three of them were in an awkward triangle. 'That's kind of you.'

'Least I could do with a murderer on the loose,' said Harry.

'Are the police no closer to catching Simon's killer?' said Ivan.

'No,' said Belinda, scrutinising Ivan's face as she spoke. 'And now we have another dead body.'

'What?' said Ivan. 'I thought this was supposed to be a quiet part of Kent. What exactly is going on in this place? Who died?'

'Belinda found Drew Matterson, one of the security team,'

said Harry. 'Vince Green seems to like the idea that it was an accident and Drew fell out of the tree, but I'm not so sure. At least it means the police won't shut the entire zoo down, only the parts they have to. As tragic as the loss of life is, Estelle will be grateful it's not another day's takings down the pan. Though all the bad publicity might stop people making bookings for the immediate future.'

Ivan stood with his mouth open, his lips moving but no sound coming out. Then he said, 'This is incredible. I'm really sorry about Drew. He seemed like a decent guy and finding him must have been horrific.'

'I'm focusing on what we can do to help,' she said. 'When did you last see Drew?'

'Wow,' said Ivan, shrugging, his eyes wide, 'yesterday, I guess, when we were talking to him after Simon was found. I'll do anything I can to help. I've already let Estelle know that I've rented a cottage in Little Challham so I can stay and help out for a while. I wouldn't dream of leaving at a time like this.'

'Oh, you're moving out,' said Belinda. She did her best to make her voice sound as light as the overpriced candy floss that had been dropped to the ground feet from where they stood, while its owner was dragged away screaming and wailing.

'Even before any of this started,' said Ivan, 'I knew that it wasn't the best idea for me to outstay my welcome in your home. I suppose I'd always known that you'd return to Little Challham, and now I'm here, I can see the attraction.' He looked over at Harry, hesitated and then added, 'What with my engagement being called off, I didn't know if I was doing the right thing staying under the same roof as you, Bel.

'I know that I kept things from you and I know I hurt you. I have learned the hard way to be up front. Whatever I can do to help, I'm here for you.'

Belinda forced her mouth into a smile. Why was this so

hard to deal with? She truly didn't know how she felt about Ivan at that moment, but her feelings weren't strong enough to put her friendship with Harry in peril. She understood that a second chance with Ivan would never give her a future with Harry. That was tearing her in two.

23

Harry knew it was time to leave the two of them to talk. He felt as if his world was about to implode with Ivan's revelation about his engagement. Perhaps he could provoke some protestors into admitting to murder. He had no qualms about leaving Belinda with Ivan. He was clearly no danger to anyone, other than Harry's pride. He edged away from the conversation, and went seemingly unnoticed back to his buggy.

He turned the buggy in the direction of the staff car park and congratulated himself for leaving his car keys and wallet in his trouser pockets for an easy getaway. His back could only put up with so much hurtling over speed humps and dodging small children running in front of him. While Belinda and Ivan were sorting things out, he promised himself that he would find out what the protestors were up to and then get back to work.

It surprised him how easily he was able to park the buggy, get in his Audi and drive out of the staff entrance without anyone stopping him. 'Terrible standards for a murder investigation,' he muttered to himself as he drove out of the gates.

A very bored-looking Stan Whiting stood at the gates eyeing him as he drove through.

'Stan,' said Harry, pulling up beside him. 'I thought you'd worked a night shift.'

'Yep.'

'Then what are you still doing here?'

'Working a day shift,' said the security guard.

'You must be exhausted,' said Harry.

'Nope.'

'How easy would it be to get into the security office and wipe the CCTV?'

Stan stared at him and said, 'I suppose nothing's impossible.'

'Well, as fascinating as this lively exchange has been, I'm off to speak to some of the protestors. Find out what I can about the murder.' Harry was reluctant to say any more. It wasn't that he didn't trust Stan, it was more that he felt as though he were being interrogated without being asked a question. It didn't sit well.

Stan looked across the road towards a gap in the hedges where Harry could make out the start of a footpath leading through the field.

'What?' said Harry, ducking his head so he could see under the sun visor.

'If you're looking for that white bloke with the dreadlocks, he left for Little Challham an hour or so ago,' said Stan.

'Over there?' said Harry, pointing towards the well-trodden path. Stan, however, had already moved away from the Audi and was heading back to his fold-out chair, strategically placed far enough from the gate to make conversation impossible.

Harry knew he had to seize this chance that James Kara might be more willing to talk to him away from Carmel and the rest of his posse.

. . .

Within a short time, Harry was back in Little Challham, his car parked at the rear of the Gatehouse, and he was on his way to the green. The shops, pubs and microbreweries were nestled around the green, and the tea room was a stone's throw from Harry's front door. He didn't usually make a habit of visiting it – he wasn't made of money and why waste it on a coffee he was perfectly capable of making in his own kitchen for a fraction of the price? He wasn't mean, yet it stuck in his craw to hand over a fiver and in return, get back a couple of silver coins and a colossal mug of lukewarm froth.

Today was different. He wanted to find out where James Kara was and whether the righteous young man had taken himself off for a pot of Earl Grey and a slice of Battenburg.

Harry picked up his step and rounded the corner, his target in sight. The large glass front of the premises revealed that the lunchtime rush was underway, something that would usually put him off, except today, he could feel himself warm to the idea of being surrounded by people. But it would have to wait – he had more important things to do.

Then he stopped dead. Across the green, on the far side of the village, he saw a figure in tweed trousers and a dark blue anorak disappearing into the post office. The clothing would have been enough of a clue, but the mousy-coloured dreadlocks were a complete giveaway. Stan's tip-off had been right: James Kara was away from his post and roaming the Kent countryside.

Harry hurried across the green, making his way past a dog walker and a jogger. The black-and-white facades of the buildings were already adorned with adverts and window displays for Halloween and Bonfire Night. Through the slightly steamy post office window, he saw a handful of customers, a few queuing at the post office counter, a couple milling around looking at magazines and newspapers, and two others in the general store part of the shop.

Harry's height and stature made it almost impossible for

him to blend in anywhere, so he knew James would see him. He decided to wait outside and watch through the window. James went to the chiller cabinet, took a few moments to decide what he wanted and then took the item to the till.

At least he's not a shoplifter, thought Harry, intrigued by what he was buying. He couldn't see what it was but James held it in one hand and a bank note in the other. Harry was aware that it wasn't a good look for a retired detective inspector to be standing on his tiptoes outside the village shop bobbing up and down to spy on a member of the public. Fortunately, years of dealing with undesirables meant that he also didn't feel at all embarrassed. Plus, James was an animal rights protester who had been demonstrating outside a zoo where two murders had been committed in two days.

James was next to be served. He exchanged pleasantries with Matilda, the very pleasant young woman who worked there at lunchtimes, and left with his change and his purchase.

The dreadlocked young man made it five feet from the shop doorway before Harry stepped into his path.

'What the—?' said James, his eyes as big as saucers. 'Why are you following me?'

'I happened to be in the village at the same time as you,' lied Harry. He looked down at what James was holding. 'You can try to hide your contraband behind your back, Mr Kara, but I see you. I see you and your Ginsters pasty. Is that one of your vegan treats?'

'I-I... What I eat is none of your business,' said James, attempting to move across the pavement.

'You're completely correct,' said Harry. 'It's not my concern, but I bet your friends – particularly the fanatical Carmel – would be none too pleased to know you've snuck away for a tasty treat that would demand many months of hairy armpits and knitting jumpers out of seaweed to offset its carbon footprint in that one artery-clogging snack.' Harry leaned forward, eyebrows raised. 'And I bet it's got meat in it. Am I right?'

'That really is nothing to do with you,' said a furious James.

'If it's a veggie one, why has your face gone a pastry pasty-shade?' said Harry.

With a flourish that would have made the Magic Circle proud, James revealed his purchase. 'See,' he said. 'It's got "vegan friendly" all over the wrapping. It's a meat-free alternative.'

Harry, slightly crestfallen but not entirely convinced, said, 'Then why did you go to such great lengths to hide it?'

'Because of the wrapper,' said James, as if he were announcing the end of life itself.

'Oh,' said Harry, 'I see. It's not combustible?'

'Combustible? What's wrong with you?' said James. 'All I wanted to do was to get away for a couple of hours and it's turned into the Spanish Inquisition. Can I go now?'

'Are you heading back to Brabourne Gardens?' said Harry, a plan forming in his mind.

'Where else would I go?' said James, picking at the packing between thumb and forefinger.

'How did you get here?' said Harry.

James shrugged and pulled a face. 'How do you think I got here? I walked.'

'I'll give you a lift back,' said Harry, hoping to subtly glean some information from him on the way back. It didn't seem that he was going to share too much on the narrow pavements of Harry's home village.

'You? Give me a lift back?' said James, the start of a sneer on his face. 'Weren't you a police officer?'

Harry gave a long slow breath. 'Yes, so it shouldn't be the first time you've been in the same vehicle as someone with an oath to the Queen and a warrant card in their pocket. Only on this occasion, my oath-swearing days are long gone. Come on, the car's this way.'

Harry had had reservations about letting on where he lived, but he was more and more inclined to think that James's clandestine pasty purchasing was the only thing he was up to. The car ride back would help cement that theory.

James was silent until they got to the Gatehouse where Harry's Audi was parked. 'You live here?' he said, gaping at the neat garden, cypress trees along one side, the last of the late-summer annuals hanging on for dear life scattered throughout the rest of the borders.

'Yes, but I don't own it,' Harry felt obliged to explain as he unlocked his car. 'I'm renting.'

'It's a pretty decent drum,' said James. 'Got any spare rooms you're thinking of letting out?'

'To you?' asked Harry with more distrust to his voice than he had anticipated. 'Sorry, I can't. The landlady would go through the roof. Besides, don't you like to live in tree houses and underground tunnels?'

James shot him a look over the top of the car. 'Don't be ridiculous. We have to live somewhere, and this seems like it'd make a good home.'

'It does make a good home,' said Harry. 'It's my home and I'm not seeking a roomie.'

They got in and put their seat belts on before heading off. Harry was on the cusp of picking his moment to find out more about the protestors when James said, 'I suppose that you want to know about everyone who's freedom fighting for the elephants to be sent home.'

'Freedom fighting?' said Harry, with a glance across at James as they came up to a junction. 'What sort of fighting?'

'It's a figure of speech. Do you mind if I eat my pasty in the car?'

'Yes, I do. I've only just hoovered it.'

'Fine,' said James with a tut. 'I want you to drop me away from my friends, anyway. I don't want them to see me get out of your car.'

'I can always let you get out here, if you'd like to walk back.'

'All right, all right,' said James. 'I just don't want anyone to see the wrapper.'

Harry bit his lip, literally and figuratively. 'So, tell me about the rest of your gang.'

'We're not a gang, we're free spirits. We roam as free—'

'That's terrific but who are they?'

'Apart from Carmel and her grandfather – he's a retired police officer – I don't know any of the others.'

'He's what?' said Harry.

'Carmel's grandad is a retired chief inspector from the Metropolitan Police,' said James. 'He happens to believe in freedom for the elephants.'

'Well, on his pension, I suppose he can afford to believe in freedom,' said Harry. 'How come you don't know the others?'

'Because I don't know them,' said James. 'They arrived at the same time as us yesterday and joined us. They're very welcome, but I've no idea who they are. Anyway, keep your friends close and your enemies closer.'

'What's that supposed to mean?' said Harry.

'I'm keeping a closer eye on the ones on the side of the elephants staying in bondage in the zoo,' said James, opening his window. 'How about I eat with my head out of the window?'

'No, you might get it knocked off by a passing tree trunk,' said Harry. 'Apart from making a mess of my motor, I'll have to walk everywhere until the police release the crime scene.'

'At least you wouldn't be polluting the atmosphere,' said James.

'How about you tell me about the other group of protestors?' said Harry, regretting his passenger. He usually enjoyed the drive along the country roads, taking in the scenery and marvelling at the views as he rounded each bend. Today, the journey was tedious and joyless. This was his payback for not staying put in the zoo and talking things through with Belinda.

'Anna Clancy knew Simon Carter,' said James, as he inspected his fingernails.

'Who's Anna Clancy?' said Harry, interest well and truly piqued.

'She's the leader of the opposition, as it were,' said James, fumbling in his anorak pocket to get his pasty out. 'They appear to be all smiles and cuddles for the elephants, but have you ever asked yourself why self-professed animal lovers would want to keep them in captivity?'

Harry heard the wrinkling of the plastic wrapper. 'Tell me more about her.'

James made a tortured sound, as if he really was in the ultimate dilemma. 'I struggle to think clearly when I'm as hungry as this. It's my blood sugar, you see. I try to concentrate but it's as if my brain cells are dying off one by one.'

Harry gripped the steering wheel. 'Eat the poxy pasty, then, but if you get crumbs on my upholstery, I'll tell Carmel you deliberately sought out food with wrapping that'll be around for longer than the Roman Empire.'

There was a sound of frantic rustling, followed by a chomp and then James chewing as if he hadn't eaten for days. 'Oh, oh, that is better.'

'You were telling me about Anna Clancy,' said Harry, as he tried to pay attention to the traffic rather than see if he could spot falling crumbs in his peripheral vision.

'Anna,' said James with a mouthful of crust-adorned meat substitute, 'is a very interesting character. She's from a very wealthy family – they're completely loaded – and rumour has it, they're connected to the zoo. The zoo that's in financial trouble, by the way.'

Harry mulled this over while James devoured the rest of his food. 'That would mean that if they succeed in keeping the elephants here in Kent, it would bring in money in the form of ticket sales.'

'Yep, not to mention the sponsorship, adoptions, zookeeper experiences, cuddly elephants. You get the idea,' said James.

'It wouldn't make any sense if they're in league with the zoo, though,' said Harry, indicating left on the approach to Brabourne Gardens. 'The zoo and the board are behind moving the herd to Africa. Why would they fight against themselves?'

Before Harry had a chance to pull the Audi to a complete stop in a lay-by, James had his seat belt unclicked and one hand on the door handle.

'Think about it,' said James, his grey eyes boring straight into Harry's, 'if the zoo make it look as though they're sending the elephants back, but have no intention of actually doing so, it brings in visitors to see them before they depart, and it makes the whole set-up look legit and all about animal welfare. Really, it's all about making money. Who's going to come and see an enclosure full of Friesian cows or wood pigeons?'

With that, James was out of the car, over the bank at the side of the lay-by and out of Harry's view.

24

Belinda hadn't realised at first that Harry had gone. It should have been the perfect opportunity for her to ask Ivan about their relationship and why he thought they could pick things up again. And as importantly, why now? Perhaps he had changed? Perhaps he was getting too old to keep starting over? It didn't give her much hope, yet now he was here, it felt like an itch she had to scratch.

Then, before she had a chance to ask, the police had arrived and took her away to one of the security offices to make the inevitable statement. That seemed to take forever – endless questions asking her the same thing over and again – until she was finally free. Belinda found herself drawn back to the giraffe enclosure, the graceful movements of the peaceful creatures something that never failed to calm her.

She knew that she needed to get things off her chest once and for all. As soon as she calmed her nerves, Ivan was next on her agenda. She walked to the viewing platform, and felt at peace. She could face up to the past and find out where she stood with Ivan.

Sabbie was nowhere to be seen but the rest of the giraffes

were contentedly moving around their enclosure, munching on leaves and generally casting a watchful eye over one another and their domain. There was no one else around so the sound of footsteps ambling along the viewing platform only gave her a second's hesitation before she made sure it was friend rather than foe. There was still a murderer out there.

Suddenly, the waft of elephant dung assaulted her nostrils. With what she knew was a sour look, Belinda turned to watch Ivan as he came along the walkway and stood next to her. He had rolled his sleeves up and done what he loved best – literally, getting his hands dirty.

'You'd think after all this time, I'd have got used to the smell,' she laughed. 'Still gets me.'

Ivan joined her in leaning on the rail, observing the magnificent creatures.

'I remember how intrigued you were when you found out that a giraffe could kick the head off a lion,' he said with a chuckle. 'I think your exact words were, "king of the jungle, my eye. It's just a big pussy cat".'

Belinda bowed her head and smiled. 'Yes, I think I did say that.' She focused her attention on Ivan instead of the giraffes. 'What you said back there earlier about always knowing I'd return to Little Challham. Was that why you did it? Why you let them kill Leonard the lion? You always claimed that you didn't think I'd find out but was it because you thought I'd inevitably leave, so it didn't matter?'

'Bel, nothing ever mattered but you and the animals.' He took her hand in both of his. She tried to ignore the stench. 'You remember how keen you were to have a giraffe breeding programme?' She nodded. 'It didn't come cheap and the only way—'

'Oh, no,' she said, snatching her hand back. 'You don't get to justify having him shot, just so we had some money.'

'No, no,' he said. 'Leonard was sick, very sick. You weren't aware, and I should have told you, I know that now. Not a day's gone by when I haven't wished that I'd told you instead of keeping it from you. Leonard wouldn't have lasted the winter.'

'Are you sure?' She knew from his haggard face that it was the truth before he even answered her.

'I would never have done anything to intentionally hurt you, Bel. If you hadn't come back early that day – yes, I would have had another lie to live with, but you wouldn't have known, we'd have had the money to breed the giraffes, and I would have treasured each and every day of you living with me.' His mouth turned down and he stared past her. 'I messed up the best thing I ever had. I'd never hurt you again.'

'I don't know what to say,' she said. Her brain couldn't process the feelings sweeping through her and she had a thousand questions, yet couldn't think of one. She and Ivan had been involved in the most intense relationship, had seen so much of the world and what it had to offer. They were virtually strangers now. Even so, his arrival in Little Challham had stopped her in her tracks.

'I like it here,' he said. 'I'll stay for a while longer, but only if you want me to.'

'I have to think about things,' she said, jutting her chin out and holding his stare.

'Of course.'

Ivan leaned across and kissed her on the cheek, allowing his lips to linger much longer than was necessary.

A movement at the bottom of the walkway caught Belinda's eye. She jerked her head away and said, 'Oh, here's Harry.' She waved frantically at him, even though he was only about thirty feet away. He waggled his fingers at her and trudged towards them.

'Are you holding up OK?' Harry asked Belinda.

'Yes, yes.' She nodded and inclined her head towards Ivan. 'We were just talking about lions and, er – I was about to ask

Ivan about the incident here yesterday. You know – the lion. How amazing Ivan's rescue was.'

She watched Harry size Ivan up and thought she saw a flash of a smile.

'It really was something else,' said Harry. 'Like something from a film. Probably about the bravest thing I've ever seen.' He clapped Ivan on the back. 'When he's older, that young boy will probably dine out on that for the rest of his life.'

Before Ivan had a chance to respond, the sound of a buggy approaching along the pathway made them pause. Estelle Samuels, grim-faced and pale, headed towards them. Without getting out, she nodded at Harry and Belinda and said to Ivan, 'I don't suppose you've got time to help me out over at the hippos? That old problem I told you about has reared up again.'

'Certainly, Estelle. Provided Belinda and Harry have finished with me?' Ivan's question was directed at Belinda who murmured her agreement and watched him sail off in the buggy.

'Have the police spoken to you yet?' said Harry.

Belinda nodded and said, 'I could do with a coffee, and I think we need an update. I don't know about you, but I've thought of a couple of things since we spilt up earlier. I'm sure you've got a few things to tell me about too.' She crossed her arms and added, 'Where *have* you been?'

'I hope these things you've suddenly recalled are matters you've already told or will shortly be telling our friendly neighbourhood police constable?' said Harry.

'Yes, yes, that goes without saying,' said Belinda, flapping her hands. 'But you're so much more important than PC Green. Besides, you've years and years of experience more than him.'

Harry puffed out his chest and said, 'Did I tell you about the time I worked on a murder and—'

'Coffee, Harry, and you still haven't told me where you've been.' It was her turn to fix him with a look.

'If you have to know, I left the zoo.'

She gasped. 'You. Left. The zoo. What new hell dimension is this, where you don't follow protocol?'

'OK, OK,' he said, frantically looking around at the deserted courtyard. 'Keep your hair on. We can go and discuss it over coffee.'

'Great idea. Wish I'd thought of that.'

Belinda hadn't processed what Ivan had told her. Her attempts at teasing Harry were nothing more than stalling for time while she made sense of what had just happened.

25

Safe in the confines of the security office, Harry made both himself and Belinda an instant coffee. 'We don't have anything near as good as Estelle does,' he said.

'She is the owner,' said Belinda. 'If anyone should get the good stuff, it's her. I could do with some milk without lumps, though.'

Harry sniffed the carton. 'Then best you have yours black. Tell you what, how about I get us the keys to the meeting room? It's in the building between this one and Estelle's office. It's got a large conference table and we shouldn't be disturbed in there. They've probably got those tiny pots of UHT milk that you can never get the top off.'

'I, for one, can't wait.'

'Is that sarcasm?'

'Yes, Harry, it is.'

The meeting room was around twenty-five by thirty-five foot with windows running along the two longer walls, a door to a small kitchen on the far wall and opposite it, a large whiteboard with marker pens.

Belinda laughed and tucked her hair behind her ears. 'Now I see why you wanted to come in here.'

Harry put his hands up in mock surrender. 'I'll admit that it wasn't all about the ropey milk. You know me – any excuse to get you on your own.'

Slightly flustered at the directness of Harry's comment, Belinda fiddled nervously with the sleeves of her top and then, glancing at the kitchen door, said, 'Coffee, we need coffee. Allow me.'

More to stall for time to compose herself than because she needed a drink, Belinda took herself to the kitchen. It was a smaller space with a sink underneath the window, a well-used electric cooker complete with filthy hob to the left-hand side, a small fridge and adjacent to that, a cupboard with a few basic pieces of crockery and cutlery. It occurred to Belinda as soon as she opened the door that someone had been in here recently and had been cooking. There was an aroma she couldn't quite place.

Belinda opened the fridge. It was empty except for a plastic milk bottle. It was half full and still in date. She put the milk back and stared around the room. Under the sink was a black duffle bag. She pulled the bag out and unzipped it. Inside was clothing, a few toiletries and a pair of white Reebok trainers. 'These are Drew's,' she muttered to herself. 'But where are the laces?'

As she crouched down to examine the contents of the bag, the rubbish bin was level with her nose. 'Pot Noodle,' she said and leaned across to pull the bin bag towards her.

'B, I thought I'd give you a hand—' Harry stopped in the doorway. 'Are things that tough at the castle, you're eating out of the bins now?'

'You're a funny man,' she said, one hand in the rubbish. 'Look, a Pot Noodle.'

'Yeah, it's fine. You have it.'

'Ha ha. No, it's the sort of thing that Drew would eat if he was sleeping in here. Young man, little to no cooking facilities. I thought that's what I could smell.'

'I didn't have you down as a Pot Noodle girl,' said Harry, seeming to give too much thought to the matter.

'Never mind that,' she said, getting to her feet. 'In the rubbish, I found a pair of white laces. They look as though they've been cut. See?' She held them out to him. 'And in this bag, there are Reebok trainers without laces.'

'Blimey,' said Harry, his face clouded over. 'Someone cut his laces.'

'Remember I told you that Drew thought someone was getting in here and interfering with his stuff? If someone did this, he would have worn different shoes, making it more likely he slipped.'

'We have to tell the police that Drew's stuff is still here,' said Harry. 'They'll want to send someone over to go through it right away.'

'OK, you call them,' said Belinda, putting the laces on the draining board. 'While we wait for them, how about we use the time wisely?' She gave him an alluring look and marched off to the conference room to the whiteboard.

Without waiting for Harry to join her, she grabbed one of the marker pens from the narrow ledge that ran along the bottom of the whiteboard and got to work.

'So,' she said, her back to Harry as he made the call to PC Green, 'who are we putting on the list?'

'We can certainly leave poor Drew off this latest one,' said Harry, as he waited for the call to connect. From the creak, Belinda didn't have to look round to know he was perching on the edge of the conference table rather than using one of the two dozen chairs. 'Why was Drew killed? If we're saying he was murdered, why him and how did this person manage to get him up a tree?'

Belinda cocked her head to one side. 'Perhaps he saw something that he shouldn't have seen. Or someone sent him up the tree for a reason that meant he would risk it in completely the wrong footwear.'

Harry folded his arms, scrunched his face up in concentration and said, 'Perhaps it was a useful vantage point for Drew. We know from Estelle and the bag of stuff that he sometimes stayed over, even if he wasn't supposed to. Maybe he saw who was sabotaging the place. Letting rhinos wander off, penguins make a bid for freedom, tripping up giraffes, that sort of thing. If Drew was a danger to whoever was behind all that, it would have been worth the risk of cutting his laces, cutting through the branch and killing him.'

'I see what you mean,' said Belinda, feeling slightly overwhelmed that someone was prepared to pick off anyone who got in the way of their plans to discredit the zoo. 'Even the incident with the boy being thrown into the lion enclosure was another attempt to destroy the zoo. It's beyond comprehension that anyone would allow a child to be torn to pieces just to have a zoo shut down.'

'Sorry, B, but there really are total sickos out there,' said Harry. 'Hang on, it's gone to voicemail.'

Belinda waited while Harry left PC Green a message to let him know about the bag and the shoelaces. When Harry had finished, he put his phone in his pocket and said, 'Are you OK to carry on with this?'

'I never back down,' she said, staring at her friend.

'So, who are we considering might have done something so abhorrent?' said Harry.

'We have the protesters,' said Belinda. She wrote 'Pro Leaving' as a heading and 'James Kara and Carmel' underneath.

'Carmel's grandad – the one with her the other day – he's a retired Met Police chief inspector,' said Harry.

Belinda spun round. 'Who told you that? Vince?'

'No, he hasn't told me anything, not yet,' said Harry from the table edge, his long legs out in front of him, crossed at the ankles. 'Whether he ever will is anyone's guess. No, the information came from James Kara himself.'

'When did he tell you that?' said Belinda, tapping her foot in irritation. 'He didn't mention it when I was with you, so why did he keep it to himself?'

'I don't know,' said Harry. 'Perhaps he didn't want to spill the beans in front of the others and seem like a grass. I saw him an hour or so ago in Little Challham's general store. He'd snuck off to buy himself a vegan pasty.' Harry gave the start of a laugh and said, 'He didn't want the others knowing that he'd bought food in a non-biodegradable wrapper.'

'This is more serious than we thought,' said Belinda, her mind working overtime.

'Is it?' said Harry. 'I'm all for reducing my carbon footprint but one piece of plastic isn't going to save the planet. I suppose if we start small, then—'

'No, not that!' Belinda stared at Harry. 'He's sneaking off to buy food, so what else is he up to? Is he sneaking in here in the night? Perhaps he was the one messing with Drew's stuff. James might have been responsible for the rope in Sabbie's enclosure. He's certainly fanatical enough to do anything to get the zoo shut down. He'd probably think that one giraffe was worth the sacrifice. How could he be so... Hang on – what were you doing back in the village when you should have been here?'

Harry's face glowed like embers. 'I – er... I have to admit that when I saw you and Ivan chatting away earlier on, I decided to bow out. I know you have unfinished business. I know that we've got two dead bodies on our hands and that'll come first every single time, but I thought I'd leave you to it and speak to the protestors. Stan Whiting told me that James was on his way to the village.'

He looked out of the window, into the trees beyond that obscured the view. 'Ivan seems like a pretty decent bloke and we know that he couldn't have anything to do with the murders. He's come all this way to help the zoo and didn't even know Simon Carter or Drew, let alone have a reason or opportunity to kill them both. I can't see Ivan being involved in any of the other weird stuff that someone's doing to discredit the zoo and bring about its downfall.'

For the briefest of silences, Belinda didn't know what to say, and then her nerve left her. Harry had left the zoo – abandoning murder protocol to give her time to speak to Ivan. Not for the first time, she felt as if she didn't deserve Harry's kindness. 'I expect that ducking out for a breather is allowed, so back to the list. What about those in favour of the elephants staying here? What are we going to call them?'

'Anything but "Remainers",' said Harry, making Belinda laugh.

'How about "Stayers"?'

'Why not?' said Harry. He cupped his chin in his hand and said, 'Stick Anna Clancy at the top of the list. She's the leader, according to James.'

'What do we know about her?' said Belinda, adding her name to the list.

'At the moment, that her name's Anna Clancy,' said Harry with a shrug. 'She's loaded, according to James, and has connections within the zoo, although I don't know who. We could be looking at an insider angle. James thinks that she's up to something because her agenda of keeping the elephants here will bring in more money than sending them on their way. Sorry. It's all I've got. I've no idea about the rest of her followers either.'

'OK, I'll add them to the suspect list. If the zoo gets closed down, the animals will be sent to other zoos rather than rewilded, so they get what they want.' Belinda stepped back and looked at the meagre list. 'As much as it grieves me to do so, I'm adding in Estelle Samuels and Rob Piper.'

'I thought that you were friends with Estelle,' said Harry with an ill-disguised yawn. 'And what does she hope to gain from getting her own zoo closed down?'

Belinda scrunched the corner of her mouth, gave his words some thought and said, 'We're more acquaintances, if I'm honest. She's a wonderful advocate for the animals – she bought the land and built the zoo from scratch after rescuing a couple of discarded pets – and it grew into what we see here today. There's no denying that she would stop at nothing to see animals put before humans.'

'And that's what's worrying you?' said Harry, as he eased himself off the edge of the table.

'That and two unsolved murders,' she said, standing beside Harry so they could both admire her handiwork on the white-board. 'We can't rule Estelle out any more than we can rule Rob out, although she'd never do anything to risk the place getting closed down.'

'How about if she thought she could get away with murdering Simon who was a financial threat?' said Harry. 'Then the problem arose that Drew was on to her. She killed him, thinking it was the only way she could save the zoo.'

'So, whoever is sabotaging the zoo is someone entirely sepa-rate from the killer?' said Belinda. 'We know that Estelle relies heavily on Rob to get on with things.'

'I agree, but he's not as invested in the zoo as Estelle is. He's worked here for about five years and has a long career in secu-rity work. That's why he's in charge. What would make him kill Simon Carter and then make Drew Matterson's death look like an accident? Drew was one of his own team, and he took me on knowing that I've got a background in solving murders. He wouldn't risk it... and what would he possibly gain if the zoo shut down?'

'The same's true for Estelle,' said Belinda, a quick glance at her watch. 'She's put everything into this place. She's not likely to have wanted a retired murder squad detective working here either if she were a killer. I know that I put in a good word for you, but she could have vetoed it. As much as I wanted you to get the job, if she hadn't had been in favour of it, I wouldn't have pursued it.'

'And yet you did?' They were standing shoulder to shoulder so she couldn't see his face. The change in the pitch of his voice gave her the impression he was merely curious rather than there being any accusation in his question.

Belinda tucked her hair behind her ears. 'I didn't want you to leave Little Challham.' She heard a dry laugh and thought it best if they plough on. 'So, is the plan that we concentrate on James and his cronies, as well as Anna and hers? They seem to have the most to gain from the place going to ruin.'

'It's a lot of ground to cover,' said Harry, mercifully going with Belinda's 'carry on regardless' attitude. 'Exactly how much do you trust Ivan?'

'At one time, I'd have said with my life. We know he's not a danger to us or anyone else.' With a firm nod, she added, 'I trust him.'

'Ivan seems to be in Estelle's company a lot, so how about you track him down and we find out all that we can about what Estelle's up to?' said Harry. 'In the meantime, I'll see what I can wheedle out of the protestors.'

'Providing we can speak to Vince soon, we can ask him what he knows about Anna Clancy and if she knew Simon Carter,' said Belinda. 'If all else fails, one of us can nip down to the gate and speak to her.'

'Tell you what,' said Harry, 'leave that bit to me while you find Ivan.'

'Sounds like a plan,' said Belinda. 'If I have anything to do with it, this zoo is going to go from strength to strength.'

Harry gave a sigh. 'The problem is, there's someone very dangerous out there who seems to be plotting its downfall. We need to be extremely careful. There are people who will stop at nothing to get what they want.'

'Then it's lucky the two best people are on the case,' Belinda said with more confidence than she felt.

26

Harry knew which direction Belinda was heading from the CCTV feed. He felt extremely uncomfortable tracking her movements, but he wanted to ensure that they covered more of the zoo. Doubling up wasn't going to help either of them, nor the two murder victims. The police were still claiming that Drew's death was an accident, which made Harry extremely uncomfortable. He was expecting that to change as soon as Drew's bag and its contents were examined. Both of the laces from his training shoes had been cut, leaving no doubt that someone had deliberately tampered with them. There was no way that the police could ignore that.

He couldn't wait any longer for Rob Piper to reappear. Before going to the meeting room with Belinda, Harry had left a note telling Rob where he was in case his boss was looking for him. Several minutes after Harry's return and Belinda's departure, the head of the security outfit still hadn't made an appearance. Harry's assumption was that Rob was off with the police. The only problem was that he couldn't see him on the patchy CCTV coverage.

Never one to shirk any sort of duty, Harry thought he would venture outside to see what the protestors were up to. He could see their antics, but he wanted to hear what they had to say for themselves. Using the element of surprise, he took one of the small vans used by the housekeeping and maintenance crews, drove it to the staff exit – it seemed that Stan had, at last, gone home – and let himself out onto the road. If walking across the fields from the lay-by was good enough for James Kara, it was good enough for Harry Powell.

Harry, unlike James, had black brogues and suit trousers on, so his idea wasn't the best one he had ever had. *What's a bit of mud between friends?* he thought as he stepped out of the van. 'Oh, for crying out f—' he shouted within two seconds of moving away from the tarmac.

In a panic, Harry looked along the road, worried that his voice had carried the distance to the gates. He would have preferred to take them unawares, or else he might simply have strolled along the dry pathway and not ended up with sheep dung hanging off his trouser creases.

Despite his personal torment, he carried on walking, slipping from time to time and righting himself, until he came upon the sound of voices. The light traffic passing him on the road stopped him from climbing back over the small bank of earth and rejoining solid ground. He would rather end up caked in dirt than dodging vehicles, so he trudged on, keeping an ear out for any sign of animosity.

As Harry drew closer, he made out the faint murmur of what sounded like two people chatting, one man and one woman. The conversation seemed to be an amicable one. He could see by the contour of the road that he would soon be entirely exposed, a little way ahead of where he had expected to be seen. Whoever it was had clearly moved several hundred feet away from the two opposing groups, presumably so as not to be overheard. They were unlikely to take kindly to Harry popping up out of nowhere.

The gentle tinkle of a woman's laughter and the deeper chortle of a man wafted on the breeze as Harry stepped into view. He was still a respectable distance away, giving them time to spring apart as if they had been caught in the act. From their surprised expressions, it was clear they weren't expecting anyone. When their astonishment began to resemble annoyance, Harry knew that he had hit a nerve.

James Kara had been chatting affably to a woman in her late thirties, whose mid-length red hair had been plaited and was resting over her shoulder. Her dress was of a simple knee-length black material, and accompanied by dark green woollen tights, black boots and a green parka jacket. She couldn't have come wearing a more obvious protestor costume if she were Mr Benn and had been kitted out by the Shopkeeper.

'Afternoon to you both,' called Harry. He watched James lean over to the woman and saw her nod in agreement. 'I expect you're wondering what I'm doing over here?'

'Not really,' said the woman. 'If you want to get covered in cack, that's up to you.'

By now, Harry had joined the two of them. They both stared, waiting for him to talk. 'You must be Anna Clancy,' he said.

'Is he the ex-detective?' the woman asked James.

'It's time for the meeting of the mortal enemies,' said James, squinting in the weak sunshine. 'Harry Powell, retired police officer, may I introduce you to Anna, staunch supporter of the herd staying in the zoo.'

Harry considered shaking her hand for less time than it took him to realise that walking in a muddy field in his work clothes was one of the worst ideas he'd had in a long time. He opted for nodding instead.

'You two seem to be in cahoots,' said Harry. 'The two rival

gang leaders caught with their heads together. Do Carmel and the rest know about this?'

'That we are capable of speaking?' said Anna. 'Or are you referring to the fact that we're on opposing sides, and yet we're having a civil conversation?'

'It's what the civil conversation was about that intrigues me,' said Harry. 'I could have sworn that I heard you say "Simon".' It was a lie, but he might as well give it a go.

Anna rolled her eyes 'You know full well that I said nothing of the sort, but nice try. I did know Simon. He was a decent enough person. A couple of hours before he was killed, he bought a tray of takeaway hot drinks for *all* the protestors. He even brought along cartons of soya and oat milk in case we were avoiding dairy. How considerate is that? Granted, he was an annoying little man. And before you start thinking you've got me *bang to rights*, I was out here the whole time with my partner Cecil. You can't miss him: he's the one with the drums.'

'Drums?' said Harry. 'Oh, splendid. Anyway, what about Drew?'

He watched her face as he said the dead security man's name. She gave a half-hearted shrug. 'Am I supposed to know who that is?'

'The second person to end up dead here this week?' said Harry.

'Really?' she said with a wry laugh. 'They employed you on the security team... was it Wednesday afternoon? It's only Thursday, barely lunchtime, and there've been two dead bodies. Heck, are they paying you? I hope not. The zoo could have fed the entire cackle of hyenas rather than give you a salary.'

'Hyenas?' said Harry. 'What made you say "hyenas" and not rhinos?'

Anna jammed her hands in her pockets and said, 'Are you for real? What does it matter? Hyenas, rhinos, wolves, bears! The point is, you're clearly a waste of resources and we want to make sure these animals are well cared for, not just so that the Brabourne Gardens Board of Trustees can make money. This should be about conservation in action, breeding programmes, making sure that these species are increasing, not being sent back to the wild and certain death.'

'The elephants wouldn't end up somewhere unprotected,' said James, his attention now back on Anna. 'The research has taken years and there's nothing that would say they wouldn't live out a long and peaceful life in the wild.'

'Except for poachers and loss of habitat,' said Anna, a vein popping out of her forehead.

'Elephants in captivity live for less than seventeen years on average,' said James, waving his arms for effect. 'In the wild it's about fifty-six years, so tell me why that's a bad thing?'

'Here, they have veterinary care,' said Anna, now completely engrossed in the heated debate, Harry forgotten. 'They won't have the same care if they're rewilded.'

'Can't you see that they're better off without us?' said James, now on the cusp of shouting. 'The death rate of captive-born elephant calves is *double* that of their wild counterparts. Double! Double! That's how much better they do without human intervention.'

'Oi,' hollered Harry. 'When you two have quite finished, can we get back to the matter of murder? Or should I say murders? Drew was found dead this morning, and he was a colleague of mine. Any thoughts I've got of leaving this solely to the police went out of the window when I realised that any one of us' – Harry pointed his finger at James and then Anna – 'could be next. Just think about that.'

The noise of a heavy-duty diesel van chugging towards them made the three of them pause.

'Here come your friends,' said James. 'Or should I say, former friends? What's it like to be outside an organisation without any clout?'

'I don't know, James,' said Harry. 'I've still got a job and wage, so you tell me. Now, this is your last chance to tell me anything that might help us, which will, in turn, minimise the police presence at the scene of your drum-banging and placard-waving.'

'I went to school with Simon,' said Anna.

'What?' said Harry and James.

'Yes, secondary school in Sandwich,' she said. 'He was a bit of a sad lad, but decent enough. We went out for a bit. It ended amicably.'

'I wasn't expecting that,' said Harry.

'I didn't want to kill him because of a relationship over twenty years ago.' Anna fiddled with the end of her plait. 'Ask his sister Jessica. I was a total coward and got her to tell him it was over. He bought me a diary as a present and the cover was... leather.' She shuddered as she said 'leather' and rapidly blinked as if the word was about to bring her out in a rash.

'Leather?' said James. 'No wonder you were peeved. Are you all right?'

'For crying out loud,' said Harry. 'It was over twenty years ago. The cow would have died of old age by now.'

Fortunately for Harry's one-man-band investigation, the police van was now behind him and drowned out any more of his outburst. He knew that he would never again have the patience for police work. The general public really did get his goat.

'Harry,' said a voice from inside the van, 'any chance you could fill me in on the voicemail message you left earlier?'

Harry saw Vince Green's face peering down at him through the window. 'I couldn't think of anything I'd rather do more, officer.'

The Sprinter van's side door slid open revealing five uniformed police officers. All appeared curious, but with that wonderful laid-back air of only feeling obliged to look because there was now a massive gap in the side of their vehicle, and they were being paid to pay attention.

'I'll catch up with you later,' Harry said to James and Anna as he hopped inside. He felt much more at home in the van's stale air than on the roadside with a brace of hostile animal protestors.

27

The second Belinda found herself alone, she gave a couple of nervous glances over her shoulder. What if the murderer were still at the zoo and watching her? She shook her head clear of such ridiculous thoughts. What were the chances of a killer striking three times in the same venue in two days? Especially with the police around. Mind you, they hadn't done much to stop poor Drew meeting a vile end, and didn't even seem to want to investigate his death. If nothing else, that should change.

Belinda set about finding Ivan as she had told Harry she would do. She trusted she could bring Ivan on side and ask about Estelle and what she was up to. If there was anything untoward going on, Ivan was bound to have noticed. He wouldn't side with Estelle, or so she repeatedly told herself. He was someone she had shared hopes, dreams and her bed with. Of course she had faith that when it was time to do the right thing, he would.

These thoughts jostling in her head, she tried to enjoy the practically empty grounds as she headed across the man-made river via the footbridge. To her right was the large pond that flowed under the wooden bridge. A pair of swans floated serenely, their majestic presence weirdly soothing. To her right hand-side was the start of the red river hogs' enclosure, a secret favourite of Belinda's. She couldn't really fathom why, but perhaps they reminded her of the warthogs that had caused her endless amusement in Africa.

For a short while, all other thoughts pushed aside, Belinda stood on the bridge, leaning on the wooden handrail, peering over at the family of hogs as they went about their business, their snouts making circular motions as they sniffed for food. Belinda always took solace in watching animals being them-selves – as long as they weren't ripping each other's throats out or trying to eat a human.

Even though she was supposed to be looking for Ivan, she indulged herself in two or three minutes of hog-watching. She was so engrossed that some time had passed before she moved her attention elsewhere. A hundred feet or so across from the snorting hogs, she could see Estelle Samuels and Rob Piper. Catching a glimpse of them wasn't the problem, it was what they were actually doing that was very much an issue.

Belinda ducked her head down so that she could see more clearly through the low-hanging branches. Rob seemed to be pleading with Estelle. It looked as though at one point, he was going to get down on bended knee. Estelle's hands flew up to her temples and she shook her head at whatever he had said. From the gesticulating and the body language, Belinda would have placed a hefty bet that she was shouting at Rob while he continued to appeal to her.

The problem was that Belinda was too far away to clearly make out their voices. Anything that might have carried to her was, in fact, obliterated by the snorting of the hogs. She thought about running around to get closer. The spot they were in, however, was remote, and she could only assume that was for a reason. They had business that they didn't want anyone else to overhear.

With the fascination of an amateur sleuth and the voyeurism of a peeping Tom, Belinda changed position several times before she was satisfied that she had the best view possible.

Peeking between a branch and the bridge handrail, Belinda watched as Rob grabbed Estelle's upper arm. Estelle opened her mouth and presumably cried out in pain. Rob yanked her towards him and Belinda knew that she couldn't leave things there. She fumbled for her mobile phone ready to make a call and race around there and intervene.

Then, from nowhere, Ivan appeared. Estelle and Rob's surprised reactions showed neither of them knew he was nearby. He stormed his way over, causing Rob to let go of Estelle's arm. Rob made a placatory gesture with his hands, but it did little to appease Ivan. In one movement, he grabbed Rob by the throat.

Words were exchanged, and Estelle stood with her hands by her sides, crying. There was something about Estelle's stance that unnerved Belinda. She couldn't put her finger on what – after all, she was a hundred feet away, and also in somewhat of a tizz. The former love of her life had come to the rescue of another woman. It had left her discombobulated, as did the fact that she had been about to call not the police, but Harry. It was his name that she had hovered over on her list of recently called. That really told her how she felt about Harry and how much she had come to rely on him. How could it have taken her so long to work out it was Harry she really wanted?

Despite all these distracting emotions, Belinda focused on what was happening on the far side of the hogs. Thankfully, Ivan had let go of Rob's throat and stood by while the other man staggered backwards, nursing his windpipe. Some more indistinct words were exchanged, followed by a lot of pointing on

Rob's part, and then he walked away. He was still shouting as he went. The only words Belinda picked up were 'nightmare', 'dangerous woman', 'your problem' before he completely disappeared from her sight and hearing.

The theatrical exit had meant that Belinda had taken her eye off Ivan and Estelle. Now, she turned her attention to the pair of them and wished she hadn't. Ivan had Estelle in his arms. She was only able to see the back of his head and none of Estelle's face. Ivan's head was tilted one way and the woman he was supposed to be comforting had hers tipped in the other direction. Surely the two of them weren't kissing. That would be utterly unthinkable. Ivan was here in a professional capacity and had made it clear he had flown to England to see if Belinda still had feelings for him. Not to mention, Estelle was technically his boss. The entire episode left Belinda reeling.

As Belinda crouched down, her legs getting cramp and her brain getting fogged, she gawked at the two of them. Then they moved apart. Perhaps she had imagined it. Ivan was probably making sure Estelle felt well enough to carry on working, that must have been what was going on. Even if it looked like a kiss.

Estelle stepped backwards, then gestured in the direction of the rest of the zoo. After talking to Ivan a little more, she waved him away. It looked as though she was dismissing him. That was most definitely a woman who didn't want someone around for the next few minutes. Not entirely convinced that she, too, should walk away, Belinda remained rooted to the spot. She knew that she didn't have long in case Ivan crossed the river and discovered that she had been studying them.

Morbidly fascinated as to what might happen next, Belinda carried on watching Estelle. Her persistence paid off: Estelle glanced left and right before producing an African Savannah Safari Experience bandana from her pocket, screwing it into a ball and throwing it into the river.

28

Harry sat in the van listening to the usual police banter and realised that he missed this part, just not the bit where he worked sixteen hours straight, got home without a decent meal, and then got the cold shoulder from the now ex-wife. Some aspects of his life were much better as a civilian.

The driver dropped him and Vince Green inside the entrance, while the rest of the crew were given tasks to do on both sides of the gates.

'I need to get you up to speed about what Belinda and I found in the meeting room,' said Harry as they started on the ten-minute walk towards the security offices.

'At this stage,' said Vince, a healthy glow to his cheeks, 'I'll take any help I can get. I'm less convinced it was a case of the poor man falling out of a tree and ending up a dead, tangled mess.' He listened while Harry told him about what they'd found in the bag and what Estelle had said about Drew sleeping in the zoo from time to time.

'So I think it was murder,' said Harry, coming to a standstill on the pathway. 'You need to get the senior investigating officer to declare this a major incident.'

'At least I've got you and Belinda on my side,' said Vince with something akin to a girlish giggle.

'It's not funny, son,' said Harry.

'Oh, yeah, I'm really sorry,' said Vince. 'It's just that you've worked more murders than me *since* you've been retired, let alone before. I get a bit carried away. Please don't tell anyone.'

Without giving the lad's request another thought, Harry said, 'We need to find out what Drew was doing up the tree. And what happened to his shoe.'

'We're, er... working on that,' said Vince, avoiding eye contact.

Harry slapped himself on the forehead. 'Tell me that you've got the chuffing footwear back from the hyena.'

'Mostly,' muttered Vince.

'By mostly, you mean...'

'I mean, no,' said Vince. 'They're very dangerous and I don't remember "pack of rabid dog training" when I joined up.'

'They're not rabid,' said Harry, 'merely dangerous. What is the police force coming to? It's vital evidence and you're waiting for what? The negotiator to talk the hyena into swapping it for a Kong toy filled with peanut butter?'

'Do you think that will work?' said Vince, getting his notebook out of his pocket.

'No, son, I don't,' said Harry. 'Get your DCI or whoever is in charge of this... charade to get that shoe away from the hyenas. This is a total disgrace. I'm going to the office and I suggest that you ask your boss to contact me, and I'll arrange for a keeper to go in and retrieve the vital exhibits in your murder inquiry. In the meantime, get the bag from the conference room kitchen seized and examined.'

Harry stomped away, not really angry with the young PC, but livid that no one had done their job properly. He would take solace in catching up with Rob. His supervisor was bound to have a list of other tasks that the police needed help with before they both went home for the day.

29

Belinda stayed where she was, safely hidden from view by the trees. When she was convinced that both Ivan and Estelle had gone, she made her way to where she had seen them talking. And possibly kissing, but she decided to blot that last part from her mind. Viewing two dead bodies in as many days was bound to have skewed her judgement. She steadied her breathing and made every effort to put one foot in front of the other without turning and running back to the safety of the police, or better still, Harry.

Just when had she become so nervy all the time? This wasn't like her at all. But then it wasn't every day you found someone at the bottom of a tree with their limbs broken and mangled. If she could get to the other side of the hogs and grab the bandana Estelle had tossed into the water, it might prove to be incriminating. Belinda knew that she didn't have time to call Vince to come and get it: it was bound to have washed away long before he arrived. It couldn't have been the one used to strangle Simon because that had still been round his neck when the body was found. Even so, Estelle clearly didn't want anyone to get their hands on it. There had to be a reason why.

Then a terrible thought struck her that Ivan might be caught up in whatever Estelle was involved in. Why else would he be so close to her when he was making moves to re-ingratiate himself with Belinda?

Belinda was so busy overthinking the events of the last forty-eight hours that she didn't notice Ivan until he stepped in front of her.

'Oh!' she said, her hand rushing up to her hammering heart. 'You scared me. I didn't see you.'

'You seemed miles away,' he said, studying her face closely. 'You look petrified. Is everything OK? Apart from the murders, I mean.' He shoved his hands in his pockets and carried on staring straight at her. 'Have you been over here for long?'

'No, not really,' she lied. 'I thought I could do with a walk. I'm just about to find PC Green and ask him if I can go home. I've really had enough today.'

'That's probably a good idea,' he said, his eyes roaming over the spot by the river where he and Estelle had been standing only moments ago. 'Everyone's tired and edgy. Who knows what'll happen tomorrow if the police don't let us open the zoo. Estelle said that we can't keep taking a financial hit if the entire place isn't up and running, not if we want to get the elephants rewilded any time soon.'

'When did you see Estelle?' said Belinda in a monotone voice, aware that it sounded odd.

Fortunately, Ivan didn't notice. 'Much earlier today, when we were watching the giraffes. It's not the first time she's told me how worried she is about money. Sponsors, in particular, in case they no longer want to be affiliated with us. She's having a very tough time.'

The overuse of the words 'we' and 'us' hadn't gone unnoticed by Belinda. He seemed very attuned to everything Estelle wanted. Under different circumstances, Belinda would delve a little deeper, only at that moment, she was battling against the river's ebb and flow. If she missed her chance to salvage the bandana, vital evidence might be lost. It was clear that she couldn't take Ivan into her confidence as she had assured Harry a short time ago. All she could hope to do was get rid of him and count on the confounded bandana still being where Estelle had thrown it.

'That all sounds such a lot for her to worry about,' said Belinda, making a show of peering around Ivan's head. 'I think I see PC Green heading this way. I don't want to keep you.'

Ivan moved in closer and put his arms around Belinda, taking her off guard. 'It's been wonderful to see you again, Bel. Please get yourself home soon. I couldn't stand it if something happened to you as well.'

Belinda felt herself stiffen. There was no way he was threatening her, it was more a friendly warning – but it still made her wonder if she really knew him at all.

'I'd best be off, then,' said Ivan as he released her from his hug. 'There's still plenty to do with the animals, and in all honesty, it's much easier to get things done without the public around. Just don't tell Estelle I said that!' He laughed, the corners of his eyes creasing, as if the whole thing really was hilarious.

'Oh, yes, ha ha,' said Belinda, forcing a smile to go with her fake merriment. 'I'll see you later on.' *He's got an enormous forehead*, she thought. *Why haven't I ever noticed that before?*

Ivan turned and walked away from her. She found it tragically sad that she knew he was still smiling from the angle of his head and the red tinge to the top of his ears.

With a quick glimpse over her shoulder to make sure he was on his way, Belinda stole along to the riverside where Estelle had cast off the piece of material. Belinda spent a good couple of minutes searching for it and even considered taking off her shoes and getting in the water. She quickly dismissed the idea when she remembered it was a nippy

September day and it was a long walk back home in bare, muddy feet.

Belinda was going to have to call it a day as far as the bandana was concerned. She would let Vince know and the police could delve a bit deeper into Estelle's background, as well as taking a look at the river. She stood savouring the peace and tranquillity of the spot: the noise of the hogs was quietened by the gentle sound of the water's movement and the rustle of the branches above her head. If it wasn't for the tragedy of Simon and Drew, she might have even called it perfection. Then, the hairs on the back of her neck stood up, as if she were being watched. She looked from side to side, through the trees and across the river, but she couldn't see anyone watching her.

Making up her mind that she really should go home, she texted her brother Marcus to come and pick her up and then called PC Vince Green. She explained what she had seen Estelle up to, leaving out the part about Ivan, and that he should speak to her immediately. He sounded worn out and weary and didn't even argue with her when she informed him, 'And I've had quite enough for one day. If you want anything else from me, I'll be at home.'

30

By the time Harry got to the office, he had calmed down considerably and regretted snapping at Vince. It wasn't the young PC's fault that his superior officers hadn't thought to arrange for something as straightforward as a keeper to enter the enclosure and get the shoe. It was basic police work, surely?

Muttering to himself under his breath as he entered the empty, and more worryingly, unlocked office, Harry went over the CCTV screens to see if he could find Rob. He didn't want to disturb him if he was busy. Watching Belinda on the CCTV had felt intrusive, but Rob was a different matter. He didn't want to go to dinner with Rob for a start.

That thought had taken pole position in his mind, causing him to pause. Too much time had passed now for him to even contemplate asking Belinda out. Any chance of a relationship was behind them. Ivan was back now, swashbuckling adventures and all, leaving Harry with no chance of a date, let alone any kind of happy ever after.

Harry tried to look on the positive side: at least his heart wasn't about to get slammed in the door again by the most wonderful woman he had ever met. He put his energy into thudding the keyboard until he got the better of the hardware masquerading as his nemesis, and the system came to life. He punched his password in and sat himself down to locate Rob. Instead of Rob, the screen to his top right gave him a clear and perfect view of Belinda standing next to the red river hog enclosure in an embrace with Ivan.

Saddened and embarrassed, Harry got up and did what he often found himself doing in times of trouble – he put the kettle on.

When Harry had a mug of strong tea in front of him, as well as a packet of Bourbon biscuits, he steeled himself to look again at the monitors. It was his job, after all. With a mouthful of tea and a biscuit already dunked, he turned back to the screen where he had seen Belinda and Ivan. Now, Belinda stood by herself, seemingly in a bit of a daze, glancing around her as if she were searching for something. Eventually, she moved around the other side of the enclosure and his view was blocked by the trees. Right now, he needed to concentrate on where Ivan had gone.

It took no longer than two more Bourbons for Harry to locate the South African as he idled along towards the main gate. Fascinated, Harry tracked his movements as he walked outside and approached James Kara. The two of them stepped away from the others – an action that was clearly noticed by Carmel and Anna. The two women exchanged glances, and if Harry wasn't very much mistaken, Anna nodded at Carmel.

Harry thought there was more going on between the protestors than their opposing views on what should happen to the elephants. Anna and James had appeared to be in conversation about something when he'd paid them a visit. And now

Ivan was off talking to James once again. Was it something they were all in on?

Harry wondered whether he should tell Belinda who he had seen Ivan speaking to, and more importantly, whether he should tell her that in the lead-up, he had seen her and Ivan in a clinch.

31

The afternoon had a manic freshness in the air. Belinda was only too pleased to climb into her brother's Mercedes at the staff entrance. She had insisted on walking up the hill to meet him because she wanted to keep moving.

Vince hadn't exactly been enthused about the bandana in the river, maybe because he didn't fancy the idea of passing the news on to his sergeant, only to have the task handed back to him with a pair of waders. Still, it could be a vital clue. When she had called in on Harry to tell him she was leaving, he seemed a tad distracted and was muttering about 'missing out' and 'standards slipping in the police'. He seemed unable to look her in the eye, which she took to be a sign of how much it was all getting to him.

'I say, sis,' said Marcus, when she slammed the passenger door shut. 'What's got your knickers in a twist?'

'Nothing,' she said with a sigh of epic proportions. 'It's been one of those days – again. Thanks for coming to get me. I didn't mean to stay as long as I did, but Harry gave me a lift here and then we had another murder.'

Marcus had started to pull away but hit the brakes, causing

Belinda to jolt forwards violently. 'Oh, sorry,' he said. 'Another murder? Who was it?'

'A chap called Drew Matterson who worked at the zoo with Harry. I don't know very much about him, but he was only thirty-something. It's so horrible. The police weren't going to declare it a murder because it looked as if he fell from a tree and died from his injuries.'

'And the police gave you that level of detail?' said Marcus with a shake of his head. 'Couldn't they have been more vague?'

'I found him like that,' she said, miserable to the core.

'Strewth,' said Marcus. 'You really have had a rotten day. And old Harry? What's he doing?'

'Helping the police to solve the deaths,' she said with as little energy as she felt coursing through her. 'I'm hoping that he'll drop by later so that we can talk suspects and strategies.'

'In the meantime, you've got me to sound ideas off,' said Marcus. 'We could be like Dempsey and Makepeace, Holmes and Watson.'

As luck would have it, there was a bend in the road coming up and a tractor just turning into a field, so Marcus wasn't able to see the look of astonishment on Belinda's face. 'Er, thanks,' she said. *More like Abbott and Costello*, she thought.

'Well, let's not forget that if it hadn't been for me, with that wine tasting last time, that scoundrel would have got away,' Marcus said.

'You did actually have hold of the wrong person,' said Belinda, 'but your help was very much appreciated.'

'I'll grant you that the chap I apprehended was completely innocent, but I don't like to admit defeat,' he said. 'Besides, three heads are better than one.'

Not when one of them is full of air, she thought, and settled back into the journey.

. . .

Belinda started to get anxious when six o'clock came round and she still hadn't heard from Harry. She was worried that something might have happened to him. He was, after all, in a zoo where people were being murdered at an alarming rate. Marcus was trying his best to soothe her nerves, but his presence was as welcome as a court jester in an operating theatre.

'I got this from the loft,' he said, heaving a huge chalkboard into the drawing room where Belinda had settled herself with a camomile tea. Her dog Horatio was next to her chair, snoozing on one of his many beds. 'When I say I got it from the loft, I mean I got one of the staff to get it. I had no idea where the loft was.'

'It's in the roof,' she said, 'where they generally are. And why have you got that?'

Belinda was curled up in an opulent green armchair, her legs folded under her, the beautiful if crisp day coming to an end through the patio doors to her left-hand side. She didn't have much time for that, or for Marcus's antics either. She wasn't in the most tolerant of moods.

'I thought that you, me and H – when he gets here – could run through the likely killers,' he said, as he brushed dust from his purple trousers. He beamed at her. 'Isn't that what the two of you do? I can help.'

Belinda's heart melted at the sight of her daft, yet well-meaning older brother. He pushed his floppy blond hair from his blue eyes and seemed genuinely thrilled. That was the problem – it shouldn't be a thrill. It was death and murder and not a game.

About to answer him, Belinda was mercifully interrupted by her mobile phone. 'Hello, Harry,' she said, keeping the relief from her voice as best she could. 'Where are you?'

'I'm outside the door. You did say it was OK to come over?'

Belinda smiled as she answered him. 'Absolutely. Park at

the back and come in through the patio.' She unlocked the doors and pushed them wide open, ready for Harry.

As she turned back to her seat, she caught her brother smiling at her.

'What?' she said, hands on her hips.

'I think, after all this time, Harry knows the way. It's good to see you so pleased to see him.'

'He's my friend,' she said, a blush creeping along her neck and finding its way to her cheeks. 'Besides, it's warm in here.'

'Yes, you have gone rather red. You're either embarrassed or else it's the men—'

She snapped her fingers at him. 'If you say "menopause", I'll volunteer you to the Women's Institute for their charity car wash.'

Marcus put his hands up in mock surrender as Harry's feet crunched their way across the gravel. 'H, old man. Thank goodness you're here. You can take some of the heat off me. Little sis is quite going to town.'

Harry winked at Belinda and said to Marcus, 'Knowing you, mate, it's nothing that you didn't deserve. What on earth is that blackboard doing here?'

'I think we're saying chalkboard these days,' said Marcus. 'Anyway, it's to help us solve the murders.'

'And the idea being that we hit the killer on the head with it or hide behind it?' said Harry. 'It's huge and there's no chalk.'

'Oh, drat,' said Marcus. 'I didn't think of that.'

Belinda slowly blew the air from her cheeks. 'You have a chalkboard and no chalk.'

'In the meantime,' said Marcus as he took a seat on one end of the three-seater sofa and gestured to Harry that he should sit down on the other end, 'how about hearing my new business idea?'

'I'm not sure that I can take much more,' said Belinda,

pinching the bridge of her nose. 'Although I suppose it might take my mind off the more unpleasant aspects of the day.'

'With a profound sense of dread, I'm all ears,' said Harry, easing into the cushions.

'The Island!' said Marcus, eyes darting from his sister to Harry and back again.

'The island?' said Belinda. 'Which island?'

'There's only one,' said Marcus.

'No, there's not,' she said, closing her eyes. 'There are thousands of them all over the globe. The Caribbean, the Balearic Islands, the Canary Islands, not to mention the Isle of Man.'

'Our island,' said Marcus. 'Kent's one and only Isle of Sheppey.'

'You actually used jazz hands then,' said Harry. 'I think it's a world first that anyone accompanied the words "Isle of Sheppey" with jazz hands. Well, I'll be.'

'It's a mighty fine place and there's only one way on and one way off,' said Marcus, glee and stupidity all over his face.

'We know, Marcus,' said Belinda. 'It's called a bridge, and actually, there are two of them.'

'How about this?' Marcus leaned forward and lowered his voice, presumably to impress upon his audience the genius and confidentiality of what he was about to tell them. 'We turn the Isle of Sheppey into Europe's largest drive-through safari. It'll have the big five: elephants, buffalo, lions, rhinos and... what's the fifth? I can never remember if it's hippos or giraffes?'

'It's leopards,' said Belinda. 'If you're going to attempt to lure people in from all over the world with a safari experience, I suggest you have the correct animals.'

'Aren't you forgetting something?' said Harry. 'People live on the island. There are shops, restaurants, a nature reserve, holiday camps, not to mention the prison cluster.'

'The word cluster did spring to mind,' said Belinda, hoping her brother would go out for the evening in the very near future.

'Mm, the prisons might be a bit of a problem, but it should deter anyone from escaping if they thought they were going to be eaten by a lion.' Marcus held his chin between his thumb and forefinger as he stared at the carpet, far too much thought going into the prison population's dash for freedom.

'It might also stop people going out at all, children going to school, people digging up the spuds from their allotments, that sort of thing,' said Harry. 'Tell you what, how about you go and see if you can find any chalk for that board, then Belinda and I can give it serious thought.' He widened his eyes at Belinda, who nodded eagerly.

'Great,' said Marcus, jumping up and clapping his hands together. 'Make sure I don't miss too much. I'll be back soon.'

'Thank you,' said Belinda when her daft sibling had left the room. 'He means well – if you don't live on the Isle of Sheppey – but I couldn't take any more of his nonsense today.'

'You look pale, if that's not a bit rude,' said Harry.

'No, I feel a little battle weary, to be honest,' she said. 'Come on, let's go and put the kettle on. By the time Marcus comes back, he'll have forgotten what he was boring us with and will have found something else to do. He's got the memory of a concussed goldfish.'

Horatio raised his sleepy head and with a sigh, lay back down, deciding it was all too much.

32

'Are you sure you're feeling up to this?' said Harry for possibly the tenth time. He didn't like the peaky look on Belinda's face. In the sparse lighting of the kitchen's under-cupboard LED lights, she appeared worryingly pale.

'I'm fine.' Belinda smiled at him. She wrapped her hands around the freshly made mug of camomile tea that Harry had put on the table in front of her. He had made himself at home opening cupboards and brewing himself a strong coffee. The modest and cosy room they had taken themselves off to was really the gardeners' kitchen, where Belinda frequently spent part of her day.

'Care to tell me what's really bothering you?' he said, pulling out one of the chairs and taking a seat opposite her. He didn't want to pry if it was Ivan-related, but he still cared greatly about her.

Belinda raised an eyebrow. 'You seem to have taken up "interrogation position" directly opposite me. I suppose you have ways of making me talk.'

'Short of plying you with Sauvignon Blanc or adopting the Home Office unarmed police defence training tactic of tickling your armpits – it does actually work, by the way – I'm going to have to ask you nicely.'

Belinda smiled again, took a sip of her tea and said, 'I saw Ivan talking to Estelle.' Harry said nothing so she carried on. 'They were down by the red river hogs. They always cheer me up – the hogs, not Ivan and Estelle – so I took a tiny detour that way, and that's when I spotted them talking on the far side of the river.' Harry nodded. 'They were talking at first, but then it looked as though...' Belinda pursed her lips and looked to the ceiling. 'I can't be one hundred per cent certain, but it looked as though they were kissing.'

'Oh,' said Harry.

'His engagement's called off, so I suppose it's nothing to do with me,' she said, placing her mug back down with a bang. 'Apart from the part where he told me he flew here to see if there was any hope of a second chance for us.'

Harry had decided to adopt a silent technique to get Belinda talking. Now, he was a bit concerned that he might say the wrong thing and suggest that perhaps Belinda was jealous. He knew he couldn't take it back if he made such a faux pas, so carried on nodding wisely.

'I know what you're thinking,' said Belinda. 'Why is she so worried if she's got nothing to do with him anymore? I, for one, am only too glad I dodged that bullet. Have you noticed what an enormous forehead he has?'

'No,' said Harry, trying to look as though he was struggling to conjure up an image of Ivan's gigantic head.

'He has, it's colossal.' Belinda traced the rim of the mug with her finger. 'The thing is, it threw me so much, I was disorientated. I don't mean his forehead, I mean what was going on. To begin with, Rob was there, talking to Estelle, only it looked as though they were rowing. I feared it was going to turn nasty at one point. Rob seemed to be pleading with her about something; he was almost on bended knee. Then Ivan appeared and broke it up.'

'I'd wondered what happened to Rob this afternoon,' Harry said, scratching at his stubble. 'It makes sense if he was on the other side of the river. The CCTV is very hit-and-miss over there. Unless someone's standing on the bridge, it's tricky to pick them out.' This was why Harry hadn't wanted to talk too much. Perhaps he should tell her that he had seen her on the CCTV talking to Ivan, and later when Ivan had his arms wrapped around her. Minutes after he'd been kissing Estelle. *And* Harry was sure Ivan used hair gel. What a waster.

'It's interesting that the CCTV doesn't stretch over to where Estelle and Rob were standing,' said Belinda. 'Rob would definitely know that the area isn't covered by cameras. And I donated money to upgrade the security system.' This Harry hadn't been aware of. 'Estelle prepared me an in-depth report detailing what was covered and what wasn't. Drew helped her put the report together. She would have an overview of it all too.'

Harry got up to pour his coffee. As he stirred the milk into his drink, he said, 'It's unlikely Estelle would have purposely chosen a blind spot to have a row with someone, especially if two people had just been murdered nearby.'

'After Ivan turned up, Rob left and then, eventually, so did Ivan.' She stared into space and added, 'Estelle took a bandana out of her pocket and threw it into the river. It was an African Savannah Safari Experience one – I could see that from the colours. Quite why she did it, I've got no idea.'

As Harry sat back down opposite Belinda, his stomach let out an almighty growl. 'Er, sorry about that. The concession stands were all closed again, so I couldn't get any lunch. Anyway, we know it wasn't the bandana used to strangle Simon. But I agree with you that her actions are bizarre.'

'Then, before I had a chance to go and look, Ivan came back.'

This was his opportunity to tell her he'd seen Ivan with his arms around her. 'Do you think Ivan came back for the bandana?' Harry was so gutless at times.

'No, I don't.' Belinda took another sip of her tea. 'He didn't cross back over that side of the river and by the time he'd gone, I couldn't see it. I did tell Vince, though. The police should have taken a look, except we don't know the significance, so we've no idea how thoroughly they'll search.'

'I know it's none of my business how much money you donated but do you have any idea how much financial difficulty the zoo's in?' said Harry. He would have liked a figure, even a ball-park one.

'I've never been given the details, only that it's not great. We'd have to speak to Estelle to find out the exact extent. I can't help thinking that the animal rights people are a bit of a mixed blessing.' She looked around the room for something to write on. 'At least they're getting news crews to turn up and talk about the rewilding project, even if it's turned into bad publicity with the murders.'

With a flourish, Belinda brought over a couple of A4 pieces of paper and a blue biro. 'Tiny make-do whiteboard time. I'd go and find something more suitable but there's the outside chance I'd bump into my foolish brother and he'd tell me about some other brainless scheme he's concocted.'

'So far,' said Harry as he leaned across the table, 'for both Simon Carter's and Drew Matterson's murders, we're still looking at Estelle Samuels, Rob Piper, James Kara and his entourage and Anna Clancy and hers. Although we shouldn't overlook whether one or both lots of protesters are behind the sabotaging of the zoo, they won't necessarily be responsible for two murders.'

'We know that Estelle is in money trouble,' said Belinda

with a frown. 'At least, the gardens, zoo and conservation projects are costing her dearly. I think she bit off more than she can chew. She might have seen Simon as a concern – he threatened to sue on more than one occasion – but Drew doesn't make sense.'

'That brings us back to the sabotage again,' said Harry. 'With so many different occurrences, I'm now having trouble accepting that all of those things and both murders were done by the same person. They don't boil down to one motive.'

Harry watched her write Estelle's name on the top of the paper and underline it twice. 'I think that we have to ask what Drew was doing,' said Harry. 'He might have seen something while he was up the tree, slipped and lost a shoe to a hyena. But why was he up there in the first place?'

'Maybe he was scoping for where to put CCTV cameras?' said Belinda, her eyes wide and a hand up to her chest. 'But why that particular tree?'

'Maybe someone sent him to that location, having already weakened the branches. We know someone deliberately damaged his shoelaces, meaning he wore entirely the wrong shoes.'

Belinda paused, pen in hand. 'There's Rob too.' She added his name.

'Agree,' said Harry. 'He's as likely to be irked by Simon's constant potential as a financial drain on the zoo as Estelle. Except he seemed to think very highly of Drew, even to the point of them being friends. Again, it comes back to what Estelle's and Rob's motives would be for the zoo shutting. They'd both be out of a job.'

'Then that only leaves the animal rights people,' said Belinda. She added the few names they knew to the list and eased back in her chair. 'They all knew Simon, despite their insistence he was a decent sort who bought them all hot drinks. If he was suing the zoo, that might mean an end to the rewilding, giving James a motive for getting him out of the picture. It would, however, mean that James managed to get the zoo shut down, which could have been his aim all along.'

'Perhaps it was always James's aim,' said Harry. 'If the zoo closes, the animals would have to be sent somewhere, and that somewhere might be back to Africa.'

'It's certainly a win-win situation for James and his supporters,' said Belinda. 'If they're behind the sabotage, too, it would tick all of the boxes. Drew would also have been a problem for James, as he was security and was busy trying to get more cameras put up and make the place safer.'

They both stared at one another, realising the implications of what Belinda had said.

'They'd have to take us all out, if that's the case,' said Harry. He was beginning to regret leaving his last job as a dog food delivery man. By and large, no one had tried to kill him when he dropped off their pet's kibble.

'Anna Clancy makes no sense, though,' said Belinda. 'She wouldn't want the zoo in jeopardy because it might mean the animals were disadvantaged. Still, Simon's attempts to get money may have meant she wanted him out of the way. The less he took, the more for the zoo.'

'Not forgetting that – providing we believe what James told us – she's connected with someone in the zoo,' said Harry. 'Perhaps that someone was Drew and he was causing her problems.'

'If Anna did kill Drew,' said Belinda, a spot of colour coming back to her cheeks, 'it might be enough to discredit Estelle and get rid of her. That would increase the chances of the elephants staying. They don't want the herd to go overseas.'

'So we could have one group trying to discredit Brabourne Zoological Gardens so that the elephants stay,' said Harry.

'Or James Kara's rival group sabotaging the place so it gets closed down and all of the animals sent home.' Belinda moved back in her chair and closed her eyes while she considered this.

Harry stared into his coffee mug. 'I need to tell you...' He looked up at her perfect face as she waited for him to speak. 'I told you that I was looking for Rob this afternoon, and I used the CCTV to try and find him. I couldn't see him; you told me why that was. Anyway, what I did see was Ivan going to speak to James. It's not the first time the two of them have had their heads together, and well, I suppose you should be aware of it.'

Harry had derived no pleasure at all from telling Belinda this, particularly as he left out the part where he had seen her hugging her ex-partner. Or had he been hugging her? There was still something that Harry didn't like about him, and it wasn't solely down to him having broken Belinda's heart. Although that was probably enough reason to hate him.

When Belinda had had a moment to digest this latest update, she said, 'OK, then. How about first thing tomorrow, we have this out with James Kara? We can find out exactly what it is that he and Ivan keep discussing before we confront Ivan.'

Deep down, Harry knew that it would make more sense to start with Ivan, but he recognised that Belinda was stalling for time.

33

Belinda slept fitfully and awoke early on Friday, with the feeling that a long day lay ahead of her. The view from her bedroom window cheered her somewhat – it was difficult to not be moved by the sight that greeted her every morning. But today, she had other places to be and no time to ponder the countryside. After showering, dressing and walking Horatio, she grabbed a coffee and got on her way.

She had arranged with Harry to make her own way to Brabourne Gardens. She didn't want to have to wait on a lift home, and besides, Harry had a job to do. She drove her Land Rover out of the castle grounds and along the country lanes and dual carriageway that took her to Brabourne Gardens.

The morning was drab and miserable: rain hung in the air, giving everything a dank and gloomy feel. Or perhaps that was Belinda's mood. Whatever it was, she sensed a tension creeping across her shoulders and up to her neck.

Probably in a bid to delay arriving, Belinda took a slightly longer approach and turned the Land Rover towards Brabourne Hill. The huge white mansion house sat proud, as if it were keeping watch on the formal gardens and zoo below.

Belinda lived in a castle so shouldn't find the mansion imposing or intimidating, yet its magnificence had always taken her breath away. Steps led down to the start of the gardens and many a bride and groom had posed for their wedding photos with the backdrop of the verdant, immaculate gardens behind them.

Like many important thoughts, this one came to her as her mind was mostly concentrating on driving. The mansion was taking a small fortune in wedding parties and other special occasions. A number of the villagers had bar, catering and housekeeping roles there and frequently spoke of how far in advance the place was booked up. She happened to know the cost of the refreshments, too, and it had made her balk. Where was all the money going? Perhaps Estelle really did have some explaining to do, after all.

Belinda reached the top of the road and drove through the gates to the mansion house. She didn't really have any intention of going in or even getting out of the car, but thought that if she viewed the zoo from a different perspective, she might just think of something that she and Harry had missed.

She pulled the Land Rover over beside a gap in the low shrubs which marked the start of the descent towards the rest of the grounds. The two-storey sixteenth-century mansion was set within twenty acres of landscaped gardens, with many more acres of parkland beyond that. It was separated from the zoo by a bluebell wood, a walled garden and a deer park centred around a lake, partly visible before the start of the vast animal enclosures that adjoined the boundary on one side – although many areas were shielded by the trees and natural contour of the land.

Belinda opened the car window and stared at the splendid views beyond. This place was perfection itself so why kill a visitor and a member of the staff? Would someone really commit murder to keep all this? Or to destroy it? It only convinced her that both Simon Carter and Drew Matterson must have been a great threat to someone with a lot at stake.

Belinda glanced towards the front of the mansion, ran an appreciative eye over the Kentish ragstone and was about to drive off when she saw the main door open. Estelle stepped out, looking extremely flustered. She raked her hands through her shoulder-length hair, dragging it into a ponytail, and raced across to a line of Brabourne Gardens vehicles. Estelle fumbled with a set of keys, got in a vehicle and pulled away with more speed than caution.

Estelle's eyes flashed Belinda's way, and on recognising who was staring at her, she slammed her foot on the brake and gave her an opened-mouth glare back. Not being prepared to leave it there, Belinda got out of her Land Rover and made her way over to the van, careful not to walk in front of it.

'Hello, Estelle,' she said, crouching down at the window. Estelle only created a gap of three inches so Belinda all but had her nose to the glass. 'Everything OK? You look upset.' She did indeed look as though she had the weight of the world on her shoulders. Her eyes were red, with dark circles underneath, and her skin had a blotchy appearance. It was a far cry from the usual healthy outdoors look that Estelle had always carried off.

'Belinda. What are you— Oh, it doesn't matter. We had an emergency board meeting to discuss the future, if we actually have one. I can't get my head around this.' Estelle let go of the steering wheel and pressed her palms into her eye sockets. 'The police called me in the middle of it to tell me that they've found another body. I can't take any more.'

'Oh, this is horrendous.' Belinda put a hand up to her own mouth, her heart hammering. She hadn't heard from Harry this morning. All she knew was that he was going into work early and she hadn't been with him. And Ivan? Where was he? 'Who is it?' said Belinda, not sure she wanted to know. A wave of nausea washed over her.

'I-I don't know,' said Estelle, one hand back on the steering wheel and the other on the gear stick. 'All they would tell me was that it was a man. I can't get hold of Rob either. I have to go, I'm sorry.'

Estelle sped off, the tyres throwing up dirt and gravel as she went.

With her heart in her mouth, Belinda rushed back to the Land Rover and grabbed her phone from inside her coat pocket. She called Harry but the number just rang and rang.

34

Driving like the very devil was chasing her, Belinda made it back to the zoo's staff entrance in record time. She opened the window and shouted at Stan without stopping the Land Rover. He was a man of minimal facial expressions at the best of times, but even he looked a tad surprised at her lack of manners. Doing as he was told, he opened the gate and stood watching her careen past him.

'Please let Harry be safe and well,' she said, aiming for the first parking space she saw. 'Please let Harry be all right. I promise that I'll tell him how I feel and won't waste any more time. Please let him be all right.' Belinda's eyes filled with tears as she turned the engine off and bowed her head forward, gathering her strength. She wiped the errant tears that were spilling down her cheeks and tried to call him again.

It rang and rang. On the third ring, she threw her head back against the headrest, her eyes squeezed shut. 'Please, please...' A bang on the windowpane jolted her back to full alert.

Harry's gorgeous, lined, worried, battle-worn face loomed at her through the passenger window. In her haste to get out and hug him, stamping on his feet as she did so, her mobile phone dropped to the ground.

'Gawd, blimey, Bel,' he said, choking out his words with her head against his throat. 'I don't normally get this reaction when I tell someone they have to move their car. We've got a delivery coming in – you can't leave it there.'

'A delivery?' She released her grip on him. 'A delivery of what? Hasn't there been another murder?'

Harry cleared his throat and patted her, encouraging her to let him go. 'Yes, it's quite horrible, but, as grim as it is, we still have to feed the animals.'

Right on cue, they both heard a small van coming towards them, driven, if Belinda wasn't mistaken, by none other than George Reid, Little Challham's village butcher.

'He surely doesn't deliver the meat here?' she said, incredulity replacing her earlier anguish. 'He only runs a small butcher's shop, there's no way he can supply enough to feed *all* these animals.'

By now, George had manoeuvred the van next to Belinda's Land Rover and jumped down to stand next to them. 'What ho! If it isn't Harry and Belinda. Love's middle-aged dream. You two get everywhere.'

Belinda gave him one of her best looks of disdain. She had been practising for a while. 'I didn't know that you supplied the meat here, George. How wonderful.'

'Not all of it,' he said. 'As you probably know, what with you having a well-manicured finger in every pie, I like to help out charitable organisations wherever I can. If there's any meat going out of date that isn't fit for human consumption – otherwise we'd donate to food banks, of course – us local butchers give it to places like this. It was something that poor so and so Drew organised. I can't believe he's dead. He was such a thoroughly lovely guy.'

For a moment, Belinda thought that George might actually shed a tear or two. He did seem to be genuinely touched.

'I'm sorry,' she said. 'I didn't realise that you knew him. He was a decent man, and it's a great loss.'

'I'll second that,' said Harry. 'I didn't know him well, but he was a good man.'

George stepped forward, nose to nose with Harry. 'I'll drop this lot off whenever the lion tamers or cheetah charmers or bare-back buffalo riders or whatever they are get here. Do me one favour, would you?' He stared unblinking at Harry.

'Go on,' said Harry.

'Find the son of a gun who killed Drew,' said George with an audible breath. 'He was genuinely good people.'

'Everything within our power, I promise,' said Harry.

'Great,' said George, clapping his hands together. 'Well, I'll be off and leave double oh three and a half and Miss Funny-Money to it. Laters.'

With that, George went to the back of the van and began to unload, as the zookeeping team arrived to take the meat from him.

Harry inclined his head towards the row of electric buggies. 'We should take one of these and find out what's happened. I'm still not completely sure whose body's been found.'

'Really?' she said as she hopped into the passenger seat, Harry ready to pull away. 'How come you don't know who it is?'

'When we get there, it'll be obvious why. All we can tell at the moment is that the victim is a man.' Harry shook his head. 'And prepare yourself, Bel. This is going to be very unpleasant.'

35

As Belinda and Harry made their way towards the scene of Brabourne Gardens' latest death, Belinda was taken aback to see so many of the general public milling around. The concentration that Harry was putting into driving the buggy prompted Belinda to wait until they had screeched to a stop before she said, 'Why haven't the police closed the zoo?'

Harry turned to her. 'To be honest with you, I'm pretty cheesed off about it. There were three coachloads of school kids here this morning from Essex – the trip was too late to cancel, apparently – and there's been pressure from the board of trustees towards the police chief. Money talks and all that.'

'But there's been a murder!' said Belinda, a lot louder than she had intended.

'Or has there?' said Harry, his eyebrows raised.

'There either has, or there hasn't,' she said, feeling as confused as she no doubt looked.

'At the moment, would you believe, they're trying to pass this off as another unfortunate accident. Come on. See what you think.'

Wondering exactly what new house of horrors was about to

greet her this time, Belinda turned her attention to the elephant house. A large crowd of zookeepers, police and a couple of the security team were gathering around the back of the restricted area.

'I've been through this way myself,' said Belinda as she tried to keep up with Harry. 'I did a couple of hours feeding and looking after the elephants. It was a publicity thing. Estelle was trying to raise money and promote the ranger experiences, keeper academies, animal encounters, that sort of thing. It was me and a couple of TV celebrities, a soap star and a children's author.'

'You never mentioned it,' said Harry as they reached the gate.

'There wasn't much to tell, but it raised a lot of money, so I was only too happy to help out,' she said, wondering why they were being allowed this close to the enclosure if there was a dead body somewhere nearby.

As if reading her thoughts, PC Vince Green stuck his head around the large metal gate leading to the elephants. 'Morning,' he said. 'Neither of you look suitably dressed for moving a herd of the world's largest land animals around.'

'Morning, Vince,' said Belinda, her attention momentarily drawn to the trumpeting going on out of her sight. 'I see you've been reading up on your elephant facts.'

'Mm, and since about half an hour ago, I happen to know a lot about their dung too,' he said, an unreadable expression on his face.

'I told you it wasn't going to be pleasant,' said Harry.

'You don't mean...' said Belinda, bile rising, the stench now taking on a more toxic implication.

'Afraid so,' said Vince. 'It looks as though someone tried to hide his body in the... you know what. I can't let you in but we've got the crime scene investigators here, just in case.'

Belinda poked her head around the gate and took in the

strangest sight she had ever set her eyes on. In the farthest corner of the yard, there was a large pile of elephant dung. In front of it, two CSIs in white paper suits, complete with foot coverings and face masks, were busy taking photographs of something on the floor, partially covered by the excrement. She couldn't make out what it was and at first it looked like a pile of rags. She gasped when one of the CSIs stepped back to get a clearer shot and saw a foot and what was clearly the bottom of a trouser leg. One of the corpse's outstretched hands was clinging onto a length of what appeared to be green rope. A man and a woman stood back from the body talking into their mobile phones, both dressed in dark-coloured trouser suits with police lanyards around their necks. They had the well-worn weariness of two detectives called along to another suspicious death, only this time, one of the most bizarre they had ever encountered.

Whoever it was on the ground appeared to have been smothered with elephants' droppings, and lots of it. Belinda craned her neck to get a better view. She was sure she remembered seeing a person in tweed trousers in the last couple of days, and thankfully, she didn't think they were the sort of thing Ivan would wear.

As one of the CSIs moved in closer to take a photograph of the dead person's face, Belinda found herself looking right at the open staring grey eyes of James Kara. The avid supporter of the elephant rewilding project seemed to have been unceremoniously buried in elephant excreta.

36

Belinda gave a very audible involuntary gasp, which attracted the attention of the two suited detectives. They both looked over and glowered at her, the woman rushing towards the gate. Harry, realising that this was not going to help either the investigation or Vince's chances of joining CID any time soon, stepped in front of Belinda and said, 'Sorry, my mistake. I'm Harry Powell, deputy head of security. I insisted I come to see what needs doing.'

Vince's feet had taken to stepping towards the senior officers and back again. From his red and flustered face, he was also finding it difficult to form coherent speech, or in fact, any words at all.

'And this young PC was only seconds away from having to arrest me to stop me coming this close to your crime scene,' said Harry, thumbing in Vince's direction.

'You shouldn't be in here,' said the woman, who was now barring both their way and their view. 'Vince, get them out of here and don't hesitate to nick them if they won't cooperate.'

'Oh, yeah; I mean, yes, ma'am,' said Vince. His posture

seemed to have returned to normal and he stood with his arms crossed to show he really meant business.

'Yes, we'll leave straight away,' said Belinda, as she made a hasty retreat, not relishing the idea of getting herself 'nicked'.

The three of them made their way back towards the public area, Vince bringing up the rear and doing a grand job of pretending he was in charge, while the detectives and CSIs looked on.

'Who was it?' said Harry, once they were out of earshot. 'I couldn't see.'

'It was James Kara,' said Belinda, her hand on her heart. 'Wow, that was horrible. What a very undignified way to go. Drew's murder was upsetting enough but if I had to take my choice, I think I'd rather go with death by falling rather than... well, you know.'

Belinda took as deep a breath as she was willing to risk, considering their location and what lay on the other side of the wall.

'We should probably move a little bit further away,' said Vince. 'Apart from getting it in the ear if we don't move, I heard the guv'nor say the entire pile of dung needs to be raked over, on the off chance anything else is hidden in there. I heard them say that he was killed and his body moved into the dung, so the actual cause of death hasn't been established. Still, I agree, it's a terrible place to end up, even if he was already dead.'

'I can get someone to check the CCTV and make sure no one else was anywhere near here,' said Harry, taking his mobile out of his pocket. 'Any idea exactly what James was doing?'

'Not this time,' said Vince. 'We've surmised it had something to do with his belief that the elephants should be rewilded. Not really sure how breaking in during the dead of night was going to whisk them off to another continent. We can only guess that he was up to no good.'

'It must have been James who caused the injury to Sabbie

by putting green rope across the giraffe enclosure,' said Belinda. 'He really was prepared to do anything to get what he wanted.'

'And someone took the ultimate revenge,' said Vince. 'Brutal, very brutal.'

Belinda was partially distracted by Harry's call to Rob in the security office. Not far into the conversation, he glanced their way and put a little more distance between himself and Vince. He continued to speak in a lowered voice with his hand over his mouth.

To help her friend out, Belinda said to Vince, 'Look over there. It seems that more of your colleagues have arrived. Perhaps they could do with your help. I'll wait until Harry's finished and get him to call you from the security office.'

She hadn't really expected it to work as well as it did. Vince scarpered off towards two plain clothes detectives and briefed them on which way to go.

With one ear listening to Vince and the other trying to decipher what was irking Harry, Belinda took stock of what was going on around her. There were groups of school children as well as families and several couples. The police hadn't announced this was murder number three, but it surely must be. James couldn't have met such an unpleasant end otherwise.

Harry ended the call and checked that Vince was still occupied elsewhere. 'That was interesting: Rob said that someone's been into the security office and messed around with the system. All of the footage is gone. Not to mention Ivan was there first thing this morning asking what cameras were on what enclosures. He was particularly interested in the elephants and the wolves.'

'The wolves?' said Belinda. 'How about we pay the wolves a visit – the outside of their enclosure anyway – and find out what Ivan thinks he's up to.'

The pathways around the wolf enclosure were mostly empty, what with the wolves not caring very much for people.

As Harry drove the buggy closer to the towering chain-link fence, a grey wolf appeared at the perimeter and trotted alongside. Harry halted the buggy. The wolf stared at him with piercing yellow-gold eyes, before carrying on with his pacing along the edge of the fence. When the animal reached the other end, he turned and walked back towards them.

'That's a little bit unsettling,' said Belinda. 'Do you think it's agitated? I don't know much about wolves.'

'I'm not sure,' said Harry, scratching his head. 'It probably wouldn't hurt if I call up the keeper once we get to the security office. I can see from here that the inner gates are locked, so I don't think that either the wolves or people are in danger. Perhaps it's a coincidence.'

'No such thing,' said Belinda, as Harry pulled away again. She couldn't resist another glance over her shoulder at the wolf. It stared back.

The door to the security office was open when they pulled up outside. They could hear Rob shouting before Harry had a chance to secure the buggy. 'This doesn't sound very promising. My new boss hollering at people when I'm only three days into a job.'

'Harry,' said Belinda, 'please don't take this the wrong way, but did you *actually* hand your notice in at Doggie Delight?'

'Funnily enough,' he said, 'the new regional manager texted me yesterday to see if I wanted my old job back.' Harry's eyebrows were raised to his greying hairline as he spoke.

'What did you tell him?'

Harry looked over to the office where Rob was now practically roaring. 'I told him that I'd call him back over the weekend.'

'You're not as stupid as you look,' said Belinda, her mouth

twitching with the start of a smile. 'I'll let you go in first. It sounds like a very charged atmosphere.'

Harry walked up the steps, his body language devoid of all trace of enthusiasm. He stopped short inside the doorway, Belinda almost colliding with him. Rob was on his own in the room and seemed to be shouting at someone on the other end of the phone. 'I'll call you back!' he shrieked into the receiver.

'Sorry, Rob,' said Harry. 'I didn't mean to interrupt.'

Rob peered over Harry's shoulder at Belinda. His face relaxed when he saw her and he seemed to bring his temper down to simmering point. 'Please, both of you, come on in. Take a seat. I was taking care of a bit of business. Nothing to worry about.'

Both Harry and Belinda edged their way into the office, although neither took Rob up on his offer of sitting down. His knuckles were still white from gripping the phone. He noticed her looking and slammed it back into its cradle on the desk.

'Everything all right?' he said, his eyes darting from Belinda to Harry. 'Apart from the people who keep coming into the zoo and managing to meet a sticky end, of course. That goes without saying. They're going to shut us down, aren't they? I don't know what'll happen to all our animals. It's tragic, simply tragic.'

'We came to find Ivan,' said Belinda, holding Rob's wide-eyed stare. 'I'm really sorry that things are going so wrong at the zoo, but we do need to know where he is.'

Rob hunched his shoulders up to his ears. 'Beats me. I don't mean to be unhelpful, but he left after waffling on about the wolf enclosure and whether it was on camera and if the elephants weren't properly secured either. I got the impression he thought that the protestors were sniffing around. They were in a funny mood this morning, but that could be because one of them had infiltrated the perimeter.'

'Any idea how James got in?' said Harry.

'Oh, yes,' said Rob, smacking his lips. 'He managed to wire

the van that you left in the lay-by yesterday. The so-called gate security simply waved him on through.'

'Oh, my good God,' said Harry, shutting his eyes. 'The van. I left it outside. How could I have been so stupid?'

'If we weren't knee-deep in dead bodies, I'd fire you for that,' said Rob. 'You have remembered that you're on a probationary period, haven't you?'

'No... I... yes.' It didn't take much to interpret Harry's mutterings as embarrassment on a huge scale.

'Was there anything else?' said Rob, as he picked the phone back up and started to punch in a number.

'No, not at the moment, thanks,' said Harry, indicating to Belinda that they should make a hasty retreat.

Once back outside, Belinda said, 'You can be grateful for one thing, H.'

'What's that?'

'You were very good at delivering dog food.'

37

Harry stared at Belinda, thinking – completely inappropriately given people were being killed at an alarming rate – that it was bad enough he was about to get fired, let alone how devastated he would be if Belinda let Ivan back into her life.

'Please don't take offence,' she said, tucking a strand of hair behind her ears. 'I was only joking. He won't fire you. Not today, anyway.'

'No, it wasn't that,' said Harry, gesturing in the direction of Estelle's office. 'It's made me think that this is a good time to pay Estelle a visit. You said that she tore off from the mansion after the abandoned board meeting, yet there was no sign of her at the elephant house. I'd say that's suspicious. And we can't find Ivan.'

Belinda had already started to make her way to Estelle's door, Harry forced to stride to catch up with her. She was a woman on a mission and wasn't going to let knocking and waiting hold her up. She was through the door and inside the spacious room before Harry had a chance to stop her.

Then they both stood stock still at the sight of Ivan and Estelle caught in an embrace, the two of them joined firmly at the mouth. The sound of unannounced visitors barging through the door made them spring apart like the very guilty parties they were.

'It's not what it looks like,' said Ivan, jamming his hands into his pockets.

'So, you didn't just have your tongues down each other's throats?' said Harry.

'In that case,' said Estelle, 'it was what it looked like.' She sighed and looked at Ivan. 'What's the point in denying it, Ivan? We've been caught.'

'And what else are you two covering up?' said Belinda. 'It's bad enough what you did all those years ago, but this? Canoodling in the office when only yesterday you were asking if it was too late for us to give things another go?'

'You did what?' said Estelle, a trembling hand at her lips. 'You didn't tell me any of that. I can't believe you lied to me.'

'Oh, he does that. A lot,' said Belinda, one foot tapping on the carpet tiles. 'Don't get me started on what he's capable of.'

Ivan's chin was on his chest. Harry would normally have relished realising that Ivan's hair was starting to thin a bit on top, but it didn't seem like the optimal moment to gloat. He thought it was best to be pacifier rather than mock the South African's follicly challenged bonce.

'Perhaps we should wait outside, Bel?' he said, reaching out to touch her arm, but changing his mind halfway through the gesture. As much as Harry wanted to be the object of Belinda's affections, this wasn't how he'd wanted things to pan out.

Belinda gave Estelle a look of pity and swept out of the room. Harry was still struggling to keep up with her. He caught up with her by the first line of staff cars. One or two of the housekeeping staff were already leaving for the day and casting concerned glances at the angry raven-haired woman charging across the tarmac.

'Bel, slow down. I'm too old to run,' said Harry.

'I'm sorry,' she said. 'I told you what Ivan did and yet, still, I gave him the benefit of the doubt. Right at the moment, I'm not even sure he wasn't in some way responsible for Simon's, Drew's and James's deaths.'

Harry stood in front of her, forcing her to look at him. 'You really think that?'

Belinda let out a protracted breath. 'No, no. I don't know what to think.' She stared over his shoulder and her face took on a hardened expression. From the noise of Ivan's boots on the ground coupled with Belinda's demeanour, Harry knew things were about to get a touch more tense.

'Let me explain,' said Ivan, with a pleading look and inflection to match.

Harry made to step away.

'No, H, stay,' said Belinda, without taking her eyes off Ivan. 'I'd prefer a witness. I've no idea what this charlatan might say.'

'Please,' said Ivan, clenching his hands in front of him as if he were praying. 'I'm not trying to give anyone the runaround. I came back here in the hope you'd still have feelings for me. It's become abundantly clear that you don't.'

'Oh,' said Belinda.

'My fiancée Tanya was a wonderful woman, but she couldn't hold a candle to you, Belinda. I thought back to the happiest time of my life.' Ivan fiddled with the zip on his jacket and avoided Belinda's eye. Harry almost felt a bit sorry for him. He was a decent enough fella really, aside from taking money for rich tourists to shoot animals. 'The closest I've ever felt to bliss was with you.'

'Naturally,' said Belinda, 'but you're too late. It wouldn't have worked out. I'm not interested.'

'No,' said Ivan, turning his attention to Harry. 'I can see that. It was obvious to me the moment I saw you two together, but I hoped I might stand a chance. I was wrong. You've made your choice.'

Harry held his stare, until he was gladly distracted by Estelle appearing in her office doorway. She watched what was happening, although made no attempt to join them, instead pulling down the sleeves of her burgundy sweatshirt over her knuckles.

Ivan grasped both of Belinda's hands in his. 'Bel, I'm so glad that you've met Harry. He really is wonderful and I can't think of anyone who would make you any happier than he does.' She looked at him, unblinking. 'I know that I could never get between the two of you. You've made that very clear.'

'So you started to chew Estelle's face off instead?' said Belinda, pulling her hands back.

'She's a wonderful woman, even if she's a bit odd,' said Ivan, lowering his voice. 'Only a second before you came in, she launched herself at me. I think she's on the rebound. That's the honest truth.' He glanced in Estelle's direction. 'Please don't think any worse of me than you already do.'

This time, Belinda let her arms drop to her sides. 'It's been lovely to catch up with you, Ivan,' she said, a slowness to her voice, as if she were talking to a child, 'but are you heading home soon? We – that's Harry and I – have murders to solve and I have a life to lead. A very good life here in Little Challham with my friends.'

With a sad nod, Ivan turned and moved back towards Estelle. 'I've been in regular contact with Estelle since she opened the zoo, advising her on what to do with the animals. I knew that the zoo was near your village and I knew you'd support it when you came home. I wanted you to have something amazing for when you came back to Little Challham and decided to spend the rest of your life here. I always knew it wouldn't be with me.'

Belinda opened her mouth to say something, but the words wouldn't come. Harry felt like a first-class interloper hearing his friend's ex-lover share a long-held secret, all the while with Estelle straining to hear.

Ivan held his hands out by his sides, his palms towards her, and said, 'It was never meant to happen with me and Estelle and it hasn't... we haven't... Well, it's in its infancy. She's been seeing someone else at the zoo and even though she's reluctant to talk about it, I know she's tried to break it off. It's all a bit messy at the moment. I should probably book a flight and leave everyone to it. I only wanted what's best for the elephants. And you, Bel.'

Harry cast an eye in Belinda's direction. He could tell from her rapid blinking that she was holding back tears. Ivan seemed choked up as he turned, once more, back in the direction of Estelle.

'Ivan,' called Harry. Ivan stopped with his back to them. 'Don't leave without saying goodbye.'

In response, Ivan gave a small wave and plodded back to Estelle.

'That wasn't how I was expecting this morning to go,' said Belinda with a forced cheerfulness. 'Still, we haven't got time to dawdle here, not when the police will be closing the zoo down for the third time in three days. At this rate, there'll be no rewilding of the herd, or anything else come to that. I suppose that the rest of Kent's zoos can take on some of the animals, others can go to different parts of the country and—'

'Stop,' said Harry. 'Stop. You've had a shock. Be kind to yourself and give yourself a minute.'

Belinda gave him a smile that melted his heart. 'We don't have time to stop. There are three murders to solve, not to mention the animals to take care of. Let's find Vince.'

She threaded her arm through his. Harry suspected it was because if they were side by side, he couldn't see her tears.

'With all of that going on, we didn't actually get a chance to ask Ivan what he was talking to James Kara about,' said Harry, as they walked away from the office.

'I need to say a final goodbye to him,' said Belinda. 'Leave it with me and I'll ask him.'

'Estelle certainly has been acting strangely, but that could have been trying to keep things quiet with Ivan,' said Harry. 'Something's clearly up with Rob too.'

'Should we speak to the protestors first before tackling the issue of Rob and Estelle?' said Belinda.

'No, I think you should speak to Ivan.' It pained Harry to see Belinda the way she was and knew that everything else going on around her was distracting her from doing what she had to do.

'You're right,' said Belinda, letting go of Harry's arm as he reached for his mobile phone, which had started ringing.

They came to a standstill beside the main concourse. The pathway leading to the main entrance and exit gate was the most in use, while a much smaller number of people seemed to be strolling around, looking at the enclosures, while the police and overstretched security team did their best to shepherd them out of the grounds.

Belinda stood and took stock as Harry spoke to Rob, who seemed to be doing most of the talking. She watched him as he nodded at his boss's instructions.

Harry ended his call and said, 'Rob is panicking. The police are stopping any more visitors coming in and sending everyone home, the vet's been called back to check on Sabbie the giraffe as she's still not back to full strength, the senior investigating officer in charge of the murders is furious about the lack of CCTV and is blaming Rob and now he can't get hold of Estelle. She was really upset about Sabbie, the giraffes mean the absolute world to her. Rob seems really worried about her. He thinks she might take it out on the protestors.'

'I'm sure she's occupied with Ivan, that's all,' said Belinda, biting her lip. She didn't want to come across as bitter. It wasn't really any of her business. 'Do you think that Rob was the one that Estelle was in a relationship with? It would explain his behaviour by the river hogs and him looking as downtrodden as he did.'

'Tell you what,' said Harry, 'I'm going to grab a burger – perhaps an emergency one for later, too, before all the concession stands close – and then I'd better get back to the office. I'll leave you to make your call. By then, hopefully Rob will have come down from outer space and have his rational head on again.'

'I'll ring you when I've finished,' said Belinda. She was already moving aside to allow one of the mobile ice-cream vans to manoeuvre past them. With a wave, Belinda was heading for the giraffe enclosure. She hated the idea of the giraffe still being injured and couldn't fathom who would want to hurt one.

Normally, she would take the time to discuss it with Harry, but right now, all she wanted to do was say a final farewell to Ivan. Before she changed her mind, she called his number and waited for him to answer.

'Hey,' he said. 'You OK?'

'Yes, I am.' Belinda paused. 'Can I see you for a minute? I'll be at the giraffe enclosure on the viewing platform in a few minutes. It won't take long.'

'Look, I've... All right, of course. I'll be there.'

Belinda hung up before he said anything else. For a moment, she got the impression that he was going to tell her that he didn't want to speak to her again.

38

Harry hadn't liked the fact that Belinda had rushed off. It was glaringly obvious that she desperately needed to speak to Ivan. It would be a relief when he got on a plane and left them all in peace. He hadn't brought much to the party, other than saving a young boy from being ripped to pieces by a lion, plus saving the very same lion from being shot by the keeper. That aside, his visit had done little to make life better for anyone. Perhaps bundling Ivan into his car and taking him to the airport himself might be a bit much, but at least he'd be gone once and for all.

Harry noticed that the crowd was getting denser as more and more people walked towards the exit. He could hear people complaining that there were better zoos in the county and more deserving charities to donate to. One man with a face that could launch a thousand wanted posters briefly stopped to snarl at Harry. 'What's the point of security if you keep letting people get murdered? We've got a family ticket, you know!'

'All tickets will be refunded or reissued at the gate,' said Harry, keen to get away from abusive members of the public. He felt his phone vibrate in his jacket pocket. He took it out and read the text message from Rob:

Any idea where the hell Estelle is???She's not in her office!

Harry watched the land train go by, even fewer people on it this time. He thought about where he should start looking for Estelle. Rob had checked the offices, so she couldn't be there; Belinda was going to speak to Ivan, so she wasn't with him. He decided to give Vince a call.

'Hey, Harry,' said Vince. 'I've just got one of your electric buggies from Rob. Where are you? I'll come to you.'

'I hope you've got both hands on the steering wheel,' said Harry, 'and you're on hands-free.'

'Er, something like that. I'm coming down the hill towards the animals.'

Harry told him where he was and started walking to where Vince would eventually appear. In the meantime, he ran an eye over the grounds and considered where Estelle might have got to. His most sensible guess was that she had gone back to the mansion house, but that didn't explain why she hadn't been answering her phone.

By the time Harry spotted Vince and climbed aboard the buggy, he had convinced himself of one of two things: either she was the next victim or she had something to do with the murders.

'Vince, has anyone actually declared James Kara's death suspicious?' said Harry.

Vince nodded and said, 'It turns out that he was strangled. The post-mortem still needs to be done, but that's what it's looking like. He had a lot of bruising on his neck and was thrown into the dung to hide the body. Whoever it was probably panicked.'

'We don't know where Estelle Samuels is,' said Harry. He pointed at Vince's police radio. 'Any chance you can call up and see if anyone knows where she is? I'm worried and it's not as if this zoo hasn't seen its fair share of people ending up dead.'

Harry sat and listened while the officer alerted his colleagues and the control room that the young woman was missing, last seen wearing a pair of chinos and a burgundy sweatshirt, and in the company of Ivan Brenner.

Belinda had gone to meet Ivan. Ivan was the last person to have seen Estelle. Harry didn't like this one little bit. He got his phone out of his jacket, hopped back out of the buggy and called her.

With great relief, she answered on the third ring. 'You can't keep away, can you?' she said.

'From you, never,' said Harry, the warmth of her voice making him smile. 'I was making sure you're all right. Are you still with Ivan?'

'No, he's gone off to look for Estelle. She still hasn't shown up, apparently. Now what are we going to do about these murders? As well as someone trying to hurt the giraffes and bring about financial ruin.'

'Please be careful,' said Harry, keeping an ear open for any update via Vince's radio. 'Our murderer's indiscriminate about who they kill. I'm worried that Estelle might be hurt.'

'I truly hope she's OK, but Ivan's bound to track her down,' said Belinda. 'The likelihood is that Simon and James were murdered because of the harm they could do to the zoo, and we haven't ruled out that Drew met a grim end because of what he saw. Oh, and that appears to be Rob down there. I think I'll go and see what the update is on Sabbie. Speak to you later.'

Harry found himself listening to silence, so put his phone away and asked Vince what the plan was for dealing with Estelle's vanishing act.

There was another pause, this one more uncomfortable. Vince said, 'Estelle isn't a high priority, and while we are concerned about her, we don't know anything bad's happened to her. They're broadcasting a message for all patrols in the area to be on the lookout.'

'Seriously?' said Harry, feeling his patience disappearing. 'That's it? Three people have been murdered here in three days, a young woman is missing, the killer is still roaming around and she's not a high priority. Give me strength.'

As he went to get out of the buggy, he felt Vince's hand on his arm. The grip was surprisingly strong for someone he'd always thought was a touch on the puny side. He stared at the officer. 'I'm in,' said Vince. 'Let's go and look for Estelle.'

39

Belinda trudged towards the private staff entrance to the giraffe enclosure. She felt very weary and knew that the day was going to stretch out and leave her entirely exhausted. It would be several hours before she got so much as a chance to rest and stop her mind from running over the events of the last few days. She had already texted Marcus to make sure that Horatio got at least one decent walk today. The thought of getting home and putting her feet up with a decent mug of tea was almost making her salivate.

Rob saw her coming his way and tried to open the gate for her from the inside. He seemed to fiddle with the lock for an age before he got the correct key, which made her glad he wasn't trying to undo the gate in a panic with a wild animal snapping at their heels.

'Sorry about that,' he said when he finally got it unlocked. 'One of the things I've been on about to Estelle is security gates with keypads. She won't even hear it. Sometimes, she drives me to distraction.' He fixed a stare on Belinda and said, 'Tell me honestly, what do you think of how this place is run and managed?'

'I'm not sure it's my place to say,' she said, easing around the gate before he closed it behind her.

'I think it is,' he said, invading her personal space. 'After all, you've sunk a lot of money into this place, helped with publicity, and you've got the ear of the board of trustees.'

'I don't think all that is true,' she said, feeling slightly uncomfortable and weirdly relieved that the vet and two keepers were still only several feet away.

'I'm sure that I could do a better job of running this place,' he said. 'I've tried to make changes and Estelle has seen the benefit. I have more ideas to shake things up too.'

'Where exactly is Estelle?' said Belinda.

'Where is she?' he said, giving an empty smile. 'Your guess is as good as mine. She's lovely – don't get me wrong – but she does this all the time: goes off on a wander and I'm left to pick up the pieces. Did you know, she actually considered going to Africa to stay with the elephants for their first six months after they've been rewilded?' He leaned in closer to Belinda. She could smell his breath, and it was not an experience she relished ever repeating. 'I told her that she couldn't simply be up and away for months on end. Who was going to take care of things here? If she expected me to do it, I would need more staff and more money. That didn't come into it, of course. It was all about the blasted elephants. What about me?'

'Oh, yes, indeed,' said Belinda. 'Terrible. Your suffering must have been awful. I don't know how you coped.'

'I coped because I'm good at my job.'

'Does Estelle think so?' said Belinda.

'She had no complaints until that ruddy South African came along,' said Rob. 'You seem to know him pretty well. Is there something going on between him and Estelle?'

'What if there is?' said Belinda, trying to read the look in his eye. She couldn't work out if the stare was interest or something a little sinister.

'Nah, none of my business,' he said. 'It's just that the board of trustees wouldn't take too kindly to her fraternising with him. He's staff, technically speaking, and other than them frowning upon that sort of thing, there's always the chance he'll lure her away. Has she told you she's leaving? If she did leave, I would do a much better job of running things.'

'But you're not on the board?' She watched his eye twitch. 'And you weren't at the emergency board meeting this morning, were you? The one Estelle was called out of.'

'You were there?' said Rob, with a fixed unblinking stare.

'No, I wasn't,' said Belinda. His reaction to the emergency meeting intrigued her. 'Drew was going to join the board, wasn't he?'

'Drew? On the board? Now, that's funny.' Rob gave a short bark of laughter. 'He was always following Estelle around with his "little boy lost" look. It was almost comical. She took advantage of him, of course. No, he wasn't on the board.'

Rob beckoned her closer, which she was keen to avoid. 'There *is*, however, a board member who's related to Anna Clancy. I don't know the full details, what with me being kept out of the loop, but if the CCTV was being wiped and Ms Clancy was connected to someone on the inside, they must have been working together. Perhaps it was her and Drew and they got even with James.' He gave an exaggerated shrug.

'I think that the vet's calling you,' she said, pointing over his shoulder, wishing she could move away from his bad breath, but the gate was right behind her, blocking any chance of a hasty retreat.

'I didn't hear anything,' said Rob.

'She waved at us,' said Belinda. 'I hope Sabbie's OK. Is there any clue as to who did such a thing to her?'

Rob's face took on a grim expression, his jaw set firm. 'They found green rope in James Kara's dead fingers. Estelle was beside herself, so someone's got even with him for that.'

'Whichever side the protestors are on, they're trying to help the animals, not hurt them,' said Belinda.

'But don't you see?' He inched closer to her. 'They can't even agree whether the elephants would be better off here or in Africa. Kara wanted all zoos closed down and all the animals set free. How can the two groups possibly begin to care when they have the same facts available to them, yet have such differing opinions?'

'I suppose that what some people find acceptable, others do not,' she said, easing to the side so as to get away from him. 'We all have different standards of behaviour.'

'Oh, yes, that's very true,' he said. 'Your friend Ivan, for example.'

'Ivan?' she said. 'What about him?'

'How high are his standards of behaviour?'

'I don't know what you mean.'

At that moment, the vet called out for Rob, leaving no doubt that he was required. Belinda saw frantic pointing between the vet and the other member of the security team who was checking the fences for any sign of damage.

'I best go and see to this,' said Rob with a sigh. 'See? They can't cope without me.' He rolled his eyes and reached past Belinda to unlock the gate.

Once she was on the other side, she took a moment to wonder exactly why Rob was unnerving her so much. Perhaps she didn't like him being disparaging about Ivan, or criticising Estelle's management style, although it could simply have been his rancid breath. Belinda put some distance between herself and the giraffe enclosure, ready to give Harry a call and let him know her concerns about Rob. He had certainly alarmed her enough to make her think he was capable of murder, but was she overreacting?

One thing was for sure, Belinda was going to speak to

Estelle about Rob's attitude. The only problem was, they had to find Estelle first.

40

Harry had to hang onto the side of the buggy as Vince took corner after corner with speeds that the vehicle clearly shouldn't have been driven at. They had taken a brief, not to mention rapid, tour of the zoo and gardens, called up to make sure Estelle wasn't at the mansion and were now left to the conclusion that she had either left the zoo unobserved or something had happened to her.

Vince pulled the buggy over towards the main concourse. 'We've looked in all of the obvious places, Harry. It's time to call it in and then start a proper search.' He made a move for his radio.

Before the keen officer had a chance to transmit, Harry put a hand over the mouthpiece. 'Listen to me, Vince. The zoo is almost empty, and we don't have long before the police completely shut the park down. You were told to leave searching for Estelle and that she wasn't a priority. Apart from getting in the proverbial for going against orders, it probably won't change anything and no one will start looking for her. Not straight away, anyway. I've an idea, though, let's head to the red river hogs.'

'I'm making an assumption that you're not taking us there for therapeutic reasons,' said Vince, making a clumsy turn on the concourse.

'Too right,' said Harry, raising his voice to be heard over the wind that had whipped up, dragging leaves and twigs along the ground. 'It's where Belinda saw Estelle talking to Rob and then later to Ivan.'

Vince took his eyes off the pathway to look at Harry. 'If something's happened to her, is our money on Ivan or Rob?'

'It does seem a coincidence that Ivan arrived and suddenly people were being murdered in alarming numbers, but I simply don't have him down as a murderer. But Ivan was also talking to James on more than one occasion.'

'And what do you think about him?' said Vince.

'What do you mean?' said Harry, bouncing in his seat as Vince took them over a speed bump that did little to slow him down.

'He's Belinda's ex-partner, isn't he? Aren't you a tiny bit jealous?'

Slightly put out that he was having his attitude questioned, Harry said, 'There's no room for the green-eyed monster when we're talking about murder. Besides, I don't think he's a killer, although I suspect he's up to something.'

'And would you have the same views if he wasn't the man who had broken her heart?' said Vince, pulling the buggy up by the bridge that led to the hog enclosure.

'Of course I would,' said Harry. He knew he wasn't being completely truthful, but this was *murder*, and it didn't pay to ignore the tell-tale signs. 'It's not clouded my view of him. If it had, I'd tell you he's a potential suspect. Only I really don't think he is.'

'Fair enough,' said Vince, giving nothing else away. He got out of the buggy, stood with his back to Harry and said, 'Where should we start?'

Harry scanned the area. The red river hog enclosure was directly in front of them, and other than snorting hogs and mud, there seemed to be little else in the acre or so that was big enough for someone to hide in – or for someone to hide a body. Vince walked across the bridge and peered down into the water and under the bridge itself. The water was only about eighteen inches deep, so unless something or someone was lodged in the bank or behind rocks, they would have been visible.

The rest of the area behind them was a vast open expanse until the next animal enclosures. The hogs were at the start of the river, mainly on their own because they could be noisy.

Frantically, Harry carried out a recce. He remembered Belinda saying that she hadn't had a very good view of Rob and Estelle to begin with. He ducked his head down so that he could peer under the lowest branches to where he guessed that the couple would have had their spat.

A short way further along the river stood a storage hut, around the size of a large garden shed. It was metal with a gently sloping roof and what seemed to be a door facing the riverbank. It looked to Harry as if it was locked tight. His feet took him across the bridge before Vince realised that he was on the move.

'Harry,' he called. 'I'll get the buggy.'

As Harry ran – which he liked to avoid at all costs – he thought he saw another figure heading off in the distance. He couldn't be entirely sure, but the person fleeing was wearing what looked like a green parka and had long plaited red hair bouncing as she went.

Vince caught up with Harry in the buggy. Harry pointed into the distance where the figure was heading into the trees, and called, 'It's Anna Clancy.' With a nod and a shout into his police radio, Vince was away across the grass, calling up for another patrol to head off the fleeing suspect.

Out of breath and out of condition, Harry reached the door.

He had been partially correct: the door had been locked but someone had forced the padlock and it hung open and damaged. In a second, he unhooked it and threw it to the ground.

He pulled open the door and after his eyes took a few seconds to adjust to the gloom, he peered around. There were stacks of bagged feed for the animals, a couple of piles of logs and an axe and in the far corner, a very scared-looking, gagged and bound Estelle Samuels.

41

Belinda put as much distance between herself and Rob as she could manage in as few minutes as possible. On the way, she spoke to a couple of police officers who were checking that the concession stands and the information booths were closed or closing. The officers couldn't give her any update on Estelle or – more likely – wouldn't give her answers to any of the questions she asked. Exasperated and worn out, she tried Harry's phone for the third time, but again, it went to voicemail. Then a very flustered Ivan came running towards her.

'What's the matter with you?' she said, her tone a little sharper than intended.

'I can't find anyone,' he said. 'I've been to the security office and spoke to a guy called Stan Whiting. He gave me next to nothing, but I managed to scan the CCTV monitors to find you. Then he threw me out.'

'No news on Estelle, then?' said Belinda.

'No, not a clue,' said Ivan, shoving his hands in his pockets, then taking them out and raking them through his hair – something that Belinda knew he usually avoided at all costs. 'Now I can't find Rob either, I'm worried. Estelle would be so angry with me for telling you this, but she had a bit of a fling with Rob and he got nasty when she tried to end it. He'd wanted to be on the board but she didn't want him having that much power. She liked the idea of Drew because she could control him a lot easier than someone like Rob.'

'Why didn't you say something earlier?' said Belinda. 'She might be in real danger. I knew you were looking for her, but I didn't realise how worried you've been.'

'The two of them weren't even in a relationship and he tried to tell her how to run the zoo. After one night together, he told her that he'd go to the board and get her fired. Estelle thought he was delusional, so didn't take his threats seriously.'

'James Kara,' whispered Belinda, more to herself than anyone else. 'If it was James who hurt Sabbie, Rob could have killed him to impress Estelle and bring further shame on the zoo. It would be a win-win.'

'Estelle told me she cried all night about Sabbie's injuries. Rob told her to leave it with him and he'd make sure it never happened again. This is my fault: I saw James outside the zoo, close to where the fence was tampered with. James was full of himself, telling me that he would do everything in his power to get the zoo closed. I only talked to him because I wanted to find out what he was up to. Now James is dead too.'

'And you told Estelle what James had been boasting about, who told Rob,' said Belinda. 'It's not your fault, Ivan. You didn't kill anyone, you only told Estelle what you'd found out.'

'We have to find Estelle,' said Ivan, frantically peering around.

'Perhaps we should go and look for her together,' said Belinda, seeing how on edge he was. 'Have you any idea where she might have gone?'

'We know she's not in her office,' said Ivan. 'Or the security office.'

'If she's thinking rationally – and I appreciate that she may well not be – perhaps she'd have headed to the concierge desk,' said Belinda.

Ivan schooled his features into the start of a smile, but he couldn't quite get there. 'Good thinking. If Estelle's in trouble, she'll head to where the most people and the police are going to be.'

It all fitted into place: Rob had killed Simon Carter because he was a threat to the zoo and then Drew when he became suspicious. He then killed James for injuring the giraffe and the other acts of sabotage. Rob wanted to control everything, including Estelle and the zoo.

Belinda had to move quickly to keep up with him as he strode across the crossroads that led to the concierge and general booking office. A little further ahead – in between the balloons and toy elephants being carried by departing parents, their children having long tired of them – something seemed to catch Ivan's eye. He half-ran, half-crouched, advancing at a speed that Belinda couldn't match. For a moment, Belinda was distracted by a flash of burgundy to her right-hand side as it disappeared out of sight into the ladies' toilets. She shouted for Ivan, but he was too far in the distance and she had no chance of making him hear her.

There was hardly even time for her to make a decision, let alone weigh up whether it was a good one or a bad one. With one hand in her pocket to grab her mobile phone, Belinda made a beeline for the toilet block. It had one entrance on the side nearest to her for men and the side farthest away for women. The doorways themselves were obscured with a raffia screen in an attempt to make the whole experience more jungle-esque.

Belinda ran to the far side of the block and into the toilets. There were only three cubicles and an empty area for the wash basins and hand-dryers. Only the door to the middle cubicle was closed.

Taking a deep breath, Belinda kicked at the door, only to

find that when it sprung back – just before slamming closed again – there was no one there. She let out a breath and turned to leave.

There, blocking her way, was Rob Piper, in a burgundy sweatshirt not unlike the one Estelle had been wearing.

The tic in his left eye and the blank stare he was giving her unnerved the usually spirited Belinda. 'Oh, hi, Rob,' she said, not daring to take her eyes off him. Unblinking, she tried to see past him without tearing her gaze away. The only way out was closed. She silently prayed that he hadn't locked it from the inside. No one knew where she was. No one was coming for her. She was sure Rob had already killed three people – possibly four if Estelle wasn't safe and well – and he wouldn't hesitate to end her life too.

'What's the matter, Belinda? Nothing to say to me?' Rob took a step closer. 'I wouldn't be so angry if you hadn't allowed that damned South African to come here and upset things between me and Estelle.'

As he closed in on her, she took a tentative step backwards.

'I've worked so hard, done what the board asked, done what Estelle asked, but does anyone care about that?' Rob stared up at the ceiling as he spoke, giving her time to watch in fascination as a crazed expression took over his features. 'I've worked here for years and I've seen the way the public abuse this place and make ridiculous complaints, like that moaning Simon Carter. What did that waste of a skin ever do for this zoo or the animals? Complain, that's what. And he had the audacity to try and sue us. Again!'

Belinda didn't fancy her chances trying to overpower Rob. He wasn't the smallest of adversaries, not to mention he was backing her into the corner of an otherwise empty toilet block. At least on the plus side he hadn't tried to kill her yet. Perhaps reasoning with him wasn't off the list.

Then he pulled an African Savannah Safari Experience

bandana from his pocket and held it in front of her face. 'I gave Estelle one of these for her birthday,' he said, voice almost a whisper. 'She used to carry it everywhere and said she'd cherish it forever. Oh, how she lies.'

Belinda couldn't remember the last time she had gulped. The ladies' conveniences in Brabourne Gardens was about to be her final attempt.

'This should be my zoo,' he said. 'I'd run it better than Estelle ever could. I've poured years of my life into this place, and for what? Simon Carter couldn't have come at a better time with his moaning and whining. I lured him with the promise of a free VIP Safari Experience Priority Pass, did away with him and then planted the pass in Drew's pocket. All so simple. I feel a bit bad about Drew, but James Kara was trying to ruin everything with his acts of sabotage. Not. In. My. Zoo.'

Rob wrapped the yellow, black and green material taut around his fingers. Belinda noticed this one was adorned with giraffes.

Giraffes can kick the head off a lion, she thought as he rushed at her with the bandana.

And then Belinda's leg shot out at a speed that surprised her almost as much as it shocked Rob's testicles right back inside his scrotum. Bringing her knee up to his nose for good measure as he doubled forward, she heard a crack, right before a scream.

Belinda saw the blood on the leg of her trousers, dared to hope it was all from her adversary, and bolted for the door. Dread filled her every fibre as she grabbed the handle with her shaking hands and pulled. The rush of fresh air to her face was almost as much of a relief as the lack of a hand on her shoulder pulling her backwards.

Help – she had to get help.

Outside in the watery sunshine, Belinda ran onwards. As she fled, she pulled her phone from her pocket, desperately trying to punch in the security code without taking her eyes off where she was heading.

When she thought she had covered enough ground, she turned to see if Rob was behind her. The sight of him lumbering onwards – an insane, possessed grin on his face – gave her all the answer she needed. The piercing cry that emanated from his lips was enough to turn her blood to ice. Here was a man totally unhinged and she was the target of his broken state of mind.

Belinda carried on, aware that as the police had completely shut off this part of the zoo, there wasn't a soul in sight.

42

Harry moved towards Estelle. She shuffled back against the wall as far as her bonds would allow. He glanced around for a light switch, turning it on as he went. 'It's OK, it's me, Harry,' he said as soon as he realised that she was also blindfolded. He made short work of untying both the African Savannah Safari Experience bandana bound across her eyes and the one used as a gag.

'What happened?' he said, guessing the answer, but thirty years of policing didn't mean that asking open questions went out of the window.

'Rob – Rob did this,' she choked, trying to get her words out and crying at the same time. 'He's insane, completely insane. I told him the brief affair we had was over and he should rethink his future at the zoo. He grabbed me and brought me here. Rob's lost it completely.'

'You're safe now,' said Harry. He hugged her to him, aware that her hands and feet were still bound and she felt cold to the touch. He guessed that she must have been there a couple of hours. 'Where's Rob now?'

'I don't know,' she said, keeping it together remarkably well under the circumstances. 'He said he'd be back to get me. Then he picked up that axe over there and said if I was lucky, he might kill me quickly. His behaviour had become so erratic and only got worse when Ivan arrived. I had no idea how much he wanted to take over the zoo. It's all about control. He said that he couldn't stand to see a woman in charge of something so valuable, especially as I wouldn't nominate him to join the board. That would have given him too much of a say in *my* animals.

'Oh, God, I was so frightened, I told him that I'd sign the zoo over to him and he could have everything, as long as he let me live. I was petrified that he was going to kill me right here, so I begged for my life in exchange for the zoo. I thought he just took his job seriously, not that he was completely unhinged. All I can think now is that he was playing me all along to get his hands on this place.'

Harry could see that she was starting to hyperventilate. Worried that she was going into shock, he got her to concentrate on breathing slowly, repeating that she was safe and reassuring her that the paramedics were on their way too. Estelle would have to live with the fact that her silence had cost so many lives, but now wasn't the time to mention it. She was clearly petrified of Rob, so keeping quiet had probably felt like her safest option.

'He's a total monster,' she said between waves of panic. 'Rob used to tell me how much he hated Simon Carter, but we all did. Simon threatened the future of every animal in here with the financial damage he was going to cause. But to kill him for it is monstrous. Rob told me how jealous he was of Drew, so he sent him off to find CCTV blind spots up in the beech trees by the hyena enclosure where he'd cut through the branches. And he strangled James, and still said that he wasn't done yet.'

Estelle flinched at the noise of Vince scurrying through the door. 'Oh, hell's bells,' he said when he saw the terrified woman on the ground. He pulled a multitool from one of his pockets, opened the blade and cut the ropes that bound her ankles.

As he busied himself with freeing her wrists, Estelle said, 'I don't know where he's gone, but Harry... he has it in for Belinda. He blames her for bringing Ivan here. Where is she?'

Harry felt as though his world were collapsing. 'Belinda isn't with me.' He looked imploringly at Vince, who nodded and went outside to call in the urgent update and get everyone searching for Rob Piper. That still wasn't anywhere near enough for Harry. If Rob harmed Belinda in any way, Harry wouldn't be responsible for his actions.

'The police will look after you,' said Harry, touching Estelle's shoulder and giving her a reassuring smile. He was up and on his feet, through the door and on the buggy before Vince even registered what was going on. 'Make sure Estelle's safe,' he called as he started up the buggy. 'I'm going to find Belinda.'

Harry was vaguely aware that Vince was shouting, but the red mist had come down and he was stopping for no one. Well, not unless they had a vehicle that could beat the twenty miles per hour of his electric buggy. Still, he pushed it on as hard as it would go, back towards the main thoroughfare of the zoo.

The last time they had spoken, Belinda was at the giraffe enclosure. Steering with one hand and trying to get his phone out of his pocket with the other, he was torn between trying to get through to Vince to pass on her last known location and calling Belinda.

Unsure where to head, Harry made for the pathway that would eventually take him to the main crossroads. Risking taking one hand off the wheel, he tried Vince's number. It was engaged.

'There's no point in leaving a message,' muttered Harry to himself and banged on the steering wheel through complete frustration. He then called Belinda's number. That too was engaged.

Never one to give up, Harry drove the buggy as far as he could before the departing pedestrians seemed determined to get in his way. He could see that the police had shut off many of the pathways, corralling the crowds through the main thorough-fare. Realising he would have to continue on foot, he abandoned the buggy on the approach to the crossroads, running the last thirty feet and standing in the centre, turning in circles searching for Belinda.

Something grabbed his attention. Ivan was climbing onto the roof of an ice-cream van. It was probably the last food truck that hadn't shut. Ivan clambered up on the roof by putting his boots on the serving hatch in the side, much to the annoyance of the ice-cream man and the astonishment of those queuing for a 99.

'Ivan,' shouted Harry. 'Estelle's safe, but have you seen Belinda?'

Almost slipping off the van, Ivan turned to Harry, scanned the pathways and then he pointed towards a steep dip in the landscape. Harry looked at where he was indicating and there, in the distance, was Belinda. She was stumbling and falling, glancing backwards as if Satan himself were chasing her.

43

Belinda's hair was sticking to her face as she ploughed on, trying to get to safety. The complete lack of people was concerning, to say the least. It was a choice between keeping on the move in completely unsuitable footwear as she tried to escape a serial killer or stopping to call for help. She was convinced she had got her phone unlocked at one point but checking the screen only meant that she tripped and lost valuable seconds.

In the end, in total blind panic, she dialled 999. Not for one second doubting that the call would connect – that someone, somewhere would work out from the GPS where she was – she forged on. A movement in her peripheral vision told her that something was approaching her and approaching her at speed. Still, she pushed on, phone in one hand as she tried to shove her hair out of her eyes with the other.

Then her feet hit a solid object and she catapulted forward, landing with a heavy thud onto her front. With a rising panic, Belinda realised she was lying on the land train tracks and the noise she had heard was the sound of the train bearing down on her.

Although it was only travelling at a moderate speed, she was lying on the ground with a twisted ankle and in total shock. Belinda stared at the grate of the train as it got closer and closer. She tried to drag herself away across the tracks in the opposite direction to her tormentor and then someone was grabbing her under her arms and heaving her upwards. Her left ankle throbbed in pain and she winced in agony.

'Sorry,' said Harry, picking her up in his arms and staring into her eyes, moments before he slung her over his shoulders in a fireman's carry. 'I'm not as young as I used to be, so excuse me carrying you like a sack of spuds.'

Despite the horror and gravity of the situation – not to mention the searing pain in her anklebone – Belinda smiled at the absurdity of it. 'Rob,' she said. 'Rob was chasing me. Harry, you have to put me down.'

'I know,' he said, heaving her from his shoulders once they were clear of the train. 'Me and Ivan saw what was happening and came to your rescue.'

Momentarily stunned, but her senses returning, Belinda glanced round. 'Where's Ivan? Is he all right? Did he go after Rob?'

The train had come to a stop, blocking their view of the ground Belinda had galloped across, and, of course, Rob. They both turned their attention to the now missing murderer, fearing that Ivan was in danger. They needn't have worried as the South African was limping towards them, a rip in his trousers revealing his right kneecap.

'How did that happen?' said Belinda. 'Did Rob do that?'

'No,' said Ivan in tones more subdued than was usual. 'That stupid kid over there dropped his ice cream and as I was sprinting to your rescue, I slipped and fell over. I've cut my knee. It really smarts.'

'Rob,' said Belinda, 'we have to find Rob. He's the murderer. He threatened to strangle me in the ladies' loos. He told me that he'd killed Simon, Drew and James too.'

'What was he doing in the ladies' lavs?' said Harry. He shook his thoughts away. 'Oh, who cares? We know he's the murderer, we found Estelle and she told us. Where's he gone?'

'Over there,' said Ivan, who despite his injury had jumped onto the side of the land train's cab and was pointing across to one of the enclosures. 'Good grief! He's heading for the wolves. Surely he's not crazy enough to let them out with all these people around?'

Belinda turned to her friend, her mobile phone in her hand, finally connected to the emergency services. But Harry was already on his way to the wolves, and he was stopping for no one.

44

Harry's heart had been in his mouth when he saw Belinda fall in front of the train. He really had hoped that Ivan's presence might mean that no matter who did the rescuing, Belinda would be safe. Now that she was, he had precious little time to relax before Ivan alerted him to Rob rushing towards the wolf enclosure.

Without giving it a second thought, Harry jogged around the train and towards the unhinged killer, right by a fenced-in area with large meat-eating canines who hunted in packs.

What could possibly go wrong? thought Harry as he neared the gates.

'Rob!' called Harry, watching as he froze. 'Don't go in there. It's suicide. They'll attack you – you know that.'

Harry's former boss turned and glowered over his shoulder. 'Who said anything about going inside?'

Total panic gripped Harry as he realised that Rob was crazed enough to let the wolves out, amongst couples with babies in pushchairs and toddlers eating Cornettos and people sauntering to the gates, stretching out their time before the police marched them off the premises. He raced towards the gate as Rob fumbled with the bunch of keys he was holding, trying his best to jam the right one into the lock. One of the wolves was pacing along the inner perimeter and eyeing them both warily.

This usually would not have given Harry much cause for alarm. What was making every one of Harry's hairs stand on end was that the inner door of the enclosure was wide open. There was only one padlocked metal cage door between the wolf and a veritable smorgasbord of goodies.

Harry's feet took him closer, while his nerves were fighting the losing battle telling him to run as fast as his legs would carry him. He couldn't. He had to stay and face the music – or in this case, the wolf.

He'd made it within thirty feet of Rob when the head of security gave a crazed cackle and swung the gate open, taking refuge in the gap between it and the fence.

Sensing freedom after probably years in captivity, the wolf made very short work of covering the distance between the perimeter and the cage leading to unknown riches. With a slightly cautious air, it trotted through the inner door and stood beside Rob, who wasn't mentally disturbed enough to realise that cowering was his best option.

All three of them were briefly frozen: Rob stood shaking behind the door, the wolf stared at Harry with a look between hatred and indifference, and Harry felt his legs begin to tremble.

Suddenly, the wolf ran outside the enclosure, straight at Harry. He stood his ground, remembering Belinda's warning about Ivan showing no fear to the lion. He wasn't sure it would also work on a wolf, but it was too late to do the research now. He could only hope. At the same time, Rob tried to make a run for freedom from behind the gate. The noise of the metal clanging distracted the animal who, unused to people and crowds, seemed more cautious than it had been. Rob ran away from the wolf with as much speed as he could muster, until he headed straight into Ivan's fist.

Fortunately, Rob was too out of his mind and Harry too focused on not getting his throat ripped out by a wolf, so neither of them had seen Ivan edge over, his camouflage gear clearly worth its weight in gold. All Harry had to do now was to focus on the grey wolf.

His eyes met the yellow-gold of the creature's own and for a second, Harry was lost in them. Then his survival instinct kicked in as the wolf stepped closer. Frantically, Harry felt in his pocket for something to throw at it.

He put his hand into his jacket and pulled out his emergency burger. It was a touch on the flat side after picking Belinda up from the floor, but now wasn't the time to worry about that. He doubted that the wolf would care either.

Harry stood stock still, aware from the background noise that a few people had gathered nearby. They were no doubt all doing that British thing where they assumed that it must be part of the show, as surely a man wouldn't head off a wolf with just a Safari Burger. Slowly, he unwrapped the food, all the while watching his adversary sniff the air.

Giving the wolf no further time to react, Harry threw the burger in an underarm movement. It landed at the creature's paws. The wolf put his head down, sniffed it, shot Harry a look of disdain and ran back inside his enclosure.

'Oh, yes,' said Ivan, appearing beside him. 'That is typical wolf behaviour: he ran away from the crowds, he must have been scared. You were never in any real danger, my friend.' He clapped Harry on the back.

'It's extremely good of you to point this out now. You know – what with you having stayed right over there, away from the action,' said Harry.

'You know me, Harry,' said Ivan. 'I didn't want to get too close in case I scared him more, especially when you had it so beautifully under control – who else carries a burger in case of carnivore emergencies? You are absolutely the hero here.' He leaned in closer to Harry. 'Don't look right now, but Belinda is only feet away from us. She looks as if she doesn't know whether to hug you or hit you for what you've done.'

'Oh, I should go and check on her,' said Harry, not sure what to make of Ivan's praise. 'What about Rob?'

Right on cue, PC Vince Green elbowed his way through the gathering masses. 'Harry, Mr Brenner. Are you both all right? How's the wolf?'

For the briefest of times, Harry felt a little put out. 'Ah right, Vince. You're a vegan. The wolf's fine, although someone should probably go and shut that gate before he tells all of his mates there's a vast feast of human flesh out here.'

A couple of people tutted at Harry's choice of words. It momentarily left him speechless until he saw Vince haul Rob to his feet and place handcuffs on him.

Vince called to Harry, 'By the way, we picked Anna Clancy up. Her uncle is on the board. Did I mention that? She coughed to smashing the padlock off the food store shelter where we found Estelle. She was up to no good, but she's in nowhere near as much trouble as Mr Piper here.'

Rob continued to mutter under his breath and cast dark looks towards Belinda, Harry and Ivan, as Vince held onto him waiting for his colleagues to arrive. When Vince had finished arresting him and listing the numerous offences he would be held for, Rob beckoned Belinda over.

'Careful,' said Harry as she took a cautious step his way.

'I expect that Estelle will tell you all about it anyway,' said Rob, his voice laden with the cold and calculated tone of the insane. 'Drew was too nice, too accommodating, so I sent him to install a new camera up one of the trees. Only I'd cut through the branch. He lost his footing when his shoe came off. Killing Simon Carter was a pleasure, but I'm a bit sorry about

Drew. James, not so much. He tried to injure one of my giraffes.'

'You're sick,' said Belinda.

Rob pulled a face of mock outrage. 'Me? You paid for the cameras. Drew only did it because he liked you and wanted to make sure your instructions were carried out.'

Harry had edged closer to make sure that, despite the handcuffs and police presence, Rob wasn't going to hurt Belinda. At that moment, there seemed less chance of that and more of her striking him. Harry said, 'He's winding you up, B.'

With a haunting giggle, Rob said, 'The only reason I didn't argue about you getting the security job was because everyone knows how smitten you are with Lady Muck, here. You were never going to get in my way.'

'Except for the bit where you're going to prison for committing three murders and a kidnap,' said Harry. 'Estelle's fine, by the way. And look, here comes your ride. Bye now.'

They all stood back and watched as a marked police van made its way over to them. An officer jumped out and opened the rear doors while Vince led Rob away and out of sight.

'That was quite a day,' said Harry, as he, Belinda and Ivan all watched the van drive slowly towards the main gate. 'Bel, we really should get your ankle examined by a paramedic.'

'No, I'm fine,' she said. 'I'm a tiny bit battered and bruised. Nothing that a drink at the pub won't fix. Besides, what could possibly go wrong with you, Ivan and Vince looking after me?'

'I have to say, Harry, that you and PC Green make quite a duo,' said Ivan. 'The two of you charging off into the distance is like watching an overweight Batman and flat-footed Robin.'

'When's your flight, Ivan?' said Harry. 'I'm happy to drop you at the airport.'

45

Belinda stared out of the misted windowpane, her view of the gardens partially obscured. She wasn't listening to Marcus as he enthused to Harry about Kent and how the county was such a rich resource with untapped potential. Horatio slumbered in his basket only a few feet from where she stood.

'Don't you agree, sis?' said her brother.

'Sorry? What was that?' She turned to face her brother, who had the usual simple yet happy smile on his face, and the slightly solemn yet friendly expression on Harry's.

'Marcus was telling me that now everything's calmed down at the zoo,' said Harry, shifting on the sofa, 'and getting back to normal, we should look at what we do next.'

Not for the first time in Harry's presence, Belinda felt her heart lighten. Harry had definitely used the plural, a good sign without a doubt. Her eyes darted to where he sat, somewhat awkwardly holding a tiny cup and saucer, looking like a giant cradling a child's toy in his hands. He looked back and smiled at her.

'I'm not entirely sure that the zoo was the right place for me after all.' He paused and set the bone china down on an occasional table. 'After Vince's latest update that Rob started on his whole sorry business by chucking a child into a lion enclosure – admittedly when he didn't think there were any lions in there – as a distraction as he murdered Simon, I thought perhaps I should seek alternative employment. I wasn't entirely sure about the Doggie Delight food delivery business but at least it was mostly mundane.'

'Apart from the dognapping we managed to get ourselves involved in,' said Belinda, taking a step away from the window.

'And not forgetting the murders,' said Marcus, leaning over the back of the sofa.

'Well, there is that,' said Harry. 'I can't say it hasn't been lively. Perhaps I should look for a job where the boss isn't trying to slaughter half of the employees. I've sent my resignation to Estelle. She's got a lot on her plate with Ivan flying back to South Africa, but I suggested Edward Logan takes over. I think I'd like a new start.'

It didn't escape Belinda's notice that Harry was fiddling with the cuffs of his navy-blue shirt. It was as if he were nervous about something. Perhaps he really was going to leave Little Challham and forget about her. He could have another life without her. He had grown-up children and possibly he'd be a grandfather one day and leave her all alone.

'Television!' said Marcus, clapping his hands, a move that caused Harry to snap his head to the right. 'Sorry, old boy. That was right in your ear, wasn't it?' Marcus launched himself away from the back of the sofa and towards his sister.

'What?' she said. 'You want to watch television?' Sometimes her brother really was too much for her.

'No, no. Not watch it,' he said, placing his hands on her shoulders and totally obscuring her view of Harry. 'Not watch it. *Make* it.'

'Not for the first time, I'm failing to understand what you're saying, Marcus.'

They stared into each other's eyes for a second until Marcus winked. She smiled. He always managed to make her laugh – apart from the times when he infuriated her to the point of making her want to shout.

'It'll be perfect,' Marcus said, letting go of her shoulders and placing his index finger on his chin. 'We can have our own reality show in the grounds. We can call it...'

'*Love Castle?*' said Belinda.

'*The Only Way is Challham?*' said Harry.

'*The Real Housewives of Kent County?*' said Belinda, worried that her brother was taking a mental note of their ludicrous suggestions.

'Mm,' said Marcus, walking over to the window, where the remaining daylight was making itself scarce. He continued to peer out for a few seconds and said, 'Security, we'll need security. That sounds like an ace job for you, Harry, especially now you've resigned from the zoo.'

Belinda knew it was another of Marcus's daft ideas, but it didn't stop the relief take hold of her as she saw Harry give the idea serious consideration and slowly nod his head.

'I suppose that I will be looking for my next challenge,' he said. 'And, providing it's all right with my landlady, I'd very much like to extend my lease at the Gatehouse.'

Aware that she was grinning, Belinda said, 'It would save me the bother of advertising for a new tenant. So, it's a yes from me.'

'Splendid, splendid,' said Marcus, rubbing his hands together. 'I'm off to find someone with some cameras, a film crew and – well, I suppose, some money.'

He left the room, the door closing behind him. Horatio looked up, yawned and went back to sleep, leaving Belinda and Harry alone.

Rather inexplicably, Belinda felt nervous. They were all alone without the interruptions of a murder to be solved or ex-partners to get in the way. It was just the two of them – and a snoring Labrador.

'Well,' said Harry, standing up and taking a step towards her.

'Well,' said Belinda, suddenly unsure what to do with her hands.

'Nice to see Marcus is still full of ideas.'

'I note that you didn't say full of good ideas.'

Harry chuckled. 'I'm definitely interested in a new job. I'll need something to do if I can't get my Doggie Delight round back.'

'I'm sure you'll find a way to fill your days,' she said, aware that Harry had moved closer to her. He was so close, she wasn't sure she could bear the intensity of it.

'We could always ask to be contestants on Marcus's new show,' said Harry.

'What?' she breathed.

'*Arrested at First Sight and Crazy About Each Other Twenty Years Later.*'

'It's not very catchy,' she said.

But then Harry's arms were around her and she forgot about anything else.

A LETTER FROM LISA

Dear reader,

Thank you so much for reading *Murder at the Gardens*. I had fun writing it and including so many animals, and I hope that you enjoyed reading it. If you'd like to keep up to date with all my latest releases, just sign up at the following link. Your email address will never be shared and you can unsubscribe at any time.

www.bookouture.com/lisa-cutts

The inspiration for *Murder at the Gardens* came after I spent a blissful two days at Port Lympne Safari Park in 2021. Absolutely no one – neither human nor animal – was murdered, but it seemed like too perfect a backdrop to resist setting a murder mystery in it. I knew that Belinda would enjoy it, having spent so much time in Africa, and it was perfect for Harry's new job.

I've loved creating more characters for Belinda and Harry to meet and investigate, and hope you've had fun meeting them too. If you would be kind enough to leave a short review for the third in the Little Challham mysteries, your time would be greatly appreciated. Feedback from readers is so important and if you've enjoyed the book, letting other readers know would introduce them to the rest of the series.

Thank you so much for reading,

Lisa

facebook.com/lisa.cutts.505

twitter.com/LisaCuttsAuthor

instagram.com/lisa_cutts

ACKNOWLEDGEMENTS

The inspiration for Harry Powell's job as a Doggie Delight rep is all due to Tony Ramskill. As a DC, I spent many hours in North Kent custody dealing with prisoner after prisoner when Tony was on duty as one of our custody sergeants. The tedium of the tasks was always brightened by Tony's presence and humour, and for that I will always be grateful. For those who have spent endless hours in a custody suite (both police officers and our 'customers'), the experience is always brightened by a helpful sarge. Tony was promoted to inspector, retired and then took up a job delivering pet food. That, along with his amusing dog-handler stories – police dogs bite their handlers with alarming frequency – gave me the inspiration for Harry Powell's second lease of life. Thank you, Tony.

The Dog and Duckers was a lifeline during lockdown and, yes, I was inspired enough to use the name for one of the pubs in Little Challham, so special thanks to Kris and Wendy, the landlord and landlady. Thanks to all who took part in the Friday night quizzes. I would like to say that my knowledge of trivia increased, but I still can't remember Postman Pat's surname.

Once again, my huge thanks to the superb team at Bookouture. Ruth Tross is a wonderful editor and I owe her so much for shaping the books and guiding and supporting me throughout the entire process. I know there is so much behind-the-scenes work that goes on in the editorial process and despite a huge workload, nothing is ever too much trouble whenever I've asked for your help. Thank you. Massive, massive thanks to Alex Holmes and Aimee Walsh in editorial, Kim Nash, Noelle Holten and Sarah Hardy in publicity, Lisa Brewster for the wonderful cover, Alex Crow in marketing, Jon Appleton and Rachel Rowlands for copy-editing and proofreading. For many years, I admired Bookouture from afar and now have to pinch myself that I've been published three times by such an amazing team.

So many thank yous to readers everywhere and to my family and friends who have supported me and cheered me on. Take care.

Made in United States
Troutdale, OR
08/15/2023